The God-Damn Fool

By L.B. Deyo

Dear Mary,

Thank you for being my wonderful sister and a joy to know! Much love. Enjoy the book!

Love
LB

Acknowledgements

Thanks to Lance Fever Myers, Juanice Myers, Peter Graff, Lefty Leibowitz, Jeremy Pollet, Graham Reynolds, Kathleen Deyo, William Deyo, Christina Deyo, Mary Deyo, Bilo Sheridan, Marjorie Costello, Kathryn Rogers, and all the other family and friends who have shepherded this book, and me, safely through the storm.

Persistence of Vision Publishing

For Ellie

Book I: Aurea Mediocritas

Chapter 1

Theogony

> Ancient Europe had no gods. The Great Goddess was
> regarded as immortal, changeless, and omnipotent; and
> the concept of fatherhood had not been introduced into
> religious thought. She took lovers, but for pleasure, not
> to provide her children with a father. Men feared,
> adored, and obeyed the matriarch; the hearth which she
> tended in a cave or hut being their earliest social center,
> and motherhood their prime mystery.

—Robert Graves, The Greek Myths

Peter Graff
Gaia
Ms. De Bono
Dr. John Harriman, PhD

Then we heard the roar of like a tornado or a freight train.
Something big was moving fast overhead, but we couldn't see
it.

And then the impact, maybe five blocks away: one of the
loudest sounds I'd ever heard, and a brilliant flash. People
were screaming now, some of them.

I had the reporter's instinct, which could have been mistaken for a hero's instinct, to start running toward the fire. People were running with me. I almost ate shit when we reached a wooden rail fence at the edge of the school's football field. Then we were hopping the fence, crossing the street. It couldn't have been nine o'clock yet, but there was no traffic. It was a moonless night. All the light that could be seen came from the impact site, which lay on the other side of several blocks of houses and small buildings. It was cold. My legs were tight and springy.

I didn't want to die.

We reached ground zero. It was a trail of fire and junk that had been some kind of commercial jet plane, plus a few row houses. No way anyone had survived inside that plane, but there might have been injured survivors in the buildings.

The air smelled like kerosene.

Some woman from the basketball game was taking charge. She was yelling at everyone to keep back, giving some instructions I couldn't make out.

I took out my phone to snap some pictures, but of course my phone was still dead. I wanted to know where the hell were the firemen, and the cops. It had been a good ten minutes since the crash. The turbines in the jet engines were still spinning out their moments of inertia. There was an extraordinary quantity of glass all over the place. The flames were so brilliant, the smoke so thick, and the night so dark that we could see nothing but a refracting yellow glare, a diffuse, kaleidoscopic specularity, like the world reflected in a shattered fun-house mirror.

I'd served in Iraq and Afghanistan, first as a soldier, then as a reporter. I'd seen crashed planes, crashed helicopters, blown-up buses and trucks and personnel carriers, hotels on fire, airstrikes, artillery strikes. I'd fought fires. But the difference in context was stark. It had been terrible overseas, nightmarish, absurd, but I'd had a definite role to play, a set of procedures to execute. I'd never had to wonder what to do.

A crowd had encircled the jet. Some people were tentatively probing toward it, but nobody could get in close with all that jet fuel burning. It really looked like the end of the world, which at the time it was.

I turned away from the heat, and at that point I saw the other fires. Whole neighborhoods were going up now, far away, too far to have been sparked by the jet crash.

Probably every adult there was thinking about 9/11, fifteen years earlier. What I felt specifically was like at that moment when the first tower collapsed, the hyperreality of it, that we were watching real people die.

Somebody asked what the hell was happening. I turned and saw an old guy with a white beard, a weird intensity in his face, his eyes.

He asked, *What's happening?*

Not realizing the answer until it came out of my mouth, I said, "We're under attack."

This book is about the gods, and right off the bat let's establish one thing: The gods are slow. Celestially slow. As in, not too swift, okay?

The story concerns itself with a lot of marginalia that barely signifies. A parade of nonsense, plus one thing that really does matter, a question that I had to ask myself, which happens to be the only question worth asking:

Should I let you live, and why?

Earth worship, which had for centuries held the West in thrall, was by the eighteenth century a footnote, and the page upon which that footnote was printed was itself burned in a factory furnace, and the factory furnace bred foul contagions over the surface of the Great Mother, and she was greatly vexed by this. And the anger that spread through and over her was mingled with the smoke of the mills, and it seeped through her soil and her bedrock, ever deeper, ever hotter, and in the greatness and astonishing slowness of her mind grew a plan. It was a sleeping plan. It was her secret, kept from the Father. She'd kept many secrets from him, but this was unlike all the others; it did not protect their children, but cast them into peril.

Ms. De Bono had insisted he should come. Though he was many years her senior, he fretted like a kid at being called into the headmaster's office.

Which, of course, he was. Not a child, no, but yes, being called into the headmaster's office. He was sitting in a chair in her little waiting area. It was one of those ambiguous chairs they had at the school. It wasn't technically a child's chair, but it was certainly more snug and low to the floor than was quite the thing for a grown man. Were his conscience entirely clear, he might have found the chair more comfortable, but while he had no exact idea what Ms. De Bono wanted, he was unable to imagine it was anything good.

"Dr. Harriman?" said Ms. De Bono, tucking her head out the door.

As the lame Dr. Harriman rose to stand, the chair rose with him a little. He shook it loose, and it dropped with a dampened clunk onto the shag carpet. Harriman held up his briefcase to his chest and asked Ms. De Bono how she did, but she'd already gone into her office. He pursued her within and asked again.

Now face to face with her (she behind her desk, he seated before it) he asked her in a very innocent and conventional way what it was he could do for her.

Ms. De Bono, who was a very elegant woman, a disconcertingly elegant woman, smiled in reply. It was a smile that expressed the real regret of an elegant woman called on to deliver inelegant news.

"Dr. Harriman, you know we're a small school. And you know that our endowment is even smaller. We compete not only with public schools like Newburyport High, but with the most well-heeled private institutions in the country. We have the charter, but not the budget, to compete with Andover or Exeter or Choate. That's just how it is."

Dr. Harriman, from behind the cloud-like mass of his beard, said he quite understood that. He omitted saying that *this had been how it was* for quite a long time—for many years before she arrived.

There was a pinch in Ms. De Bono's smile.

"Our faculty is the cornerstone of our reputation, and as such the basis for our continued existence. This fact isn't lost on me, Dr. Harriman. Nor is it lost on me that Latin has played a central role in what they call the Western canon. In the course of my responsibilities, I'm reminded more frequently that you might—even you, Dr. Harriman—might think, that the Western canon remains even today a preoccupation for some of our most important alumni."

Dr. Harriman said that he expected so. He was only half-listening. Or more accurately, he was listening as hard as he could, as hard as an engulfing wash of anxiety and a catastrophic hangover would let him. The room, for Dr. Harriman, was not quite spinning, but it had begun listing to starboard more sharply than he'd have liked. At such moments, his eye would roam around in search of threats. A yoga mat lay at the left of his chair. The lightbulb in her lamp was a fluorescent twist that pulsed in time with the blood in his temples.

"Ms. De Bono, dear, we are an institution of the liberal arts. Latin," said Harriman, "is the bedrock on which the liberal arts are built." The timbre of his words, a sort of croaking wheeze, undermined the effect of magnificent defiance he was going for. "I'm quite sure—"

"Latin is safe for the present, Dr. Harriman." She was smiling, but her own eyes strafed increasingly between his face and her phone's screen.

"And I think you'll be pleased to hear that your job is also safe. Because despite my own feelings about your subject, and despite the very real pressures that the coming fiscal and academic year have brought on me, I've worked with the board and we've carved out a solution. Rather than hiring a replacement for Mr. Brown, whom we released from his contract some time ago, we'll be adding his duties to your schedule."

The anxiety raging through Dr. Harriman was slightly diminished, and in its place arose a feeling of indignation.

What anxiety remained, however, was focused on a certain conviction that he should know who Mr. Brown was. Dr. Harriman was the only Latin instructor left for grades nine through twelve, and there was no Latin in the lower school at all. Mr. Brown's name was not even slightly familiar. "His duties? Which duties, exactly?"

Ms. De Bono, who had blonde hair, paused for a moment before smoking out Dr. Harriman's confusion. The smile returned to her face, broader now than before.

"Well, Dr. Harriman, Mr. Brown's duties are simply the duties of any coach in any private secondary school in the country. You will remain on the grounds after classes finish for the day, until 6:00 p.m., to coach the boys basketball team. You'll coach each of the season's 14 home games at Filibuster Gym, and travel with the team to the various Nine Schools Association schools for 14 away games."

Harriman blinked. "Do we *have* a basketball team?"

"Not at the moment, no," replied Ms. De Bono. "Nobody has signed up to play for a couple years now. Hence the termination of Coach Brown. Not having a team is a problem because the alumni, whom we depend on for donations, have been asking why we don't have a team. You may recall that in the 1970s and '80s we were well known for the excellence of our basketball program. Part of your role will be to recruit players so we can field a team this year."

They stared at each other for a few moments, and then Dr. Harriman cleared his throat.

"Ms. De Bono, are you taking the piss?"

Ms. De Bono assured him she was not.

Chapter 2
Biogenesis

Dr. John Harriman, PhD
Lefty Davis
Jackie Polish
Zero Bardoff

This was 2016, by the way.

Last days of Obama, not too long before the inauguration of Donald Trump. So that has to be borne in mind. Things change very quickly, so the reader may need a few reminders of how things were.

In those days, e.g., autonomous driving was still strictly experimental. Effectively every car on the road was driven by a human being, with predictable consequences. If you heard someone had died unexpectedly, your first guess would be 'car accident.'

Most things were run by human beings. Everyone had a smartphone, as they were called, and there were some rudimentary speech interfaces, but for the most part people interacted with computers via text input. More importantly, computers were still tools. You used a computer to do specific things. There was a set of discrete tasks that you knew were computer tasks. Editing text, sending email, playing a video game, editing a photograph. That kind of thing. "Going online." In a real sense, you were not always "online." There was a meaningful distinction between being online—operating a computer of some kind that was actively connected to the internet—and *not* being online.

Objects on earth were inert and mindless. A window, a tree, the huge preponderance of things were non-computational: blind, deaf, and dumb. Computer processing happened exclusively through the medium of semi-conductive silicon chips. The capacity to turn arbitrary substances—solids, liquids, gasses—into processors, was on the earth's surface still unheard of. The idea of whole astronomical bodies being computers was scarcely thinkable.

Everyone worked. Many, probably most, jobs had been replaced by automation, but those jobs had been replaced by other human jobs. It was absolutely understood that a person who had lost a job for that, or any, reason would go and get a different job. It would not have occurred to our heroes that as specific jobs had vanished in the past, the whole notion of having a job would itself go away. Work was simply fundamental. It was, for most, the core of one's identity. Even if you were unemployed, you were an unemployed *something*. An unemployed short-order cook, an unemployed college professor. A job was not only what you did, it was who you were. You wouldn't say, "I lawyer." You'd say, "I am a lawyer."

Pets were dumb animals. They were intellectually comparable to wild animals in nature preserves. A dog, for example, had essentially no linguistic ability. He might be conditioned to respond to a few dozen verbal commands, more or less as one of Pavlov's would respond to a bell's ring. But a dog could neither read nor speak, nor think in any but the most primitive conditioned/instinctive ways.

Despite or because of this, pets were of the greatest importance to their owners. A creepy extremity of this was the current fad of referring to oneself as a pet's "mommy" or "daddy." In this twilight of sexual reproduction, many had already taken their pets as mute, short-lived surrogate children.

People were not much brighter than the animals they loved and ate. Intellectual augmentation was scarcely an idea. Indeed, most people, if they had even considered such a possibility, would have been repelled by the thought of a brain-computer amalgam. A person who could multiply two five-digit numbers "in her head" would be considered a prodigy and might be featured on television. A chess player who could see twenty moves ahead was a grandmaster.

To put ourselves into the subjective framework of a 2016 person, we must imagine being unable to recall the names of most persons we'd met, not knowing the names of many countries, many species, many historical personages and events. Imagine being unable to perform a statistical analysis without the aid of a machine, or being ignorant of technical terms outside of one's field. A doctor might know the human anatomy, but would likely have no idea how to try a civil lawsuit, rig a ship, defragment a server, or build a cabinet.

In 2016, the first and last word out of a person's mouth might be "dude."

People communicated using grotesque cartoon hieroglyphics called "emojis." Science was little understood, if widely admired; many believed it was a body of knowledge rather than a method of investigation. Superstition was rampant almost beyond belief. Most grown adults believed, for example, in astrology, which the ancient Greeks had recognized as nonsense thousands of years before. Belief in ghosts was not only ubiquitous, but considered praiseworthy and known by the lofty-sounding name "spirituality."

Human beings felt, rather than thought, most of the time. It must be remembered that this was not their fault. They had dignity and deserve our respect and our sympathy. But it can't be whitewashed. A human being in the early twenty-first century was little more knowledgeable, and had no greater ability to process information, than his ancestor in the tenth or first century.

Are you a freshman in high school? If so, and if you'd like to enjoy an afternoon beer in a bar, you're advised as follows: Avoid the bulbous middle of the pricing curve. Dwell in the outer tails. You'll find your satisfaction at the extremities, as so often in life. On the right side of the distribution you've got your upscale, country-club-type establishment. Every customer they see is a potentially influential potential complainer, so they're gonna seldom challenge the confident drink order. "A beer, garçon, if you please." That kind of thing. Okay? And then on the left side of the spectrum you've got your true hole in the wall. That kind of place, you're looking to run into a real dead-ender who can't be bothered to give a damn how pathetic a forgery your license is. Now, Lefty and Jackie were not without means, but Zero was a beggarly day student. So that left out the high end.

There they were, shooting pool in the back of the Carousel Lounge. It was such a dive that none of our brave young swains had ever dared venture into the john. The Carousel Lounge, like many a truly sordid watering hole, was brightly lit with fluorescent lights.

It was two in the afternoon, on the one day of the week when Lefty, Jackie, and Zero shared a free period. The fair-cheeked Lefty had just sunk the six ball and was rounding the corner to line up another shot. He and Jackie were discussing baseball as they played. Zero wasn't interested. He drifted toward the bar to think.

Zero, for some reason, wore a suit. He did so pretty frequently. It wasn't a school requirement, or the style with his fellow students. It was just one of the weird things he did, like having red hair. (Probably as good a place as any to acknowledge that, too. Red hair. A pale redhead, his skin kissed by freckles. This dork looked like Huckleberry Finn dressed for church.) Maybe he wanted attention. Maybe he was compensating for his financial difficulties.

He was the worst student in the school.

He did no homework. He didn't study. This would seem to suggest that he didn't care about his grades, or was rebelling or trying to fail out. But in fact he was extremely concerned about his grades. They plagued him with worries.

Somehow in early childhood, he'd formulated some rather unhelpful notions about his scholastic life. The first was that the point of school was to persuade his teachers that he was smart. As opposed to, like, learning the material. The second was that since he was legally required to attend school for many hours each day, and since he was fulfilling that requirement, he could be under no reasonable obligation to continue with anything to do with school after the last bell had rung.

Homework, in other words, was a flagrant violation of his contract, an intrusion on time that was rightfully his own. If the other kids wanted to waste their free time on school, that was good for them. He'd have none of it.

But again, this insistence on his rights had nothing to do with any lack of concern about his grades. Far from it. The beer that he now ordered was his third, and the abstracted look on his face was grave. Indeed, each time a teacher called on Zero it plunged him into panic. Each time homework was called to the front, the impious Zero would mentally remove himself.

Now Zero faced away from the bar, through the saloon and beyond, through the fiery window pane into the sleepy streets of Newburyport, Massachusetts.

He sipped at his beer and felt pitifully low. He didn't even take out his phone to look at it—a sure sign of psychic distress. Some movement at the front door caught his eye, and Zero turned to see a familiar figure limp into the bar. "Boys," he hissed to Lefty and Jackie, "I think we're busted."

The figure was that gray iniquity, that huge fat gross beery swine, that cocker of one eyebrow, the bullish and harried Dr. John Harriman.

The boys recognized him instantly, and would have even if they weren't in his 8:30 a.m. Latin I class.

Harriman was an institutional figure at Garrison, the kind found in every secondary school faculty who's somehow at once revered and laughed at. There was no laughter in our boys' hearts now.

Harriman was ordering. He sat down heavily at the bar, heavily as only a fat old crank can sit. The bartender was fly, and had the drink in Harriman's hand in a flash. The boys, paralyzed, watched with nauseated fascination at the way Harriman tucked and smoothed his huge white beard to clear a path for the whiskey. The old man had a cheerful tic in his eye when he sipped. Looked like he was winking. Zero was just beginning to formulate an escape plan when Dr. Harriman looked up and recognized him.

So here was a Mexican standoff.

For it now occurred to both man and boys that on 2 p.m. on a Wednesday, on the third day of the fall trimester, Dr. Harriman had little more business drinking in this dump than had the three freshmen. Zero and Harriman stared at one another for a moment. Then Harriman, with a dashing flourish, raised a glass to the boys in a toast that they were too stunned to return.

None of them noticed a small symbol carved into the side of the coin-operated pool table. It was the international symbol of danger: A triangle with an exclamation point in its center.

Next day. It was lunchtime, and the scoundrels Lefty Davis and Jackie Polish were in the cafeteria, scoping the girls and playing gin rummy. Lefty was up 45 points, and that meant 90 cents. But Jackie was one fortunate draw away from his comeback.

The cafeteria!

That bright, sunshiny purgatory, that salon of the academic elite, that bulwark of nobility, where the most well-to-do were waited on by the wretched of the earth, and the baked mozzarella was so bad no one could say who'd gotten the worse end of the deal.

Lefty and Jackie, neither popular nor unpopular, neither the best students nor the worst (though Jackie was pretty far from distinguished). Lefty in his gold-rimmed spectacles with his curly black hair, Jackie in his baseball hat with his generous nose and sleepy eyes. Jewish guys, you know, the grandsons of immigrants. Sandy Koufax types. A little bit hip-hop, a whole lot punk rock. All-American.

Jackie, breaker of guitars, played a deliberate hand of gin rummy. A ponderous, meditative hand. Not for him, the hurried impulse. He shrewdly considered the universe of options before him, weighing both tactical and strategic factors.

"*Come on, GO!*" said Lefty. Lefty liked to read the school paper while he played cards, especially against a tedious slow damned player like Jackie.

Let's go ahead and note here that Jackie wore an eye patch. Sometimes on one eye, sometimes on the other. People hardly noticed it anymore. One kid had been so "woke" he'd tried to shame Jackie into taking it off, talking about "mocking the disabled" and some kind of "privilege."

Jackie had told him to fuck off, and off he'd fucked.

It was weird, though, the eye patch. It, along with his Red Sox cap, made him look like Bazooka Joe.

"You can try to rush me," Jackie smiled into his cards, "but I can't be rushed. Not with money on the line. Not in this man's cafeteria."

And who should arrive at this delicate moment, sporting a suit and tie and a black overcoat in the heat of early September? None but the redhead Zero Bardoff, the very playboy of the Western world.

"Boys," said he, taking a seat in a backward-facing chair, "the insanity continues."

Lefty's eyes didn't stray from his newspaper, nor Jackie's from his cards.

"What?" said Jackie.

"We had our share of disputes, you two and me, concerning if maybe Garrison Academy is a little light in the loafers, masculinity-wise. Right?"

Lefty looked up. "So?"

"So I think we can pretty much consider my position confirmed." Zero pulled from his pocket the same school newspaper Lefty'd been reading. "It says here the basketball program, our only remaining team sports program, will be canceled for the second year in a row due to lack of student interest."

Jackie laughed. "Hell you care, Zero? You hate sports."

"It's a point of pride, for Christ's sake," Zero shook his head. "What the hell kind of a high school doesn't have a basketball team? And on account of student god-damn *lack of interest?*"

Lefty nodded. "It is pretty hurting. The locals at Newburypoint High are gonna have a field day with this."

Jackie, without putting down his cards, stood and addressed the whole cafeteria. "Hey! Listen up! I want everybody's attention here!"

"Shut the hell up!" called out a second-grader.

"The nabobs who run this place are trying to cut basketball again. Do you nerds even care?"

Before he'd completed this impressive address, Jackie had lost his audience. The buzz of young voices had rebounded to full volume. Jackie sat back down. "There's your problem, right there. Nerds."

"Yeah?" Zero leaned in. Zero had a way of whispering that made him seem like he was orchestrating a short con. "Well, I say this is bullshit. I say the basketball program stays. Gentlemen, *we* are gonna be the basketball team."

Lefty smiled. "A basketball team has like 14 players. Five of them have to be on the floor at all times. What are we gonna do, us three?" He looked at Jackie and cracked up, pointing his thumb at Zero. "This guy! I love this guy! Ha ha ha ha ha!"

Zero considered the matter.

"Okay, five guys, huh? Okay. We'll have five guys and just won't sit out. Now are you clowns going to tell me that there ain't two other kids in this whole god-damn school we can get to sign up?"

"Outta these clowns? I ain't counting on it," said Jackie, still studying those blasted cards.

Lefty, when he contemplated some profundity, had the habit of actually stroking his chin. "If you're serious, Zero, I can think of a couple of guys who might be down. A couple of guys name of Kosoko and Mazi Wright."

Zero thought about it. "Yeah. Well. They're good athletes, but they're short. And their father's the damn mayor. Good luck getting them to listen to us."

Lefty smiled. "Yeah? You just leave it to me, friend. Kosoko happens to be my lab partner in biology. He and his brother Mazi are gonna learn to love it, because it's the best thing going today."

Jackie drew his card at last.

"Speaking of basketball, boys, this here is *Sweet Ginger Brown*." He fanned out his cards in triumph.

"Georgia," said Lefty. And the look on his friends' faces told him they had no idea what he was talking about.

An hour later, Lefty sat there in biology class, right behind and to the left of the great Kosoko Wright. Kosoko Wright, as noted, was also the small Kosoko Wright, though he wouldn't remain so. He was also very good-looking, as the reader will soon be tired of hearing. A little bit disturbingly good-looking.

Anyway, the teacher was talking about clay. Yes, in biology class. Clay. Clay hydrogel, which apparently was a very hot topic in biology. This is something that sounds really boring, but actually Lefty ought to have been paying close attention at this moment instead of planning his pitch to Kosoko to join the basketball team.

It seems that this clay hydrogel was interesting because it evolved. That is, the clay didn't evolve, but the shape, the patterns, the ripples and such as like crystallization of the clay actually evolved as the earth was cooling. Certain shapes, it seems, were favored by the environment, and self-reinforced themselves and replicated themselves, just like life forms do.

Can you picture that? Like a certain kind of channel would form in the clay and it would "succeed" in the sense of directing the flow of the clay, and in so doing it would create other channels and like cavities and crystals that were like it. And the wildest part was that this clay had evolved over time into not only the medium of its own natural selection, but also quite possibly the medium of life.

Are you hanging in with this? It's important.

Yes. So the same channels or crystals that increasingly defined the shape of the clay also formed little cell-membrane-like structures, and the little membranes created pockets in which various organic chemicals not only could form, but could be segregated from other organic chemicals that would otherwise have destroyed them. In other words, the clay was like an artificial cell, and these biochemicals were able to form because of the patterns in the clay, and then presumably the biochemicals formed more complex biochemicals, nucleotides, what have you, that themselves joined together into genetic structures and then to actual biological life, which of course then itself evolved, and so now we have bacteria and people and horses and TV. Biogenesis, for which there really doesn't happen to be any other decent theory.

Right.

But again, Lefty wasn't really paying attention.

A good student, you know. Not bad. But nobody's perfect. And unable to wait for the end of the lecture, Lefty went ahead and leaned over and tapped Kosoko right on the shoulder.

Chapter 3
The Gift of a Whistle

Dr. John Harriman, PhD
Lefty Davis
Jackie Polish
Zero Bardoff
Kosoko Wright
Mazi Wright
Birdie Love
Maj. Kim Jigu
Kim Jigu's subordinates

"I hate all sports as rabidly as a person who likes sports hates common sense."

— H. L. Mencken

And so it was. Dr. Harriman had expended what political capital thirty years of loyal service had won him, and still failed to evade this coaching assignment. He'd been thwarted by three damned punks.

It was early October, near the start of the basketball season, and it was time for the first practice of the Garrison Liberators.

A bleary Dr. Harriman stood before his team, they being Lefty, Jackie and Zero, who were like brothers, and Kosoko and Mazi, who *were* brothers.

Dr. Harriman, who owned neither a tattered gray sweatshirt nor a baseball cap, wore his accustomed tweed and bow tie.

"Coach Harriman," Jackie called out, raising his hand.

Coach Harriman. The surreality of it echoed through Filibuster Gym.

"Coach, we got you something." Jackie rose from his folding chair and approached Dr. Harriman. "Well, it's a whistle."

Dr. Harriman, who was not drunk, winced through his white beard.

"Thank you, Mr. Polish," he said, accepting the whistle and looping its chain over his head. "I shall treasure it."

Jackie sat down in his folding chair again. It squeaked through the gymnasium.

The exertion of bringing the whistle chain over his beard now triggered in Dr. Harriman a fit of coughing. It was a long few moments in passing, and Zero had almost risen to help the old man when it stopped.

"Gentlemen," said Dr. Harriman, who had a booming bass voice when he spoke up. "If my standing here before you as coach of the Garrison basketball team seems to any of you to be a farce..." He began to cough again, but brought it under control. "A grotesque buffoonish god-damn farce, then you have better judgment than I gave you credit for."

Kosoko and Mazi didn't snicker, or even stifle a snicker, but amusement was so evident in their eyes that it spread to Zero, who couldn't resist laughing once, loudly.

"The man you see before you," Harriman went on, "was at one time as arrogant and entitled as any among you. That arrogance, that hope, that pleasure in life, has been ground away. Oh, yes, my boys. Ground to powder by three fucking marriages, a war, the insolence of my students, the contempt of the faculty, and the god-damn and blasted rise of *politics* in academe."

He somehow managed to bend over and pick up a
basketball from the wooden gym floor. He unconsciously
rested the ball on his more than generous midriff as he spoke.

"I hold now in my ancient hands the token of my last
decline. This—this leathern ball..."

For a moment the old man seemed unable to go on, but he
found his courage.

"This god-damn *bag of air,* this *Wilson,* is the last nail."

There were tears on his florid cheeks.

"And you must never think, you god-damn brats—you must
never think it could escape my notice that *it is you have
swung the hammer."*

The boys looked at one another with an innocence that was
perfectly genuine.

Dr. Harriman had been an unlikely choice for basketball
coach. Unlikely in the extreme. But none of them had realized
he was here against his will—that the job had been forced on
him by a parsimonious administration.

As if to confirm this suspicion, Harriman said, "Your
headmaster, Ms. De Bono, for reasons too asinine to list, has
placed her trust, and the trust of this institution, in me. And
though she did it as an insult, infallibly so—as sure as I'm a
man— as a black cunning cruel disgrace—in spite of this (and
it is, *ha!* It is a miserable fucking damned contemptible
disgrace. A disgrace!) I nevertheless gratefully accept my
charge as sacred. *Aegrescit medendo.* The charge of your
health, and, I suppose, your prospects for victory in the
contests ahead, ah, this charge I take up willingly and without
complaint. Now then."

He bounced the ball once, and tried to bounce it again, but
on the second try it struck the toe of his shoe and caromed into
the locker room.

"Yes! Now. Who of you has ever played basketball?"

Lefty raised his hand halfway. This was fitting, because he had only halfway played. And as he considered it now, he realized he hadn't, in any strict sense, played at all. He lowered his hand. He and Jackie and Zero, no less than Harriman himself, were startled to see that neither Kosoko nor Mazi had *his* hand up either.

"What, *none* of you?" Dr. Harriman implored. "But surely the traditions of—that is to say, the American—well, one of you must have had *at least* a hoop in his driveway."

Kosoko spoke up.

"Coach, Mazi and me had a hoop. We've played some, but mostly not much. We figured we're too little to hoop. Mostly we play soccer and swim."

Harriman looked green.

"But you know the *rules,* I'm sure. You're familiar with the *conventions.* That is, you've *played the game*, for God's sake."

"Coach?" said Mazi, the youngest of the boys. "Haven't *you* ever played basketball?"

Ten minutes later, our lads were wringing wet, clutching at their chests, choking on their own CO_2. They were hobbling around an elevated track mounted along the wall, one story up from the gym floor. The disrepair into which the track— indeed, the entire gym— had fallen spoke of the Garrison Academy's famous emphasis on academics. There was old dust on the handrails of the track, as Jackie learned by grabbing them for support. Kosoko and Mazi were bringing up the front, but even they were by now cursing their parentage.

Mazi almost stepped on Zero, who lay facing the wall, motionless but for the sobs racking his frame.

"Pathetic," growled Harriman, sealing the cap of his flask. He then blew for the first time into his whistle with the full capacity of his fat-bound lungs. "Hit the god-damn deck and commence pushing up!"

"How many push-ups?" said Kosoko.

"Well," said Harriman, "let us say two hundred."

Kosoko, the strongest of the team by far, managed eight push-ups. Lefty hit the record for his gang with four. Zero still lay whimpering against the wall.

Harriman, blowing another weak shrill alarm, found he was beginning to savor this whistle.

"Avast pushing up!" he hollered. "We shall now begin with your training. Follow me below."

He led the shattered youths downstairs to the court.

"Now then." He thrust the basketball, which he'd retrieved from the locker room, into the chest of young Jackie. "Let us see who among you is the best hand at tossing the ball through the ring!"

It would have given the boys tremendous satisfaction, irresistible satisfaction, to inform their coach that the term of art was *shooting,* not fucking *tossing the ball through the ring,* and that what was more, this bombard Dr. Harriman was a fat ludicrous ignorant drunk and a bastard of a fool.

And they would have told him so, too, if they'd had the wind.

instead, they formed a line at the top of the key and began shooting free throws. In all fairness, Harriman had not been far wrong in his choice of words after all; the boys *were* more or less tossing the ball, though not through any ring.

An eighth-grade girl had been out on the football field watching the entire time through the window, smoking cigarettes and laughing herself sick.

Now the practice was over, and the team filed out through the gym's double doors into the warm Massachusetts night.

They were dead on their feet, whipped as any cur, but they held up their heads. It had been brutal, but they'd made it through.

"Hey," said the eighth-grade girl.

Zero looked up with a half-smile. "Yeah?"

"You suck," said the girl. "Faggot."

The girl was Birdie Love of the wildlands, one of only a few dozen black residents of Newburyport, Massachusetts. She was a townie, just like Zero, and she'd just matriculated at Garrison. She loved cigarettes, kissing boys, history, and a great deal else. But she hated as strongly as she loved.

Kim Jigu was born in Kwanliso no. 25, a political internment camp in the northeast of the Democratic People's Republic of Korea, to a mother who was well on her way to death by starvation.

By the time she was six, Jigu was working on an assembly line, wrapping packages in brown paper, subsisting on a few handfuls of soybeans each day.

She was teased by her peers and the adults alike for the way she dug through the snow to scratch at the soil, which she ate in fistfuls. She chipped her teeth on little rocks and the shells of snails. The inmates started calling her Kim then.

When she was eleven, she was raped for the first time by a prison guard who for whatever reason liked to pick on her father. Catching the interest of the guards always meant trouble. Just weeks later they accused her father of stealing food, and shot him.

The difference between Kim Jigu and an animal was that an animal is unaccountable for its actions, whereas Jigu was highly accountable, not only for her own crimes but for those of her fellow inmates. Every night after hours of studying the camp rules, she and her cohort were led through a series of accusations and confessions; your fellow prisoner would accuse you of some malfeasance, and you would confess.

It was a game, and Kim Jigu was an expert player.

She knew whom to accuse, what charges to level, and how to make it seem that the accusation was more painful for her than for the one to be condemned.

She had no toys, no other recreation, so this game became the focus of all of her genius and imagination. Before she was released at the age of 14, she had developed a fearsome reputation. From then on she was never hungry even in the worst years of the famine.

Today, an adult woman, Major Kim Jigu of the North Korean People's Army Strategic Rocket Force strode into the silo to inspect first the KN-08 nuclear ICBM and second the crew responsible for it. She was base commander for this underground launch site, hidden in the Paektu Mountain silo complex. Jigu was as feared as ever. The silo went silent as she entered, and every eye turned to her.

"Why hasn't this missile been checked today?" she shouted at them.

They protested that it had been, as it was every morning.

"Let me see the report!" she said, seizing it from the hand of a lieutenant. She scanned it quickly. "This is shoddy work! You are the worst crew in the whole complex! What would the Great Leader think of this?"

The Great Leader had been dead for decades, but remained North Korea's highest authority. Even in life he had inspired no more terror than he did today.

"You selfish brats!" she cried, throwing the report down the silo shaft. "You disgrace yourselves. You don't cherish the Great Leader enough to serve him properly. You will—"

Kim Jigu stopped short, putting her hand to her forehead, pushing back the brim of her cap. There was a pain ringing out through her scalp. She closed her eyes and willed it away, but it grew stronger. Then she realized she was growing dizzy. She opened her eyes to orient herself.

"You will all be punished—" she said.

She was sweating and her face was hot.

"And I—"

Kim Jigu, who moments before had held mastery of all her strength and faculties, now collapsed to the deck, too weak to break her own fall.

As she lay there, she thought of her childhood in the camp. She recalled the weakness of extreme hunger, a weakness still felt by hundreds of thousands of her fellow soldiers every day. She thought of her mother, whom she could not remember but who seemed to her to be holding her hand at this moment. And then the new memories arrived.

A pool of water, swelling in rainstorm beside a cliff, will expand with imperceptible slowness for hours before it finds a channel, but when it does it will plunge from the cliffside with all the power of its mass, taking soil and plants over the side with it. So did the memories surge into the mind of Kim Jigu. Memories that had not been her own. Memories of uncountable eras, of primeval violence, of the agony of birth. Of a son who was also a husband and the father. Of a proud, vain sun, of Olympian majesty, of the planets.

Chapter 4
You Tread Upon my Patience

Mayor Frank Wright
His administrative assistant
Various staff, and members of the city council

Newburyport City Hall is a Yankee building, with a face of flat red brick and just enough stonework to look important. Its construction was finished in 1851, more than two hundred years after the town's founding, and about a hundred years after the completion of what was still America's oldest Coast Guard station, over on the waterfront.

This afternoon the City Hall building seemed to be on fire, with heat shimmering off the brick and sunshine flaring off the windows. Inside, in the office of the mayor, it was cool enough to breathe. But breath came haltingly to his honor, slumped in his great chair before his great desk. He was a handsome bastard, but furious this morning in his aspect.

"Do you know," said the burly Mayor Wright, "what pisses me off?"

His office was filled with staffers and some members of the City Council. No one said anything. He could have been addressing any one of them, or none at all.

"It pisses me off," said the man, rising to his feet, "that I have to send my sons to a private school, when we have one of the oldest and most distinguished public schools in the country right down the damn street. It pisses me off when, in a city founded on the struggle for equality, I have to send my sons to Garrison Academy if I want them to see any black faces among their peers."

Mayor Wright was black. He was referring to his sons Kosoko and Mazi.

The group, each of whom was white, held silent. What, they could (with some justice) have asked, did he want *them* to do about it? Did he expect them to bus African Americans in from Boston? Were they supposed to be social workers, or what?

"Relax," said the mayor, who knew their minds as well as he knew his own. "It's nobody's fault, I suppose. Anyway, that's not what I wanted to discuss when I called y'all in here. But god-damn it!" he slammed his hand down on the desk, like somebody in a movie. "God-damn it, it makes me tired."

The mayor slumped back down in his chair.

"Hell, you know what I want to talk about."

"Sir?" said his administrative assistant.

"Yeah, that's right. I want to talk about my old friend Hart."

Hart was a man from Quincy. A very capable man, by every account. Working man, blue collar, self-made. Impeccably liberal, more liberal than the mayor, even. Not handsome like his honor Mayor Frank Wright, but solid. Dignified. If such a thing as a dignity contest could be held, it would be a close-run thing between Mayor Wright and this man Hart. Elijah Hart, working man. Man of iron. And Elijah Hart wanted to be mayor of Newburyport.

"Why the hell does he want to be mayor *here?* Man doesn't even live here! Why doesn't he run in Quincy?"

"Quincy's locked down, sir. They're solidly behind Mayor Smythe. Anyway, sir, he lives here now. Bought a house on the river. Even got his kids enrolled at Newburyport High."

"Newburyport is solidly behind me!"

Mayor Wright had quit cigarettes eight years ago, and his hand still went to his breast pocket at times like these. "This town—shit, why here, though? Doesn't want to run in Quincy, that's his affair. Why come here?"

"Plum Island, sir. Wants to save the Great Marsh."

"Ecology, huh?" Mayor Wright shook his head. "That's a good starter, but it's no finisher. The Great Marsh, you say?"

"Yes, sir. And he wants to clean up the Merrimack. And, sir, he wants to clean up this city. He's alleging corruption. Throwing out insinuations. Hinting."

"When I was re-elected almost four years ago, I thought I would have my chance to do some lasting good for this community. A museum to honor the brave men and women, black and white, who fought for the abolition of slavery."

"Sir," nodded a council member.

"And I'm going to do it, by God, if it puts me in the ground. But that's going to have to wait. I have to deal with Hart, a man I've known and liked going on fifteen years, a man I trusted completely. Hell, a man I've had to my house for coffee."

The thought of Hart's treachery set the assembled heads to shaking.

"God-damn it."

The mayor suffered from acid reflux disease, also known as GERD. When it came on it felt less like a burning in his chest than like an arsenal of swords impaling his trunk from acute angles.

Now he felt the first gentle stab in his upper back, just below the shoulder blade. He knew that if an attack got started there was nothing in hell or creation that could stop it or mitigate it in any way.

"All right. Get out of here, all of you. I need to think."

Chapter 5
The Judge of Men

Dr. John Harriman, PhD
Mrs. Vite
Lefty Davis
Jackie Polish
Zero Bardoff
Kosoko Wright
Mazi Wright

Coach Harriman, MA (ancient Greek), MA (classics), PhD (Latin), stood in Douglass Library.

After some weeks of indecision, Harriman was resolved to accept the reality of the role he'd been unable to get out of. The decision gave him purpose. This was strange for so complacent a man, but it agreed with him.

He cut a portly, dignified figure, walking the stacks. No one would call him fat, he believed, but his belly spoke of prosperity and a rich life.

On such a combustive autumn day, Harriman could have nothing much to complain of (other than his edema, and his psoriasis). And his bursitis, and the hypertension (hadn't bothered him in months), and of course a very slight touch of the male pattern baldness. A little hint of rosacea, particularly around the nose and cheeks, was a minor enough inconvenience. He was pretty deaf, pretty blind, though perhaps not more so than many a robust man of his own age.

Mainly what troubled him was his leg, gimpy from an old war wound that really smarted when the weather was damp. His morbid obesity didn't do the leg any favors.

Harriman had the gout.

And, yes, he had fatty liver disease.

He was sclerotic, arthritic, somewhat prone to raving and confabulation and talking in his sleep.

And he had insomnia. And sleep apnea. And nightmares.

He happened to be infertile, though neither he nor anyone else knew or cared. He suffered some slight nervousness occasionally, which was less serious than his intermittent bouts of confusion, vertigo, difficulty swallowing, and excessive sweating.

Given his social habits, it was no surprise that he from time to time contracted the clap; he may also have had syphilis, though if so it was in the very early stages and troubled him not in the least.

Harriman couldn't touch his toes. He could barely touch his knees. And he was vexed by tinnitus, while others were vexed by his Tourettic spasms, tics, and explosive profanity.

He itched.

His teeth looked like the skyline of Berlin in 1945. His breath wasn't great. He smelled of rubbing alcohol and Bengay—basically like a nursing home. His eyelids drooped. He had frequent headaches.

In the corner of his twinkling eye he now spied Mrs. Vite. He whirled to face her and, in doing so, struck a book cart with his abdomen and sent it crashing. With infinite self-possession, he stepped over the toppled cart as lightly as a sprite and made his way to the librarian.

"Mrs. Vite, you're a grateful sight. I hope you can assist me."

Mrs. Vite looked up from the spray of books. "I hope so, too, John. But first maybe you could help me with this mess you've made."

A few sweaty minutes later, Dr. Harriman rose from his knees and placed the last book back on the cart.

Mrs. Vite, shaking her head, said, "Please be more careful, John," and started off.

"Mrs. Vite! Wait! I had sought your assistance!"

He told her he was doing a bit of scholarly research—
Americana and the nineteenth century—and of all things
wanted to know the rules of basketball.

His smile vanished when Mrs. Vite told him she'd heard
he'd been made coach. This sent her into a bit of hushed
tittering as she led him to the card catalog.

"Basketball. Basketball," she said, thumbing through the
cards. "Ah! Here we go. *The Rules of Basket-Ball* by Dr. James
Naismith. It's just this way."

"Great God!" Dr. Harriman's oath carried through the
whole floor as he held up the pamphlet. "What a damned thick
file of rules."

Actually, there were only thirteen. The thirteen original
rules of basketball, composed by Dr. Naismith in 1891.

Naismith was a wise-enough looking fellow from his
picture, beneath which read the caption, "The invention of
basket-ball was not an accident. It was developed to meet a
need. These boys simply would not play 'Drop-the-
Handkerchief.'"

The rules began like this:

*The ball may be thrown in any direction with one or
both hands.*

*The ball may be batted in any direction with one or
both hands.*

*A player cannot run with the ball, as he must throw it
from the spot on which he catches it, with allowance to
be made for the man who catches the ball when
running at a good speed.*

...

Harriman's lips moved as he read. This was a nervous habit, nothing more. He even pronounced the odd phrase out loud to aid in memorization. Harriman didn't intend to check the book out, obviously. Who wanted the responsibility of returning a library book?

"*The umpire shall be the judge of men,*" he read, nodding, "*and shall note the fouls, and notify the referee when three consecutive fouls have been made. He shall have the power to disqualify men according to rule five.*"

Harriman looked up from the page and whispered, "The umpire shall be the judge of men. That's a fine phrase. A very fine phrase."

Dr. Harriman thought the rules quite sensible, and as he read on through the short history of Dr. Naismith's life, he found himself impressed.

"The only invented sport. Remarkable!"

That evening, Harriman arrived on time and sober for practice. The boys, filing in, were amazed to see the old man in Chuck Taylor sneakers and a sweat suit, vigorously bouncing the basketball with both hands, and with neither pipe or flask in evidence.

"You boys simply would not play Drop-the-Handkerchief!" he laughed. "You simply would not!" And with this he threw the ball toward the goal, so that it nearly reached the bottom of the net. "Now!" he clapped his hands loudly. "Let's dispense with the calisthenics just for this evening. I believe we're ready for our first trial game."

What followed was a lengthy dispute interrupted by brief moments of sport.

"Oh, no, no!" said the old man, who had mastered the whistle and could now pierce the sky with it. "You may not run when you have the ball!"

"Coach, I can dribble!" said Mazi, perplexed and hostile.

"You must *throw* the ball from the spot on which you catch it!" Harriman's face shone pink through the white of his beard. "How the hell can you learn the rules if you refuse to listen?"

"He can dribble, Harriman," said Lefty. "As long as he doesn't pick up the ball, he can keep dribbling while he moves."

Lefty was still getting comfortable around Harriman, and when Lefty was talking to an adult he wasn't yet comfortable with, his voice became very soft and a little high—kind of womanish—which lent a sweet aspect to him. This cherub of a lad, with his dimples and his gold-rimmed spectacles and his curly hair. Don't be fooled, though, as so many adults were. He was the Eddie Haskell of Garrison; he was a bad kid.

"Dribbling!" the old man scoffed.

The boys persuaded Dr. Harriman to suspend practice, and led him to the boys' student lounge. There, on the TV, the Boston Celtics were playing the Denver Nuggets.

"Look at Isaiah Thomas," said Kosoko. "See what he's doing? Bouncing the ball? That's dribbling, Coach."

"I'm amazed," Harriman said. "Astounded. I have the rules word-for-word right here in my head. I promise you there is no mention of this dribbling or bouncing anywhere in the text."

This coaching business was proving a bit deeper than he'd counted on. The next day found him in the Douglass Library again, and this time his disposition toward Mrs. Vite was far less cordial.

"Madam," he hissed, leaning in to face her across the counter. "What the devil have you been about? Making sport of a poor scholar? Holding him up to the ridicule of his charges?"

"Dr. Harriman," she said, "I don't know what you're talking about. You told me you were studying nineteenth century history, and I sent you straight to the original rules of basketball. If you want the current rules, I suggest you look online."

Online. That was fucking likely.

Dr. Harriman had been a decade learning the rudiments of email; he read only physical books and his house was stacked literally to the ceiling with newspapers and magazines.

"Mr. Polish" he said the next morning as his students filed out of class. "I have an assignment for you. You're to find me the current rules of basketball and print them out so I can read them."

"Okay, Dr. Harriman," said Jackie, shaking his head.

Chapter 6
Here is Garrison

Birdie Love
Naomi Echeveria
Ms. De Bono

> "Just six months ago, some academics dismissed EMP Commission warnings and even, literally, laughed on National Public Radio at the idea North Korea could make an EMP attack."

—Statement for the Record

Dr. William R. Graham, Chairman

Dr. Peter Vincent Pry, Chief of Staff

Commission to Assess the Threat to the United States from Electromagnetic Pulse (EMP) Attack

To

U.S. House of Representatives

Committee on Homeland Security Subcommittee on Oversight and Management Efficiency Hearing

"Empty Threat or Serious Danger: Assessing North
Korea's Risk to the Homeland" October 12, 2017

The William Lloyd Garrison Academy might have been
called venerable.

It was founded in 1891, which is a hell of a long time before
our story here. But she was a latecomer by the standards of the
Nine Schools Association. Phillips Andover had already been
around for over a century when Garrison opened her doors.
Deerfield had stood since 1797, and Exeter since 1781. At all
events, Garrison looked older than she was. The buildings on
her campus had been built in a very old style, and with details
like buckshot in the bricks to make them look ancient even
when they were new. This effect had never been very
convincing until the 1970s, when the Opec oil embargo largely
wiped out the school's endowment.

Through Garrison's halls and field walked some nine
hundred students, and for every five of these students was a
teacher.

Some of those teachers, including Dr. Harriman, were old
enough to remember the oil embargo and had never since
cherished their Arab brothers in respect of fellowship. This
was a disgrace, a beggarly weak hateful disgrace, but when has
there been an institution free of such taint?

Garrison had, at least (in keeping with its namesake) been
racially integrated all along. Today its website proudly told of
its 45-plus percent "Students of Color*" with the asterisked
footnote indicating that this figure included "biracial and
multiracial students." One student who resented the "of color"
designation was Birdie Love, who called herself "blacker than
the twelve at midnight."

Birdie was walking with her lighter-skinned but equally
black friend Naomi Echeveria towards Stowe Hall, where they
were about to begin American History class.

They strolled through the falling leaves of late October, laughing and chatting. They looked as though they might have been caught in a photograph for a Garrison Academy brochure. Getting students to pay $45,000 per year for tuition, room, and board was more difficult now than ever before. The school itself was forced to contribute substantially to cover most students' shortfalls. Birdie herself, e.g., paid no tuition. Naomi, on the other hand, paid every penny (that is, her parents did), but she was one of a vanishing several dozen.

Some things must fall by the board in lean times, and as a glance around would confirm, twice-weekly garbage collection hadn't survived the stroke of Ms. De Bono's red pen.

De Bono, who would have seen Birdie and Naomi through her office window if she'd been looking, had discovered a hundred ingenious ways to cut back. She'd found, for example, that by turning down the thermostats by just three degrees in winter she could save thousands of dollars per year. Going all-digital with textbooks had been obvious, and even with the school paying for most of the tablet devices, she came out well ahead.

International students were a reliable income stream. Kids who could afford to study here from overseas were far more likely to pay the full price of admission. And whatever hits Garrison's reputation had taken domestically, Ms. De Bono could still market the school abroad on a slightly stale reputation. The school boasted students from eighteen countries, some of them the children of shahs and princes.

There had been economies in the cafeteria, too.

As recently as the 1990s, they'd offered selections for every dietary restriction, food fad, or other eating disorder. Omnivore, vegetarian, vegan, pollotarian, flexitarian, pescatarian, fructitarian, Jain, low-fat, low-carb, full-blown Atkins, South Beach, paleo, anorexic, bulimic, Kosher, Halal, Hindu, Catholic, a galaxy of intolerances, aversions, and allergies; no matter what your fucking problem was, dinner was served.

No more. Now, if you didn't want bacon, you could pick it out of your own damn salad. Most of the food these days came in powdered form, as at Taco Bell, in huge plastic sacks that would outlast the sun.

Birdie was telling Naomi about the basketball practice she'd watched and making Naomi promise to join her tonight at Filibuster Gym for another show.

"Come *on*, Naomi. It'll be hysterical. If I can stay and watch, you can too. I don't even live on campus, for Pete's sake."

"All right, all right!" Naomi laughed. "If they're as spastic as you say, it'll be worth failing history for."

"Like you gonna fail history, right?" Birdie was laughing too as they entered the building. "Miss 'it was Nathan Hale who was caught and executed by the British on September 20, 1776...'"

"September 22," Naomi said seriously. "You know Ms. Berkeley is a bitch for dates. This isn't public school, Birdie. You gotta study. For real."

"Bitch, I know it was September 22! He was hung—"

"—*hanged*."

"*Hanged* for treason on Manhattan Island. He was 21 years old, pretty, handsome, and fine."

"What were his last words?" Naomi smiled.

"I only regret that I have but one life to lose for my country, *bitch*." Birdie laughed, settling in behind her desk.

Mrs. Berkeley, who was indeed a bitch for dates, walked in and started class.

"Naomi!" whispered Birdie.

"What?"

"Don't fuck with me on Nathan Hale."

Chapter 7
Vulnerabilities in the Grid

Mazi Wright
Kosoko Wright

The Federal Energy Regulatory Commission may not be a household name, but its policies touch on some aspect of nearly every American's life. The agency oversees hundreds of thousands of miles of interstate natural gas pipelines and the bulk electric power grid.

FERC "has details of some of this country's most sensitive infrastructure," Geoffrey Berman, U.S. attorney for the Southern District of New York, said at a press conference Friday unveiling charges against the Iranian residents. . . .

What, if anything, might have been siphoned from FERC's headquarters in Washington, D.C., to the Mabna Institute, an alleged front for the state-sponsored hackers in Tehran?

"My fear is that FERC has done these pretty detailed studies on vulnerabilities in the grid," said Earl Shockley, founder and president of the InPOWERd LLC consultancy and a former senior executive at the nonprofit North American Electric Reliability Corp., which oversees operations and security of the nation's interstate power grid. "Who knows if [hackers] have any of that material?"

—Blake Sobczak, E&E News, "Iranians Hacked FERC.
What did they want?"

"Hey, Kosoko?"

Mazi, unable to sleep, was whispering from the top bunk of
their dorm room.

"Yeah, what?" replied an annoyed Kosoko.

"Big game tomorrow."

"Just a scrimmage, kid."

"We're gonna lose pretty bad," said Mazi.

"Yeah, I guess so," Kosoko smiled.

He knew they were in for a beatdown, but he wasn't too
worried about it. He was excited to play in his first refereed
game, even if it was an unofficial game. Newburyport High
was a public school, not part of Garrison's Group of Nine
Schools Association league.

Kosoko thought of all the people who'd be there watching
him, and in particular all the young ladies, and he drifted
toward sleep in a pleasantly sexy frame of mind.

"Kosoko?"

"What, Mazi? Shit!"

"Kosoko, can I ask you one thing? For real?"

"Yeah," said Kosoko. "Of course."

"If I die, I want to be buried near you. I don't want our
bones to be far apart."

"You weird, son."

"Kosoko? I'm serious."

"You ain't gonna die, Mazi."

"I'm not playing, Kosoko. I don't want my body to be
alone."

"You ain't dying."

"I'm serious."

It soon enough transpired that Elijah Hart, the fiend of
Quincy, that hater of sunshine, had joined the club.

His honor Frank Wright, father of young Kosoko and Mazi, naturally wasn't informed about this.

Why would anyone bother to tell him? He was only the mayor. He was only a longtime member of the club in excellent standing, a member who'd never allowed any temporary financial difficulties to prevent him from paying his dues on the first of every month, cash on the barrelhead.

No, Frank Wright had to find out when the serpent was already in the damn garden.

In he walked this fine evening to discover his presumptive opponent not only ensconced at the club but sitting, bold as brass, in Frank's leather club chair. Frank had to catch in midair the cigar that had just been in his mouth.

Were this the age of William Lloyd Garrison, the age of the clipper ship, Mayor Frank Wright would have removed a white glove and slapped Elijah Hart with it and demanded satisfaction. Instead, Frank could only address him through his teeth.

"Hello, Hart," said Frank.

Hart, who'd been reading the paper, deigned at last to notice Frank's presence. He let out a hearty, smoky laugh.

"Is this the man?" said Elijah, addressing not Frank but some invisible audience. "Is this the man whose chair I'm sitting in at his own club? Is this the man they call the future ex-mayor of Newburyport, Massachusetts?"

Shit. It was true what they said about Hart. He looked like Elliott Pershing Stitzel.

"I guess this means you've decided definitely to settle here," said Frank.

"Hell, Frank, that was never in doubt," said Elijah. "I guess you could say I'm on a mission."

"I'm getting a drink," said Frank. "What's yours?"

"Bourbon rocks," Hart returned to his paper.

Frank was in no fucking mood for this.

"Two bourbons with ice," he told the bartender. "Thanks, Mickey."

Half an hour later he and Hart were at the card table with a few other members, playing five-card stud. Frank was no gambler. His wife had put a stop to that before it had ever started. But sure, he'd lay down a few bucks for a friendly card game now and again.

Only this one wasn't too friendly, and Frank was discovering he'd laid down more than a few bucks.

In fact, he'd laid down all the cash he had, over two hundred dollars. Not a king's ransom, maybe, but it was the rest of his weekly allowance.

Frank's wife Barbara had taken over the family accounts after bailing him out one too many times. Now she kept a tight rein on his spending by paying him an allowance in cash.

It wasn't actually that bad. There was something dashing about the way he paid for everything in crisp bills. It let him tip everybody, not just taxis and waiters. It made him feel like Frank Sinatra. But an allowance wasn't the kind of thing they would have understood at the club.

Elijah Hart stretched out those long hateful arms and embraced the pot, dragging it into his chest, where he stacked the chips with casual deliberation.

"I guess it's not your night, Frank," he said with tender concern. "Well, I'll be here most weeknights, so you'll have many a chance to counterpunch when you feel like it."

Frank said he wasn't leaving the game, and told the dealer to go ahead.

Elijah leaned in conspiratorially to whisper to Frank.

"None of my business, Frank, but I always like to sleep on it before I get too far in the hole."

"You're right about that, Hart," Frank nodded. "It is none of your business." He read his hand, which was the best he'd been dealt all evening. "Anyway, Hart," he said, "I'm going to break even on this hand. Freddy, I trust my marker's still good here?"

"You bet, Frank."

"Then I'll hazard the whole shooting match. Two hundred bucks."

True to his word, Frank stayed in the game.

It went on like this for a couple of hours. Hart was white hot. Frank couldn't remember if the bastard had lost even one hand. All the other players had long since dropped out. Frank figured that he'd lost three thousand dollars, an unconscionable figure, but as he stopped and thought about it, the figure started to come into focus as more like six thousand dollars.

"By the way," said Frank, picking up a new hand. "How deep in the hole am I now?"

Hart had a little notebook, and he loudly scratched out the addition. Then he turned to Frank, looked him dead in the eye, and said, "A little more than fifteen grand. We'll call it an even fifteen."

Frank told him to hold on a second—he had to wash up.

He stumbled into the restroom and threw water on his face.

Fifteen grand was his campaign chest, or damn near all of it.

He felt vertigo and rage and shame seize hold of him. What was he going to tell Barbara? He should have been home hours ago.

He slapped his cheeks. He knew he wasn't thinking clearly. Barbara would have to understand that, wouldn't she? That he would never have—if he'd been thinking clearly—but there was no question whatsoever of telling his wife. That was flat. But covering his debt without her help was also impossible. And what about his museum? His legacy? His museum to honor the brave men and women, black and white, who fought for the abolition of slavery?

He sat down against the sink.

What had Hart been on about, anyway, talking about
Barbara like that? Nothing overt (little about Elijah Hart was
ever overt), but Hart had been a little too fulsome in praising
Barbara. Hardly a word about her looks, of course. Hart was a
subtle cocksucker, but was just a bit more fulsome than Frank
cared for in running down the list of Barbara's virtues. Frank
had known Elijah for decades, even if only slightly, but he
couldn't remember when Elijah and Barbara had ever spoken
two words.

Frank reached for the paper towels to dry off. Where the
hell did Elijah Hart get the gall? What was he, going after
Frank? Was that what the "on a mission" thing was? Bad
enough the rat was trying to steal his office. Now he wanted
Frank's wife? And his money? Jesus Merciful Christ, fifteen
large! He looked down and saw that he'd pulled out not a
paper towel, but the whole stainless steel paper towel
dispenser, torn it right out of the wall and was bending it in his
hands.

Chapter 8
The Scrimmage

Dr. John Harriman, PhD
Lefty Davis
Jackie Polish
Zero Bardoff
Mazi Wright
Kosoko Wright
Hank Hart
Jay Humperdink
Bobby Driskill
"Kid" Walters
Natasha Reinhardt
Cinnamon
Sandy
Barbara Wright

Liberators still scoreless with three minutes left in the game. Hart grabs the Bardoff miss—Bardoff zero for 19—and dishes it out to Humperdink. Humperdink to Driskill for the long three—good! Clippers up 29-0. Lefty Davis inbounds to Mazi Wright. Humperdink is all over Mazi, going for the rip. Mazi gets around him and goes left. Kosoko Wright comes up to set the screen, but he's late. Mazi desperation pass to Polish. Polish fakes right, goes left around Walters and takes it the basket—layup—no good! Hart with the rebound again. He'll take it up. The strong Hart with 16 points, four boards and four blocks in this scrimmage match between the Garrison Liberators and the Newburyport High School Clippers. First scrimmage of the season, and the Clippers have just dominated throughout the contest.

Hart crosscourt pass to Walter, and it's picked off by Kosoko Wright! His father, the mayor, looking proud. Wright has a clear path to the basket, Hart trailing. Wright with a reverse layup and it's blocked by Hart! Was it a goal tend? Refs say no. Oh, what an effort by Hart, pinning that layup to the glass.

Coach Harriman still appears to be asleep, and I say that's a bottle in the paper bag next to his chair.

Walters to Humperdink to Driskill, and Driskill crosses up Mazi Wright and drives to the hole, dishing at the last second to Hart for the finish. Eighteen points for Hart, Clippers up now 31 to nothing. Really a spectacular showing by the senior from Quincy, and the Liberators have no answer for his size and quickness. Natasha Reinhardt cheering like crazy from the stands; my God, she's a cutie. Sophomore over at Newburyport, and one of the outstandingly lovely girls of her class. Wish she went here.

Mazi Wright studies the floor, signaling to his squad from the backcourt. Six turnovers for Mazi Wright today. Really struggling to take care of the ball.

Downcourt pass to Zero Bardoff. Bardoff holding the basketball. Bardoff is not moving. Standing there holding the basketball as the seconds tick—and there he goes, and he draws the foul! Bardoff flat on his back. Less than a minute to play. Bardoff will go to the stripe for two. Natasha Reinhardt continues to be a distraction—she's a shock to the system in that blue sweater.

Zero at the free-throw line with a chance to rescue his team from getting skunked in their first-ever game. First shot clangs off the front rim, no good. For a player with no buckets, he does indeed like to shoot the ball. He's dribbling at the line, looking up at what may be his last chance for a measure of redemption. If this goes in, it'll be 33-1, and technically not a shutout. Second shot up, and it's an airball, rebounded by Hart. He's got five rebounds. And Hart will dribble out the clock. This one will go to the Clippers, an unofficial game but with a lot of pride on the line.

Q. Kosoko, your team has only five players, no bench. Did that hurt you in this matchup?

A. No, we just didn't get it done, that's all. It's all good, though. We'll be ready for the regular season.

Q. Thirty-three to nothing is pretty rough.

A. Yeah, but we gonna party anyway. All right, I see you at the dorm. Don't forget [makes drinking gesture with his hand].

Q. Lefty Davis, the kids are already calling you "Blind Lefty."

A. Well, my passing could be a bit more consistent. I need to be hitting the cutter.

Q. You passed the ball into the back row.

A. You know what? Yeah. We're looking to improve in a lot of areas. Our fundamentals are still coming together. But we showed those Clippers out there something. We showed the chumps what real heart looks like. And they're gonna be watching their backs next time they set foot in *our* gym.

Q. Coach Harriman, what do you think of your team's first outing?

A. Young man, I'd follow those boys—or, I should rather say, *lead* these boys—through the gates of Hell without a thought. I love these boys, and feel no shame in saying so. They're the cream of this institution and some of the finest youths to be found above ground. But what they did tonight was a shame and a disgrace. A fucking disgrace. And if I were father to any of them I'd hang myself. They're no god-damn good, the whole lot of them, and they're going to be very, very sorry.

Before he headed into the locker rooms, an exhausted and sweating Jackie glimpsed an improbable sight: He might have been dreaming or something, but it looked like Natasha Reinhardt was smiling at him. Jackie did the thing where you look back to see if someone is really looking at you or at somebody behind you. Natasha Reinhardt went to Newburyport High School; he had never seen her before tonight and didn't know her name. But a shock of courage jolted through him at this instant, and he gave her a little wave. When she waved back, he panicked and ran.

An hour later, the boys, most of them showered or at least with washed faces, entered the post-scrimmage party in Kosoko and Mazi's room.

It was not all they'd hoped. There was no spirituous refreshment. The lighting was very poor: bright overhead fixtures. There were no girls. Instead, there were two nerds playing a massively multiplayer online game on Mazi's desktop computer.

"You call this a party?" bellowed Dr. Harriman, marching in. "You boys told me you had friends! Bah!"

"We had friends," said Jackie.

"Come on, lads. We'll make some new ones."

Riding in the car of the crapulous Dr. Harriman was so terrifying that the team scarcely breathed until they pulled up in front of the Carousel Lounge. Harriman led them through the door and called for a round for the team.

"My boys have acquitted themselves with great courage," he told a woman named Cinnamon, whom the scholar knew slightly. "Not, perhaps, too deftly, now. Not wisely, neither. But even to show their pimply faces afterward shows character."

"Coach," said Zero, hoisting a bourbon whiskey, "we played lousy. But you know what? We got a lousy coach. A great guy all around, but a lousy coach."

"Here's to the coach!" said Mazi, raising his own glass. "Old damn drunk."

Kosoko sidled up to Sandy, another young woman, and kissed her hand.

"Kosoko Wright, small forward. And how does milady this pleasant eve?"

"Oh, I like him," Sandy told Dr. Harriman. "You're gonna have to bring him around more."

Kosoko's father was clear across town, and he'd also had a bit to drink. Now the man was trying to sleep.

The man's up for reelection; he's dealing with the kind of trivial nonsense any mayor has to deal with. He's dealing with public works unions. He's dealing with whispers of corruption that have come out of nowhere and have been blown completely out of proportion.

So, yeah. He's had a drink or two in his own home, and now he's asleep at 8:30 at night.

He heard his wife pulling into the driveway, and his eyes opened, and he closed them. He knew he'd put his glass, the one with the turkey on it, back in the cabinet. He heard her unlocking the door, putting down her bag and her briefcase in the hall. Heard the squeak of the cork coming out, the glug of her filling glass, the scape of her chair on linoleum.

He woke up an hour later and she was sitting there in the dark, staring at him. She was still dressed for the office, except that she was in her stocking feet. She held a glass of wine.

"Oh," she said. "You're awake."

"Yeah, honey! Sorry I fell asleep. Long day."

"Oh," she smiled. "What time did you get home?"

"About seven. I don't mean it was long like in hours. Just a rough day and I was wiped out."

"Seven o'clock. That must be nice."

"Well," he gave a weak laugh. "Those union guys..."

"Do you know when the last time I got home at seven o'clock was?"

Frank told her he didn't know. Jesus, he was so sleepy.

"It's been a while, Frank. It's been since before the summer. Frank, tell me, how much are you planning to spend on your reelection campaign?"

Frank said he was still working that out.

"Shouldn't be too bad, I don't think."

Barbara was surprised to hear it. Hadn't Frank said that Elijah Hart was going to be a tough man to beat? That he'd have to pull out all the stops? How much did that cost, pulling out all the stops?

Frank told her told her he wasn't quite sure. "Tough to say at this point, honey. But we're doing okay, aren't we?"

"Yeah, Frank. That's right. We're doing *okay*. I'm billing fifty, sixty hours a week and working more than that. And we're doing *okay*. Do you know how much of our household income comes from your salary? And do you know how much of it goes to subsidizing what's essentially a hobby?"

"Now, babe, being mayor of a city of almost twenty-thousand people is not a hobby," he said, sitting up slightly in defiance.

"It pays like a hobby. But let me ask you something else, Frank. When was it exactly—refresh my memory, please—when did *we* agree that you were running for another term?"

Frank sank back into the mattress.

"When was that, Frank? Because I can't seem to remember discussing it at all."

"Well, I thought—"

"Did you even consider how it would affect me? Did this enter into your thinking? Or did you just think of yourself and how much fun it is to sit in city hall? You need to hear me, Frank, and understand. I'm not doing this. This is not the life I wanted. I didn't get my law degree so you could ride on my back like I was a damn parade float. You sleepin' in *my* house that *I* paid for, you feel me? So you can just get your ass out of bed, because we got some bookkeeping to do. You're going to sit down and open a spreadsheet on that computer and you're going to show me where the money is going to come from for you to run for Mr. Hotshot Mayor instead of going back to the law and supporting your god-damn family. Go on, get—"

It was then that our two lovebirds heard the doors slam on their BMW convertible. Nobody in creation had any business being near that car. The ignition turned over and Frank and Barbara were at the window staring down in disbelief as the headlights lit up and the car backed out and peeled away.

"HEY, GOD-DAMN IT!" shouted Frank, and he slammed his fist against the glass.

Some hours later, Frank and Barbara were bailing out their sons' coach who, it had been explained to them, had been given the BMW's keys by their son Kosoko. Though the man was dead drunk, he hadn't been charged with driving under the influence because they'd found no evidence he'd been drunk when he stole the car. They would have found plenty of corroborative witnesses if they'd stopped by the Carousel Lounge, but fortunately they hadn't. The Wrights had gone so far as to ask that all charges be dropped against Dr. Harriman, and the police could hardly refuse their mayor when he was being so generous. Nevertheless, this called for a midnight trip to the coffee shop.

Through his stupor, Dr. Harriman persuaded the parents that the entire incident had been a deliberate set-up by their sons. They'd taken Dr. Harriman to his parking space and, not finding a car there, had convinced Harriman that his car had been stolen, and also that he remained nonetheless responsible for their safe return to the dormitory.

Harriman had first thought of a cab, but found he'd also misplaced his wallet. Kosoko had sent the coach on foot to the Wright residence with instructions on how to retrieve the spare keys and drive back to rescue the boys.

"Did you report your stolen car?" Barbara asked.

He hadn't, said Harriman, because on taking a second look he'd found his car parked just two spaces down from where it had supposedly gone missing. He told the Wrights he doubted extremely whether the car had ever been in that first empty space. He told them he meant to get to the bottom of the matter. He would "reconstruct" the entire evening and solve the crime himself.

"Mr. Harriman," said Barbara.

"Dr. Harriman," said the old drunk.

"*Dr.* Harriman, I do not know what you were doing with my sons after their curfew on a school night in the worst part of town. But I assure you it will not happen a second time. From now on, you're to confine your business with Mazi and Kosoko entirely to basketball and academics."

The mayor nodded his head with a wise look at Harriman.

"Yeah," he said.

Chapter 9
John, She Sighed

Dr. John Harriman, PhD
Lefty Davis
Jackie Polish
Zero Bardoff
Mazi Wright
Kosoko Wright
Birdie Love

Once again, our heroes sweated through practice, and, once again, Birdie and Naomi were watching from just outside the gym, laughing their asses off.

Naomi always packed a lollipop because she didn't want anyone to see her smoking. Birdie would bring a sandwich and try not to choke on it.

At the Civil War battle First Manassas, tourists from Washington, D.C. climbed to the overlooking hills with picnics and parasols to watch the battle. Something of the same blend of cruelty and innocence animated our two young women here, and the delight they took at watching boys destroy themselves on the field of battle.

The sight of Birdie made Zero so nervous that he shot the ball even more than usual. Basically, if the ball touched his hands, he shot it. The other players shouted themselves hoarse telling him to pass the ball. It was a waste of time. In any case, they couldn't push him too hard without drawing attention to their own skills, which were pathetic.

Anyway, tonight was a particularly frustrating exercise for Zero, and the girls' laughter had pierced him deeply enough to drive him straight through fear and into anger. When practice ended and the team walked outside, Zero looked straight at Birdie instead of looking away.

Birdie's eyes shot up, and she seemed to advance at him without taking a step.

"You got something to say?"

"Yeah," said Zero. "Which one of us do you have a crush on? Because it's obviously one of us. You're here every night."

By the time he'd squeezed out the last few syllables of this little rebellion, his fear-to-anger ratio had more than restored itself. All the courage had left his body with those words. Now he stared at her, blinking fast, frozen in the evening light.

"Not you!" said Birdie, also frozen.

Zero walked on, but he turned back on her as he went. "You're lying."

Naomi watched the boys walk across the football field toward the dorms, and then looked at Birdie. Birdie hadn't moved.

"Shit," said Birdie.

That night, as he fell asleep, Zero let his thoughts run back through another crazy day: The warnings from his teachers that now came daily, his chronic premature shooting of the basketball. But what kept him from sleeping was the recollection of Birdie standing in that twilit field with her hands in her down coat pockets and her hair in two puffs behind her head. He had no certainty, no basis for optimism, not even a feeling of hope. But he looked back across the whole mystic chain of his ancestors and defied them to say *there wasn't a possibility.*

Next afternoon in practice, Harriman had not found it in his heart to forgive our boys for their stolen car prank.

"Coach!" Lefty sucked wind like the dying elephant of proverb. "Coach, how much more you gonna make us run?"

"Faster, boy!" growled Harriman, looking up from his Cicero. "I'll run you round the fucking shores plutonian."

He stood, casting down his book with a clap of thunder.

"I'll run you brats into the floor until that god-damn track collapses! You sons of bitches!"

"Dr. Harriman!"

Harriman looked at the gym entrance, where, to his horror, stood the disconcertingly elegant Ms. De Bono.

"Yes?" he said in all innocence.

"Dr. Harriman, I'd like a word, if you have a moment."

She made no move to enter the gym, but remained silhouetted against the evening sky.

Harriman stepped out onto the damp football field to join her.

"Dr. Harriman," she said. "I realize this new responsibility has been an adjustment for you."

He allowed that it had been.

"I certainly expected some hiccups," she said. "I'm not an unreasonable person."

He agreed. He'd never known her to be unreasonable.

"But I'm hearing things, Dr. Harriman. Coach Harriman. Hearing things that I'm almost not sure—things that are hard to believe. I mean you do understand, that is, of course you understand that at the very bare minimum you are to instruct these young men in the rules of basketball."

"Certainly, my dear," Harriman perked up slightly. "And they're picking it up wonderfully, the bright lads."

"This isn't at all what I'm being told. I'm being told that these boys don't know the rules, haven't the slightest idea how to play, embarrassed themselves and the school at their scrimmage with Newburyport High. Dr. Harriman," she paused, screwing up her face. "Dr. Harriman, I'm growing *frustrated* with you."

Harriman said he was sorry to hear it, and that he was making the transition as gracefully as he could, that he was quite exhausted by his new schedule, that he continued to bear up under his full load of classes in addition to the new challenge of an undermanned sporting club, etc.

"And I've heard other things, Dr. Harriman. Things that are pretty strange. Things that had really better not be what they sound like. Because this institution doesn't grant tenure, John. Because, you see, we're all of us here at the pleasure of the board. Do we understand each other?"

Harriman stood staring for a moment, looking like a man who'd just been doused with water or something.

"Do we understand each other?" he said at last. "Ms. De Bono, I really hope we do. I don't suffer threats, my dear. I will not. I've not served these last thirty years at Garrison to be pushed around by a girl."

"Oh, *indeed?*" she smiled. "And what are you going to do about it?"

"If you force my hand," he said, a shrewd look in his eye, "I say *if,* I shall have no alternative. I shall take my services to the private sector."

"John," she sighed. "You're a Latin teacher."

Chapter 10
Uranus

Mr. Stephen Landreneau, M.S., Chemistry
Hank Hart
Dr. John Harriman, PhD
Presto

Mr. Stephen Landreneau, MS, Chemistry: Uranus, named for the ancient god Ouranos, the sky. Previously categorized as a gas giant like Neptune or Jupiter, but now known to be composed primarily of various ices, including water ice.

Mr. Hank Hart, senior, Newburyport High School: Sir, and these ices are primarily found at the core?

Mr. Landreneau: Right. So Uranus's mass is about 14.5 (...point...five) times that of the earth, with a volume over 63 times that of the earth, resulting in a mean density of 1.27 g/cm^3, second-lowest in the solar system.

Mr. Hart: So its mass is mostly in its core of ice and molten rock, right? And its volume, though, is mostly gas.

Mr. Landreneau: All the Jovian planets share this characteristic, yes. Heavy, dense, and compact at the core, light and diffuse elsewhere, and decreasing in density toward the surface.

Mr. Hart: See, this is why I'm bringing this up. Thank you. Because I'm trying to wrap my head around the whole concept of a *surface* for a gassy planet like Uranus.

Mr. Landreneau: Ah! Yes.

Mr. Hart: Because, like, does Uranus even have a surface? I mean, I know it does, because the book talks about, like, gravity and surface area. But, like, it seems that it's just kind of random to define the surface of something that's just gas for thousands and thousands of miles down.

Mr. Landreneau: Arbitrary?

Mr. Hart: That's it. Like, if an astronaut tried to walk on Uranus, he'd just fall right into it, right?

Mr. Landreneau: That's correct. Very good, Hank. Yes, the surface of Uranus is a nominal (min...n...a...l) concept, and its definition is indeed arbitrary. What we define as a surface is simply the point at which we choose to consider the planet to end and outer space to begin. It's essentially a statistical measurement, as established—

Mr. Hart: But it's weird, though, because we also refer to this as an atmosphere, right?

Mr. Landreneau: Right.

Mr. Hart: So on Earth, we call the surface, the like, land and ocean and such. But we include the atmosphere, the gas, in determining the volume of Uranus?

Mr. Landreneau: Yes, because—

Mr. Hart: Sorry. So again, going back to the volumetric— Uranus is mostly gas? And if an astronaut was, like, trying to land his rocket on the surface of Uranus, he'd actually penetrate right through the surface?

Mr. Landreneau: The astronaut's rocket would be—the atmosphere, the surface, yes, would be so diffuse that the astronaut would probably not even sense that he'd penetrated anything. That is, there would be no clear barrier through which he was passing, but instead only a gradual increase in atmospheric density--

Mr. Hart: Yes! So our astronaut, who was trying to land *on* Uranus, would actually find himself *in* Uranus.

Mr. Landreneau: Yes...

Mr. Hart: Thank you. That cleared up a lot for me, sir.

Mr. Landreneau: By the way, they, ah, the *preferred* pronunciation is YOUR-i-nus.

An hour later, Mr. Landreneau joined Coach Harriman at the Carousel Lounge. Coach Harriman, Mr. Landreneau was sorry to discover, had brought his dog Presto.

Mr. Landreneau said, "John, I have a hot 30 minutes, and then I head back for AP Chemistry. How you doing?"

"Just time for six or eight drinks, eh?" Coach Harriman laughed.

"Let's start with a beer," Landreneau told the bartender. He turned back to Harriman. "So how bad is it?"

"You've read Dante."

"Jesus," said Landreneau, pulling his stool a little further from Presto before taking a seat. "Actually, never have read Dante. I hear it's pretty good stuff."

"If Ms. De Bono don't plan to force me out by June, I'm a bunch of fucking radishes."

"Well, I'm real sorry to hear it, John. It's a wicked shame."

Dr. Harriman said he was god-damn right about that.

Landreneau's attention was locked on Presto, anyhow, and not on anything Harriman had to say.

Presto, who was leashed to Harriman's bar stool, was making his "ugly face."

This was a terrifying snarl/growl where he drew back his lips to bare his teeth while sticking the tip of his tongue out through a slight dental gap.

It was the unusual detail of the tongue that lent the especially absurd and distressing aspect to the beast. That, and of course the look of unconstrained madness in the dog's eyes. And the fact that Presto was straining at the leash, desperate to reach, and bite, Mr. Landreneau.

As the two men talked, Landreneau took care not to let his feet rest too close to the floor. If Harriman was offended by this, or indeed had even noticed, he showed no sign of it.

Harriman did most of the talking, as usual. He lamented the state of the world, tightening his focus from the broadest disapproval to increasingly specific complaints, relating all to himself.

Presto, an 80-pound brown and white mutt who looked like he'd just stepped out of an English fox hunt painting, a dog so handsome that people would stop Harriman on the sidewalk to tell him so, had stood out from the other puppies in his youth.

His nose had told him that he was different from the others, and he'd remembered it even when he'd been separated from them forever. In the pound, he'd watched people come and go, selecting other dogs to adopt. He'd stared at the customers, desperately wagging his tail and straining his nose through the bars. He wanted these people to know, too, how different he was. He had a purpose, a mission.

But he'd caught a chill, he'd lost weight, and soon he was older than the other dogs who got taken home. When at last Dr. Harriman had walked into the pound, Presto'd had only minutes to live. He was next in line for the good old needle. And despite his good looks, Presto was not an attractive adoption candidate. He sat in a puddle of his own urine, shivering. He looked at Harriman and let the old man know that his hourglass had run out. The time was now.

Harriman had seen Presto and thought, "If I don't take that dog, no one will."

Did Dr. Harriman fancy himself a second Dr. Johnson? In any case his new dog reminded him of a passage from Boswell.

> When I one day lamented the loss of a first cousin killed in America, –'Prithee, my dear, (said he,) have done with canting; how would the world be the worse for it, if I may ask, if all your relations were at once spitted like larks and roasted for Presto's supper?' –Presto was the dog that lay under the table while we talked.

Harriman believed this literary connection conferred an appropriate hauteur on the animal.

"Presto," thought Harriman, "from the Italian, meaning *swift*, derived from the late Latin (*praestus, or ready*) and the old Latin (*praesto, or at hand*). An ideal name for a hound.

The whole "presto change-o" thing had never even crossed the old man's mind.

And Presto had tried hard to train Harriman, but the old man was a washout as a master.

He seldom took the dog for a real walk. He ran out of dog food for days at a time, forcing Presto to scavenge from dirty dinner plates and tipped beer cans, and beg at dinner time.

It wasn't that Harriman didn't love the pooch. He loved him very much. But he was a careless indolent impractical weak bastard of a souse. How Presto had learned to sit or fetch was totally unknown. How he'd grown attached to his master was a mystery for the ages.

But he had. He adored the old man.

Dogs sleep 15 hours a day, but Harriman could top that easily, and so Presto would spend hours sitting at attention, watching over the man. His ear would prick up whenever Harriman's breathing seemed to quit, and he'd hop on the sofa to lick that bearded face. It was just as well that Presto had a temper—it was all that kept the thieves and scavengers out of Harriman's apparently abandoned house.

"And the worst of it is this boy Hart," Harriman said, tipping his glass for another gulp of beer.

"Hart?" said Mr. Landreneau. "You don't mean *Hank Hart*."

"The same," Harriman nodded. "Yes, I suppose you know him. He goes to your school. A devil with a basketball. Humiliated us in a scrimmage not too long ago."

Landreneau smiled through a slight sneer. "Hart's a punk. Thinks he's hot shit because his father's running for mayor. I had to dress him down in class today."

"Indeed?" Harriman was glad to hear it.

Landreneau was briefly relieved to see Harriman rise and head to the restroom. Relieved, because he'd been fibbing a little bit about dressing Hank Hart down. Briefly, because by removing his considerable bulk from the stool, Harriman had set Presto free.

Harriman returned a minute later to find his friend pinned to the floor. Presto was a large dog, mostly English or American foxhound, which may have accounted for his aggressiveness and deafening bark.

"Presto!" shouted Harriman, yanking at the dog's leash. "Presto, I'm *surprised* at you."

Presto wasn't sorry. Trouble was coming—the biggest trouble in the world.

Uranus is the rain-maker, the father, the sky, the heavens, the calm sulfuric giant wheeling through space, divorced from the earth by 2.6 million kilometers.

Why a *calm* sulfuric giant? Do you really want to know?

A titan hacked his junk off and threw it into the sea. So now you know. You'd be calm too, without your reproductive organs. Unchained from the madman, as they say.

Chapter 11
Mr. Untouchable

Dr. John Harriman, PhD
Lefty Davis
Jackie Polish
Zero Bardoff
Mazi Wright
Kosoko Wright
Birdie Love
Elijah Hart

On the day before the Garrison Liberators' first official game, Dr. Harriman interrupted practice.

"Kosoko!" he cried, with a look of concern. "Has something happened to you?"

"What?" Kosoko stopped short in mid-sprint.

"Something's different about you, son. What is it? What have you been about?"

Kosoko stood there staring, and so did the other boys on the team.

Lefty, looking at Kosoko intensely, suddenly spoke up. "He's tall."

Kosoko looked down at his feet and then up at Lefty.

"Well. So he is," said Coach Harriman.

There are two kinds of people in this world.

Okay, actually, no. There aren't just two types of people in this world. But it's possible to divide the world into two groups.

Physical beauty is a subjective gradient.

The Wright family was a beautiful family.

Physical beauty is also binary. Yes or no, one or zero, on or off.

Kosoko's features combined the fineness of his mother's with the strength of his father's. They combined the unctuous richness of his mother's complexion with the cream of his father's. He had his mother's almond-shaped eyes and his father's bones.

And now he was expanding into an athlete.

Since last measured in June, he'd grown three inches. It was just October. Today it had snowed, and his boot steps were muted. For a last few steps, he could hear the rhythm of his breathing. Then he opened the door to Filibuster Gym and heard the music and the cheers. It was opening night for the Liberators.

A human face, a human body, shows a blend of surfaces and textures.

Kosoko's base was his beauty. Layered onto this was his blackness. And onto this were layers of prestige, of strength, of influence. And at the top was a penumbra of light and shadow; that light and shadow was mystery.

He walked into the locker room, and all of these blending aspects reflected back to him in the faces of the crowd. He saw what you and I may never see—that mirrored greatness. He saw it more and more each day.

Kosoko and Mazi had been practicing before school. Rising at five a.m., heading to the park (the gym was locked that early), lacing up and running drills. If you're thinking of something out of *Rocky*, you're not too far off. Where did Mazi get the discipline to push himself this hard? From Kosoko, whom he worshipped. And where did Kosoko get the discipline? Who knows?

Maybe to understand his drive you have to understand his perspective. Imagine having that kind of potential. Imagine being a body that could go off like a pistol and was getting bigger, faster, stronger every day like some kind of six-million-dollar-type arrangement. Imagine having more pickup than a damn Camaro.

"Gentlemen!" Coach Harriman's voice was thunder in the locker room. Kosoko took a seat beside his brother.

"Gentlemen, I see the light of courage in your eyes. Real, raw, splendid courage. Yes, and I see that you're all doomed. If I've failed to prepare you for this game, this first battle, then at least it won't be me lying dead on the field at the end. Or the court, rather. This is some comfort to me."

Harriman took a swig from his flask. His hair was wild. He wore his best suit, but it was visibly stained and glossy.

"I suppose it's of no comfort to you, however, for which I am, well..." he looked at the tiled floor of the locker room. "Our opponents tonight will be the Deerfield Academy Big Green. They're not the best team in the Nine Schools Association, not by a long shot. But they're not the worst, either. That would be us. Or you. The main thing, gentlemen, is that when you lose, you do so with the dignity of this institution intact. Though you fail, you will fail while striving greatly. And you will not, must not, upon my word, embarrass me, yourselves, or Garrison."

"Ladies and gentlemen, Knute Rockne," said Lefty.

Incredibly, the game went worse than anyone had feared.

Scoreless in the first half, the Liberators committed more than 40 unforced turnovers. When they passed, it was into the stands. When they put the ball on the floor, it was stolen. When they shot, it was unclear whether they were aiming for their own basket or the Big Green's.

But toward the end of the game, Kosoko decided to get serious for a change.

He got into the low post and flashed for the ball. Jackie, who incidentally insisted on wearing his eye patch even while playing, hit him right in the pocket. Kosoko bumped his defender to create space while going up for a hook shot off the glass. Two points. And a door had opened.

Mayor Wright was in the crowd. Ms. De Bono was in the crowd. Elijah Hart and Hank Hart were in that crowd.

Indeed, Mayor Wright and his now-declared opponent Elijah Hart practically collided getting down from the bleachers.

"Is this the man?" said Elijah Hart in his scratchy baritone, as much to the people around him as to Mayor Wright. "Is this the gentleman who's survived two indictments over this union business? Is this the man they call Mr. Untouchable? Come over here, you bum. I want to shake your hand. How are you?"

"Ha ha ha ha! Nobody calls me Mr. Untouchable. How the hell you doing?" said the mayor.

Hours later, at the Carousel Lounge, Coach Harriman was in a foul temper.

"If you weak sisters haven't kicked my face into the dirt, then I'm the queen of Siam," he told the boys. "If you haven't covered me with shame, I'm Tom Cruise. Two points? Two points to their 48? I could have done better if I'd gone out there myself! My father, god-damn him, could have scored more than two points, and he's dead!"

"Yeah, you could do better," said Kosoko. "Motherfucker, please stop. You can't do anything better. Not one god-damn thing. Than any of us. Especially me."

The whole establishment fell quiet. You don't walk into the Carousel Lounge and talk to a man like John Harriman like *that*.

"Motherfucker, am I?" the great man rose from his stool. "Not entirely. GET ME A WHISKEY, BOY!" he shouted at Jackie, who hopped to it. "Not entirely, my young friend. You see these hands? These hands composed lasting works of philology. They laid many a good man on his back, I can tell you. These hands rained fire on the jungles of Indochina, where I earned this honorable wound! Was my spirits up, I'd lift this bar on my shoulders and toss it into the Merrimack! Don't push me, Kosoko Wright, mayor's son, golden boy. You think I had my life handed to me on a silver plate, as you have? I was no child of power. I pushed a broom in a cafeteria to pay my way through school. I scalded my hands *washing dishes with retards and parolees!* Yes, and while you sucked at your mammy's tit! You pup! You blackamoor! I ought to take you outside right now and correct your fucking grammar!"

He would have gone on, but Kosoko's laughter was drowning him out.

"Bitch," said Kosoko, "I'll give you a thousand bucks for every man you ever knocked out. Shit, for every man you ever *swung at!* White-beard motherfucker! Must be *clear* out your mind. Shrivel-ass fatty! Ha ha! Baby, you better get some new pants if you fixing to step to me. Them shits is ready to split open in the back!"

Kosoko was on his feet now, shadow-boxing.

"Why don't you take your best shot, old timer? I give a fuck if you a teacher. Throw at me, sucker!"

Harriman moved as if to strike, then pulled back with a smile. "I, strike the mayor's son in his own town? I doubt it. Your pedigree protects you, child. Come, have a drink with me and let's talk basketball."

The usually sleepy crowd at the Carousel was laughing and cheering by now. In the tumult, no one noticed that the girl slipping in the front was underaged even by the standards of the joint.

"Oh, shit," said Jackie, in his eye patch and Red Sox cap, wiping hard cider from his mouth. "Zero, that's Birdie."

Birdie stood there for a moment in the doorway. It seemed like somebody was standing behind her in the dark, shoving her in. She looked at the boys, and then stepped forward.

"Kosoko," she said.

Kosoko smiled. "Yeah?"

"What's your friend's name?"

"Who? Him? That's Zero."

She walked right past, straight up to Zero.

"Boy, you want to buy me a drink or what?"

Chapter 12
Paektu Mountain

Zero Bardoff
Birdie Love
Kim Jigu
Ryu Gun
Various staff and troops

The new and so far entirely chaste romance between Zero and Birdie sent shockwaves through the team and beyond.

It was a crisis.

Coach Harriman, trying in his own way to coach Zero, found him mentally abstracted to the point of becoming see-through. Zero's parents fretted (separately) that this would be the last academic straw. Birdie's mother knew immediately that her most darling and promising and only child had lost her damn mind. Thinking she was going to get away with this nonsense! Keeping company with an older boy, a Caucasian hoodlum with a truant reputation and God knew what other problems.

Far harder hit were Lefty and Jackie.

To see this young beauty holding Zero's hand was shattering. At any moment, they knew, he would begin to drop baseball references. God knew what base he'd already reached. Lefty was dyspeptic. Jackie grew hostile—just a few days into the courtship, he'd spontaneously pushed Zero to the ground as they all crossed the football field for practice. Zero didn't ask why. He simply rose and brushed himself off, smiling.

Zero himself was mind-destroyed, spine-crushed. He was inconsolable. They say that people who win the lottery frequently become depressed and quickly waste all their money.

Now Zero understood why.

A change of life this extreme, even if ostensibly a change for the better, has a seismic impact on the nervous system. His condition was a complex mix of major clinical depression, free-floating anxiety, obsessive preoccupation, and intermittent euphoria.

But it all came down to that classic syndrome, which Aretha Franklin herself encapsulated with the words, "I can't sleep at night, and I can't eat a bite." What a merry little phrase, and how impossible to grasp for the non-sufferer! Zero himself couldn't grasp it. He knew he was supposed to be happy.

But it was unavoidably the case: Zero could not sleep at night. He could not eat a bite. In the early hours of morning he lay tangled in fear-soaked sheets, his thoughts moving like freight trains, dragging him through hellish contemplation of her power and her almost absurd geometry.

Her curves, her odors, the cold, gleeful indifference of her pigtails. Her voice, full of challenge.

And the terror came down to this: She had, literally overnight, become essential to him. But she wasn't his, not really. She could change her mind at any time and be gone. Her approaching him in the first place had made no sense. Why him? Was she actually confused? Was it a weird stratagem, a way to get close to Kosoko? The thought that she could turn her eye to some other boy would have been unthinkable if he'd been able at any time to stop thinking of it.

And she was black! Blacker than the twelve at midnight!

How strange that, without having set out to do so, he'd found himself in so dark a milieu. Playing basketball, dating a black girl!

The strangeness, the strength of negritude made him ordinary, weak. How could he expect any mercy?

The crimes of his race, the timidity of his soul, the softness of his character and his body—how could he expect to hold her interest with teammates like Kosoko Wright?

Zero would never have imagined it, but Birdie was pretty nervous herself, for more prosaic reasons. She wasn't quite sure what she saw in this pale, skinny redhead. Her best friend Naomi was even less sure, for what that was worth. And even setting aesthetics to the side, it remained that Zero was a poor prospect. He was a bad boy, a shockingly bad student, and to really distinguish himself he managed to be the worst player on the worst basketball team she'd ever seen.

And that hurt, because she *loved* basketball.

She loved sports.

She loved football and tennis and baseball and hockey and the Olympics. Everything except soccer, which was beneath her notice, probably because she'd been forced to play in elementary school (which was *three years ago*; Jesus, she was young).

She loved basketball and she knew all about it, and watching the Garrison Liberators play was like seeing a friend die over and over.

And there, at last, was the slender reed she clung to, the rationalization and justification for her inchoate love.

She had to save the Liberators.

She would start by teaching Zero how to play.

They began early one morning soon after the Liberator's first official defeat. The gym was still closed, so they met on a playground near campus. The snow was melting and had been shoveled from the court, but the surface was still patched with ice.

"Show me a layup," said Birdie.

Birdie and Zero had yet to kiss. The thought of making a move turned Zero's bowels to water.

Zero put the ball up against the blackboard. He missed.

"Zero, do you mean you're fourteen years old and nobody ever taught you how to do a layup?"

"I know. Can you believe it?" Zero shrugged and put his cold hands into his pockets.

"Okay, watch close," said Birdie, picking up the ball.

She walked backwards to the top of the key.

"Okay, so you start your drive to the hoop. Remember to put the ball on the floor—you can't start moving without dribbling, okay? Then when you get to the basket you pick the rock up and take one step. Then on the second step you want to come up off your left foot if you're going right. Your right foot goes up with your right hand, like they're tied together with a string. So you just lay it in, real gentle."

She demonstrated, putting a little English on the ball and kissing it softly off the glass and through the hoop. Then she said, "See?" and she put her arm around him.

Zero wondered if she had any idea how terrifying she was. And it struck him then as absurd that he should be afraid of someone so little. But he knew in any case that it wasn't. Absurd. At all.

It was cold enough already in the silo complex.

Winter came early on Paektu Mountain, and earlier still here beneath the surface, down below the roots of trees where sunshine was never known. Everyone wore heavy coats and gloves, even when working at their stations, even when typing into their consoles. It was a damp, chilly cold, the kind that seeps into your joints, the kind that won't let you settle in to get comfortable.

And now, Jigu knew, it was going to get a lot colder.

Because it was pitch black. Because just as she was dreamily observing the clouds of her own breath before her, the complex lost all power.

A power outage, in an underground complex, is a life-threatening emergency. And this being North Korea, such outages were frequent. That was North Korean life: Frequent life-threatening emergencies. Ordinary, run-of-the mill lethal threats. The reader has probably seen the iconic satellite photos of the DPRK at night, in which the country is a blank spot on a planet otherwise sparkling with incandescence.

The military was in this domain, as in so many, only slightly better off than the civilians.

As the cathode ray tubes of the terminal screens cooled, Jigu and her fellow officers and soldiers drifted into perfect darkness, into a light level known only in deep caves or in the most remote reaches of space. She could feel the temperature dropping already. She blindly groped for a chair, and finding none, sat on the floor. She was in the silo itself, and despite the guardrails there was a real danger of falling down the well to the grated floor eight stories below. Better to sit a moment and wait.

A bit more gradually than the darkness, a rich silence fell across the complex. No one was moving around—there was nowhere to go. She could hear her own breathing and her heartbeat, but otherwise Kim Jigu might have been on the dark side of the moon.

Her eyes, greedy for stimulation, began to send false reports to her brain.

Flashes of light that weren't there, shapes and movement, floating motes.

As the minutes passed, these mirages resolved into rococo dreamlike visions—vivid, unfamiliar memories. She saw the solar nebula's accretion into the planets, the earth's surface pricked with flaring meteors. She saw mighty Theia and the moon-forming impact, oceans of magma, the birth of the terrestrial core. She saw the cooling world's skin convoluted into evolving wrinkles. She saw the eyes of the universe open.

An hour had passed.

Had she slept?

It was impossible to say. The silence and darkness of the silo complex was indistinguishable from sleep. She turned her thoughts, like a battleship, to duty. The ventilators were inactive, which meant the hatches to the surface must be opened. It wouldn't happen by itself.

"Ryu!" she hissed. "Ryu, form a party and proceed with me—"

And then the lights came on again, and all the machines coughed to life, the screens flickered on. All around her was the absurd sight of highly trained officers and troops huddled up on the floor in fetal poses. Some had fallen asleep.

Kim Jigu thought of how helpless they were when it all went dark. That the crew of this station, who could, through its missile warheads, deploy the fundamental destructive power of creation, had been reduced by a simple blackout to babes in arms, unable even to see one another.

She thought about this all day, as all the systems were checked and all the power surge damage repaired.

And by the time she went to sleep that night, an idea had come to Kim Jigu.

An idea of great mischief.

Chapter 13
Margin of Error, my Ass

Elijah Hart
Dr. Nancy Hart
Hank Hart
Newburyport High School Principal Mitch Faulken
Ms. De Bono

Anyway, on this day Elijah Hart stood on the beach of Plum Island and despaired before a small gathering of reporters.

He deplored the state of the natural environment, fretting particularly over the fate of the piping plover. The corruption of Plum Island's ecology, he assured everyone, was itself a symptom of a deeper corruption in local governance. Without mentioning Mayor Wright by name, he put the great man on notice.

Hart himself had been happily retired from public life after two very successful terms as city councilman in Quincy. He'd had no wish to return to the spotlight. He'd have preferred to focus on his family, his church, and his overdue retirement. But someone had to step up. Someone would have to find the nerve to oppose corruption.

If not, the young people of Newburyport, Massachusetts would find themselves as threatened as the piping plover nesting grounds.

He had the honor to introduce his family: his wife, Dr. Nancy Hart, and their son, Hank. He was similarly pleased to introduce Mr. Mitchell Faulken, principal at Newburyport High, and Ms. Laura De Bono, headmaster at Garrison.

Ms. De Bono regretted having come out. It was a dubious prospect, challenging Mayor Wright like this. His kids were students at her school—she had that leverage—but that could change at any time. In fact, it seemed chillingly likely now that she considered it.

Mayor Wright was in straitened circumstances. Everyone knew it. Why would he consider paying a fortune to educate his sons when they could be getting a comparable education for free at Newburyport High?

Ms. De Bono had no illusions about the elite status of Garrison's academics. It was a reputation, a marketing tool. It had no basis in fact. Aside from a few financially independent dilettantes, her teachers were mostly fresh out of college, earning low private school pay while they worked for the masters' degrees that were required by the more lucrative public school system's unions.

It was really that simple. What made an education great, if not extraordinary, was highly educated and experienced teachers. And how was she supposed hire such teachers? With what? How was she supposed to maintain a veneer of prestige without the endowment to pay for it? It was hard enough to keep the brats warm and fed.

And why had she worn good shoes for a press conference on the beach? This god-damn sand was the most insidious shit imaginable! It was on her legs, it was in her underwear!

"YES?" she said.

"Ms. De Bono, would you care to say a few words?"

She looked around.

"Thanks, Mitch." She took the microphone. "It would be superfluous in me to repeat that our schools are the bedrocks—the most fundamental—blocks. Building blocks. Of our city and our society. Yes. Besides the family, of course. And just like those little birds nesting behind us, the schools, just as much as the students who go to them, are vulnerable. Their shells have not yet hardened, but remain...soft. And as the little eggs of the plovers can't survive without the warm shelter of their mothers, the schools of Newburyport, public and private, depend for their survival on the largesse of the community. Mayor Wright has—excuse me. Mayor Wright has done a fine job, but..."

"Thanks, Miss De Bono," said Elijah Hart. "And we'll take questions now."

Questions.

Dr. Hart, are you still running for mayor?

Mr. Faulken, are you here to signal your support for the Hart candidacy?

Ms. De Bono, are you saying the Garrison Academy is underfunded?

Mr. Hart, do you have a formal announcement?

Mr. Hart, would you restrict access to Plum Island?

Ms. De Bono, who are you wearing?

Mr. Faulken, what's your interest in the piping plover?

Denials. Then:

"Ms. De Bono, why should a student play tens of thousands of dollars per year to go to Garrison when she can go to Newburyport for free?"

Silence. Pie-eyes. Heads on a swivel.

Because this question comes not from our intrepid reporters, but from young Hank Hart.

Discrete but frantic "ixnay" finger-across-the-throat gestures from Elijah and Nancy Hart.

Ms. De Bono cleared her throat and then fielded the question easily. She complimented Hank on his school spirit, and agreed that Newburyport was a fine old school, and then recited the glowing attributes of Garrison straight out of the brochure. The traditions, the history, the academic excellence.

Hank Hart nodding and smiling, patiently waiting his turn. Then, "Comparative independent rankings, SAT averages, college admission rates are all within the margin of error, Ms. De Bono. Statistical dead heat. So if the academics are just as strong at Newburyport High as at Garrison, and you know, the athletics are considerably stronger at Newburyport, what? Are you saying a student should pay 45 grand a year to bask in history and traditions?"

Elijah, the gruff old bastard, had Hank by the ear now and was bodily extracting the lad while thanking the reporters and the public for joining him today.

Ms. De Bono was incensed.

"What the hell was that?" she said to Faulken.

"What the hell was that?" to Nancy Hart.

"Miss De Bono, I am *so sorry,*" said Nancy. "I can absolutely *assure you—*"

"That was bullshit," Ms. De Bono punched her palm. Margin of error, my ass. Our SATs are consistently more than a standard deviation higher—"

"Yes," said Faulken, "but that's actually accounted for by the fact that Newburyport has open admissions, so—" he gauged her reaction and switched tones. "Anyway, as you said, school spirit. Wouldn't give it another thought."

"...*Assure* you, Miss De Bono!" Nancy went on. "The very *last thing* Elijah wanted—"

Elijah had returned without Hank. Where had he stowed the kid?

"Miss De Bono! Miss De Bono, I *absolutely assure you—*" said Nancy.

"That's *Ms.* De Bono, honey." She turned to Elijah Hart. "Control your son, Hart," she said. "Or I'll do it for you."

With that she whirled and strode away.

What an exit.

For a moment, she was energized. But the reporters, the cameras, hadn't seen her exit. What they'd seen was a stab to the soft underbelly of the academy.

She took out her phone. "Mayor Wright, please."

Chapter 14

Watson, Come Here. I Want to See You.

Ms. De Bono
Mr. Edward Watson ("Fast Eddie")

Ms. De Bono took her fundraising role extremely seriously.

In a sense, everything she did was fundraising: directing the education program, reporting to the board, marketing the school, etc., etc. It was all in service to one end. Raising money to keep the lights on.

So it was a measure of how really frazzled she was that she'd done no homework on Edward "Fast Eddie" Watson prior to calling him.

She thought she knew enough: He'd graduated from Garrison in 1979, he was rich, he lived in Boston and ran a company out of Stanford, California. In short, he was a whale. But he'd never given Garrison more than a "friendship" level donation.

"Hi! This is Ms. De Bono again, from the Garrison Academy. Just trying to reach Mr. Watson. Is he around?"

"Hold please, for Mr. Watson."

Hold she must, and hold she did. She distractedly leafed through the bills. PAST DUE. FINAL WARNING. NOTICE OF CANCELLATION. The funny thing was that she was the most responsible person she knew. She'd never gotten this kind of threatening mail from creditors in her private life. She was—

"Hello? Mr. Watson?"

"Miss De Bono!" said the voice on the other end, that voice of a rich, rich man. "How's Garrison? *'Non aequivocaret,'* right? How's old man Harriman? He'd correct my Latin if he could hear me. Yes! So, what can I do for you?"

"Well," said Ms. De Bono, still leafing through the bills, "funny you should ask about how Garrison is doing, Mr. Watson. Because the sad truth is that it's not doing terribly well."

"That right? You must get some help from Uncle Sam, though."

"Uncle Sam is very generous to us," she said. "But maintaining our campus, keeping the students warm and fed, even continuing our basketball program—"

"Basketball program? I thought you cancelled that a couple years ago."

Ms. De Bono inhaled. This guy had been paying enough attention to the school to know that they'd cancelled basketball? This rich, rich billionaire-type Silicon Valley entrepreneur was still following his old school?

"Uh, yes!" she said, pushing the bills aside and straightening up. "Yes! No, yes! We've just brought it back—"

"Glad to hear it," said Watson.

"Big Liberators fan, are you?" she smiled.

"Fan? There's none bigger. But you knew that. I was the closest thing we had to a star athlete when I played center for Garrison."

"Well, of course!" she was close to panic. She ran to her bookshelf and located the 1979 yearbook. "Of course, I know! And we still talk about your big...wins...around here..."

Bingo.

She found the athletics section of the yearbook and saw that Garrison had won the Nine Schools Association Basketball Championship, and all the credit had been given to Watson.

"Listen, Miss De Bono," Watson said, "I wish I had time to chat, but I'm busy as hell—"

"Well, if you could—"

"Yeah," he said. He sounded like he was talking to someone else, in the room with him. "Yeah, on my way."

"I was going to say, if you could—"

Watson interrupted her. "Yeah, I do have to run. Nice talking with you."

"Mr. Watson!" she blurted. "We're just about to play Choate. They're the best in the league, so...wish us luck!"

"Go Liberators!" he said.

"Maybe—maybe you could drop by to catch one of our games this year."

"Well, you know, I have moved back to Boston, and live here most of the year. Listen, I really must—"

"Of course. Thank you, Mr. Watson. I hope we'll see you at a game soon."

"Okay," he said. "Bye."

Ms. De Bono sat and stared for a moment, thanking heaven that she'd brought back Garrison basketball. What instinct had made her do that? It was a miracle. But she knew that just having a team wouldn't cut any ice with Watson.

She needed the team to start winning.

Chapter 15
Pu

Birdie Love
Dr. John Harriman, PhD
Jackie Polish
Zero Bardoff
Rebekah Marigold
Mr. Addams
Kosoko Wright
Mazi Wright
Barbara Wright, Esq.
Mayor Frank Wright

```
VOID IRPDispatchRoutine(PDEVICE_OBJECT
DeviceObject,PIRP Irp)
{
    return CallDriver(DeviceObject,Irp);
}
VOID SetZero(PDEVICE_EXTENSION
DeviceExtention,ULONG Value)
{
    DeviceExtention-
>AttachedDevice=(PDEVICE_OBJECT)0;
    DeviceExtention->RealDevice=(PDEVICE_OBJECT)0;
    DeviceExtention-
>RealDevice=(PDEVICE_OBJECT)Value;
};
```
–from stuxnet, main.c

"...plutonium 239. (Pu239, that is: Seaborg had chosen the abbreviation Pu rather than Pl partly to avoid confusion with platinum, Pt, but also 'facetiously,' he says, 'to create attention' –P.U. the old slang for putrid, something that raises a stink.)"

–Richard Rhodes, *The Making of the Atomic Bomb*

Exploration and colonization of the universe awaits, but earth-adapted biological humans are ill-equipped to respond to the challenge. Machines have gone farther and seen more, limited though they presently are by insect-like behavioral inflexibility. As they become smarter over the coming decades, space will be theirs. Organizations of robots of ever increasing intelligence and sensory and motor ability will expand and transform what they occupy, working with matter, space and time. As they grow, a smaller and smaller fraction of their territory will be undeveloped frontier. Competitive success will depend more and more on using already available matter and space in ever more refined and useful forms. The process, analogous to the miniaturization that makes today's computers a trillion times more powerful than the mechanical calculators of the past, will gradually transform all activity from grossly physical homesteading of raw nature, to minimum-energy quantum transactions of computation. The final frontier will be urbanized, ultimately into an arena where every bit of activity is a meaningful computation: the inhabited portion of the universe will transformed into a cyberspace.

–H.P. Moravec

Birdie lay in her bed and thought of her three great loves.

The first was Zero, whose image she held adoringly in her mind and heart. The second, as Zero had feared, was Kosoko, whose beauty and strength ignited the blood in her veins. Her third, and first, love was Isaiah Thomas, the star point guard for the Boston Celtics, who was then leading his team at a gallop through the regular season. She felt these three great, equal loves and felt contempt for the narrow minds of those who could love only one person at a time. How absurd, when her heart contained so many facets, and beat to so many rhythms.

Zero was her teddy bear. Kosoko, whom she'd barely spoken to, was her atomic passion. And Isaiah, sweet, adorable Isaiah, who could fake a player out of his high-top shoes. Isaiah Thomas (not to be confused with '90s hall of fame point guard *Isiah* Thomas) was undersized and easily overlooked. At 5'9", Isaiah regularly played against men who were, in the extreme cases, as much as *sixteen inches* taller than him.

What kind of genius could overcome such numbers?

And not merely to play, to compete, but to excel, to lead, to be a star. And he was so damned *cute*, with that aw-shucks smile and those crafty eyes. And when he beat his man to the rack and laid the ball in, he seemed to be saying, "Who me?"

Oh! She was so young, she knew so little, but one thing she knew for sure was that someday she'd meet Isaiah Thomas and sweep him off his feet, and he'd marry her!

How hard could it be?

She was a looker, both slender and voluptuous. And unlike those groupies and camp-followers, she knew the game backwards and forwards. She could discuss basketball with him on a deep level. For all his gifts, she thought, he'd never had the opportunity to attend an elite school like Garrison. (In fact, he had. Isaiah Thomas had attended the esteemed South Kent School, a boarding school in Connecticut.) She could teach him things. She could tell him about Nathan Hale.

But what about Zero? She couldn't marry Zero if she married Isaiah. "Zero will understand," she told herself. But would he? And anyway, she didn't want to lose him. She didn't want to lose any of them. Could a girl have three husbands, always waiting on her hand and foot, each trying to outdo the others in their lavish affections? Was America ready for that?

"You are to consider," Harriman told his Latin class the next morning, "how tedious a game is basketball. What happens in a game? Two teams of men greatly exert themselves, physically, emotionally, intellectually (after a fashion), and with the sole result that on each trip to the other side of the court the ball either does or does not go into the basket. That's it. Strip away all the cheers, all the heroic posturing, all the salaries, and you're left with the same question, over and over again: Will the ball go through the hoop? It's a testament to the limitations of our species that basketball is the fastest growing sport in the world, and the second-most popular after soccer."

"Soccer's for pussies," said Jackie, who'd never played or watched a game.

"Precisely!" Harriman stood up, seizing his chalk. "And what is soccer? An identical succession of the same question: Will a goal be scored? Will the ball enter the net? *Ad oculos!*"

Rebekah Marigold raised her hand.

"Jackie," said the teacher, "apologize to Miss Marigold for your damned language."

Rebekah shook her head.

"Dr. Harriman..." she turned to indicate the classroom windows, which overlooked the football field. "It's Mr. Addams."

There on the field, alone, stood Mr. Addams, a popular English instructor.

This was one of those occasions when a scene that should have been perfectly ordinary instead projected menace. There was no reason Mr. Addams should not be on the football field. He crossed it a half a dozen times a day going to and from class. There was something in his hand.

"Children," said Dr. Harriman. "Return to your seats."

Class resumed as normal, though everyone's attention stayed on Mr. Addams.

Inevitably, as it later seemed, two uniformed police officers arrived and marched out to greet Mr. Addams. Addams backed away from them slowly for a moment, raising his hands. But he went quietly. Zero would later recall how brilliantly the officers' shoes shone in the cold sunshine.

An announcement came over the loudspeaker—Ms. De Bono, telling everyone that class was suspended for the day and there were buses arriving to take the day students home. Night students were instructed to go to their dorms and remain indoors as a precaution. There was no danger. She didn't mention Mr. Addams or the police.

Later she would repeat to parents and students alike that Mr. Addams had suffered from personal problems, that there'd never been any danger to students, and that the matter was closed.

Word spread quickly, despite the official silence.

Addams had been armed with a pistol and had threatened to shoot himself.

Kosoko, who'd always been a good and well-mannered boy, was stuffing his face. This was the weekly dinner when he and Mazi returned home to dine with their parents. Kosoko being something of a golden boy even at home, his parents were hesitant to correct him. But it was a bit bizarre.

Frank and Barbara stared at each other, communicating a rising panic through their expressions. Finally, Frank spoke up. "They're still feeding you at school, aren't they, son?"

Kosoko looked up with his eyes but kept his face down by the plate. He mumbled something and carried on with his feast.

"Mazi," said Barbara Wright, "how's your algebra coming along?"

"Good," Mazi brightened up. "Solid B-plus." It was an exaggeration, but a slight one. "Did y'all hear about—"

"If you're averaging a B-plus, that's *not* so good," Barbara shook her head patiently. "A B-plus does not *distinguish* you. Black men who make it in this country aren't the ones who do well enough. They're the ones who distinguish themselves through excellence. And we've talked about STEM subjects being particularly—"

"—but Mom, did you hear about—"

"We heard about Mr. Addams, if that's what you mean," said Frank. "And believe me, we're looking at the problem very seriously. The future of that school, and your future at that school—"

"Frank, they don't need this kind of distraction," said Barbara with a look.

"He's a faggot," said Kosoko.

The whole family stopped short. The room fell silent.

"What in the *world*—" Barbara said. "What have we told you about using that word?"

"Not my word," said Kosoko. "It's what Chuck said."

"It's true," said Mazi. "Chuck Harerras ran into the cafeteria last week, all crying and acting like he wanna fight. He kept saying, "He's a faggot! He's a faggot!" He was talking about Mr. Addams."

"Now," Frank cleared his throat. "What your mother and I mean is, boys, we appreciate the seriousness of the situation. And we're 100% here for you." *Here for you* was the standard phrase for this sort of thing. Absolutely the correct phrase. "And nothing's more important to us than your safety. We know you'd never—"

"What your father's saying is that we know you'd tell us if you were in any trouble..."

"But at the same time, boys, we don't any of us want to go off using that kind of language. That's the kind of language—"

"Your father's saying we raised this family in a nice community, a nice town, and sent you to a very fine school to keep you *away* from that kind of hateful—"

"And even if he *was*," Frank said, "A you-know—"

"*Jesus*, Frank!"

"Even if he was a, you know, *faggot*—"

"*Frank*, what the hell's wrong with you?"

Kosoko had long since stopped listening. He helped himself to more linguini. Mazi sat there, beaming like the sun, waiting to be excused.

Mazi, born to be an alpha, was a beta when Kosoko was around. And when their old man was in the house, Kosoko was the beta, so that made him—what? Gamma.

And if the old man was alpha most of the time, he was beta to his wife. So that bumped Mazi down to delta.

Mazi didn't mind a bit. His time would come. It was all good. The growth spurt that was carrying Kosoko heavenward had left Mazi below, but what did that matter? All his favorite players were guards. And nobody was going to fuck with Mazi because that would mean dealing with Kosoko.

Anyway, nobody did fuck with Mazi. Mazi was a nice kid. He always had a smile for anybody. Mazi liked pop and hip-hop, but he also liked the old man's jazz. That was weird, but Mazi didn't mind being weird. Mazi liked math. He'd get his A. Math came easy to him. Most things did. He smiled, pulling the blanket over his head. Shit, it was all good.

In the days that followed the Addams incident, a few things happened.

First, Addams really disappeared from the school's public consciousness. Nobody wanted to talk about him, and they sure as hell didn't want updates on him or his case. The cops came around once more to discretely interview Ms. De Bono. Whatever they talked to her about stayed within the walls of her office.

There was one exception to this conspiracy of forgetting, and that was Harriman.

He could think of nothing else.

The students saw him walking the grounds with his head on a swivel, highly vigilant, scanning the buildings and the landscape. He had his little notebook, into which he ought to have been taking notes on basketball or Latin. Instead he scribbled observations and even little drawings and diagrams of the campus.

At last satisfied with his survey, he dropped in on Ms. De Bono and told her he would require changes for the good of the school. Onto her desk, before her stunned face, he unrolled a series of hand-drawn schematics.

"Barricades," said he. "Here, here, here, and here. A fence along the entire perimeter. These basements to be fortified, with secure doors, as emergency shelter. Look here at these unobstructed fields of interlocking fire. They will be disrupted like so..."

She stood and stared. She'd never seen him like this. Her thoughts, which had begun with the old fool's absurdity and then turned to the absolute financial impossibility of his proposals, ended on a certainty: He was right.

"Okay," she said.

Chapter 16
Behind Her Serene Face

Kim Jigu
Ryu Gun
Various staff and troops

In the weeks following the power outage, Major Kim Jigu found herself increasingly interested in her role in the command structure. This being, you know, to receive and check launch orders, and having done so, relay them to the missile crew. She stood as a safeguard against any invalid command to launch the missile at the United States.

The last safeguard.

On the other hand, she was also supposed to launch if anything happened to the leader in Pyongyang, e.g., if he were vaporized, and there were no launch order. This was a very routine responsibility, one she'd almost certainly never have to carry out. It was, nevertheless, a rather awesome one.

Kim Jigu felt a bit like a woman who stands on a high precipice and feels the urge to jump simply because she can. And she would even catch herself feeling that impulse. To launch, without orders, because she could. This was an absolute impossibility, obviously.

But she really wondered: Was it an accident that she'd been given this role?

The people who had put her in charge of this silo complex had known of her exemplary record of service to the North Korean army. But they'd just as certainly known how this country had treated her. She had been raped dozens of times, mostly in the internment camp, but also as a private soldier and even as an officer. She had carried out her duties throughout the famine of the 1990s, and even now was badly underfed, as were all women in the military. She had done without, as they all did, basic sanitary products. She had stopped menstruating for half a year at a time because of malnutrition and intense exertion. In all this time she had never complained, never squealed, never even commented on any aspect of her life. But they must have known. They must have known that behind her serene face was a scream of rage.

Chapter 17
Maps

Lefty Davis
William Lloyd Garrison
Jackie Polish
Zero Bardoff
Presto
Dr. John Harriman, PhD
Elijah Hart
Ms. De Bono
Naomi Echeveria
Brett Sanger
Andy Tangent
Milo Potter

Current Progress in Geographic Pedagogy: A
Teleological Free-Association

by Caitlin Upton

I personally believe

That U.S. Americans are unable to do so

Because some people out there

In our nation

Don't have maps.

And I believe

That our education like such as in

South Africa

And

The Iraq,

Everywhere

like

such as

and

I believe

That they should

(Our education over here in the U.S.)

Should

Help the U.S

Or should help

South Africa and

Should help

The Iraq

and

The Asian countries

So

We will be able

To build up our future

For our children

Lefty was in a transitional phase, as all his homeboys were. He was simultaneously building and searching for his identity. There were several serious concerns in this process. One was musical taste. Most of your current musical options at this time were about equally execrable, but the point was to find a genre that said what you wanted it to say about you. Lefty was cynical. He had a tough style. This had led him to 1980s hardcore punk.

Another transitional biggie was sex. Not much point in dwelling on that here, since for him there was none. No sex. But a major concern because he was 14 years old.

Now, you're invited to look at a 14 year old kid sometime just to refresh your memory.

Fourteen year old kids are *babies*. They look just about old enough to walk, but surely not to even think about sex. Parents of children not much younger than Lefty actually deceived themselves that their little boys were too young to "notice girls."

Lefty had never been too young.

And now, at 14, he thought about sex so continuously he almost made himself sick. He looked at persons around him, particularly female persons, and he really wondered whether he saw any whom he wouldn't "do" if given the chance. He had a math teacher named Mrs. Glick who was so ugly her cats wouldn't go near her, and still, in his darkest moments, he wondered whether he'd be able to turn her down.

A closely related preoccupation, but more general, could be summed up pretty well as "coolness." It was critical that he be cool. But cool in which of the dozens of senses of that word? He was a good student. Being smart could be cool, especially if it meant getting over on chumps and suckers. To be adult was also highly desirable, as it is to all 14-year-olds and no adults.

Anyway, being cool, being adult, meant setting aside Dungeons & Dragons.

One of the many things he'd loved about Dungeons & Dragons was its mathematical naturalism. Dungeons & Dragons was a storytelling game, a collaborative storytelling game with player and non-player characters interacting in a human way (e.g., killing each other). The outcomes of these interactions, e.g., who killed whom, were based on probability. And the probability was defined by durable properties of these characters, expressed as numbers.

So all characters would have, for example, the property of *strength*, a variable with a value. Wignar the Wise might have a strength of 10, while Brock the Barbarian had a strength of 17. If these two were to arm wrestle, each would have a probability of winning when the die was cast, but Wignar's 10 strength would give him a 15% lower probability of victory than Brock's 17 strength. Got it?

Strength was one numerical probability of six. A character would also have non-quantitative properties, like her name. But for the purpose of calculating outcomes, it was the numbers that mattered. A character, effectively, was a collection of properties with numeric values.

Having left all this behind in the eighth grade, Lefty was surprised to discover that computer programming was based on the same principles. He hadn't chosen to take freshman Object-Oriented Programming, but he found it appealed to him. In object-oriented programming, pieces of data are called objects, and they have properties, just like Dungeons & Dragons characters. So you might have a piece of data called a *string* ('string' meaning string of alphanumeric characters, e.g., a word or sentence). The string object would have several *properties*, one of which would be its length. So if you had a string, *myString*, equal to "foo," its length would be three, for "f" "o" "o." You could then access that property, reading it using "dot notation." As in, "a=myString.length." And then you could use that information in your program.

```
string myString = "foo";
int a = myString.length;
if (a>0)
{
    print a;
}
```

... and the screen would read, "3."

Objects, as sets of properties, were reusable and fungible. Even an object that had been dereferenced and purged from memory could be reincarnated as a new instance of its class. It would have a new memory address, but if its properties had the same values, it would in all other senses be the same object. This logical metempsychosis extended beyond the realm of logic and computing into what is called the real world.

This was, as Lefty saw it, sort of interesting. And kind of fun. Like a wizard in Dungeons & Dragons, a programmer could create things simply by putting the right words and symbols together in the right order and invoking them. Lefty wrote a simple text-based computer game that randomly selected from a list of 30 or so characters and had them fight. It wasn't much to look at, but the computer would tell you "Dark Lord Cypher wins" if you had Dark Lord Cypher fight with a character whose properties matched up poorly and the "dice'" had gone Cypher's way. The computer would evaluate both characters:

```
//darkLordCypher
darkLordCypher.agility = 16;
darkLordCypher.strength = 15;
darkLordCypher.intelligence = 17;
//weakPhil
weakPhil.agility = 11;
weakPhil.strength = 9;
weakPhil.intelligence = 18;
```

The numbers were plugged into a formula, some randomness would be factored in, and the computer would announce the result of the fight.

Lefty didn't show this program to anyone, because it was nerd stuff, and he was through being a nerd. But he kept working at his programming, and ideas kept occurring to him. It wasn't long before he was thinking about basketball in an object-oriented way. Zero had an agility of 6, a strength of 10, and a shooting accuracy of 5. Jackie had an intelligence of 11 (this was Lefty's wise-guy opinion), and a jump of 14, and a height of 5'9". Then there was Kosoko.

kosoko.agility = 17;
kosoko.strength = 14;
kosoko.basketballIQ = 18;
kosoko.height = 5'11";

Based on these estimated figures, Lefty could apply a formula and calculate the outcome of, say, a game of one-on-one. His formula was pretty much crap, but it did accept all the properties and spit out a result, and Lefty was pretty sure the result was accurate, because it almost always said Kosoko had won.

And Lefty further generalized beyond basketball.

Though he'd never taken physics (it was taught in the eleventh grade), Lefty started thinking of physics in that object-oriented way also. If a thrown rock had mass x and velocity y, it would hit Jackie in the nuts with force f. So he could program simple physical events. He looked up the formulas, basically Newtonian mechanics, online, and combined the formulas to create increasingly accurate simulations.

And so it was that Lefty, without much formal training, inferred on his own what has been called "the unreasonable effectiveness" of math in describing the world. And it made him think a lot of philosophical thoughts when he was falling asleep at night. Determinism, free will, that kind of 101 shit.

But not totally unoriginal.

Like people think that determinism and free will are opposites. Lefty could see that a system could be as non-deterministic, contain as much randomness, as you liked, and still not have any trace of free will. So the tools used to simulate the world could be reversed to help him understand and predict the world. It made him think, as he strolled through campus, looking up at the buildings and the birds' nests and the falling snow, of the sense in which the universe was a computer program in mid-execution. Or a game of Dungeons & Dragons.

(NOTE: Strictly speaking, the game Lefty played is called *Advanced* Dungeons & Dragons. So, another reason to be impressed with old Lefty.)

(NOTE: Might as well mention here that Lefty was not left-handed. Long story.)

And everywhere like such as and a quick survey, or map, may be helpful at this point.

William Lloyd Garrison, the great abolitionist, is having breakfast (plain toast, strong tea) with his wife in Newburyport, MA ca. 1839. One knows he's right, certainly. He does rather go on. But of course he's quite right. "Be faithful," said he, not buttering his toast, "be vigilant, be untiring in your efforts to break every yoke, and let the oppressed go free. Come what may - cost what it may - inscribe on the banner which you unfurl to the breeze, as your religious and political motto - 'NO COMPROMISE WITH SLAVERY! NO UNION WITH SLAVEHOLDERS...'"

A bit high-flown, a bit supercilious, a bit didactic. But absolutely true, one must admit. Absolutely in the best possible spirit, very advanced, very courageous.

Jackie, in his perennial eye patch, is having dinner in the cafeteria in Newburyport, MA., ca. 2016. It's almost time for Christmas break, and he's finding it hard to concentrate on his studies. He's also high, which doesn't help.

Lefty's having dinner with Jackie. He's reading the sports page as he eats. Celtics are looking good. Real good.

Zero's having dinner with Jackie and Lefty. They're just a few meters from where Garrison is eating breakfast 177 years earlier. Zero doesn't usually eat with Birdie, though she's pretty officially his girlfriend. It's a little reality that just emerged, and he hasn't had the nerve to bring it up. Presumably she likes to dine with her friend Naomi. Anyway, she does so.

Zero and Birdie have kissed by now, but done little else in that department. The thought of Birdie created a complex physiological and psychological syndrome in Zero. The syndrome involved borderline-unsafe levels of adrenaline and cortisol, triggering standard fight/flight arousal, to wit: blood flow to the extremities and major muscle groups, away from the digestive system and even growth processes. This, accompanied by stark, horrifying fantasies of Birdie falling in love with another boy, usually Kosoko or Mazi but sometimes Lefty or Jackie or some unspecified stud.

What's going on behind the scenes: The brain senses the high levels of adrenaline/cortisol neurotransmitters and becomes vigilant, searching for a threat that could explain why these levels are so high. It finds the scariest explanation (in this case that Birdie is cheating or will leave him), and then assumes it's true. This assumption triggers further release of the same emergency neurotransmitters and still greater physiological arousal. This sequence, this positive feedback loop, continues throughout each day until his body runs low of the chemicals, at which point he collapses in exhaustion but feels a ray of hope that lasts until the next morning, when the recharged glands start juicing away at full blast.

If you've never gone through it, maybe imagine something like this: You go into your house and find your family there, murdered. So you're horrified, desolated, bereft, appalled. But then you hear something. The killer is still in the house. So your feelings of overwhelming sorrow are now mixed with an equal portion of terror. So, yeah. Zero's nominally having dinner with Jackie and Lefty, but he's actually just sculpting his food and trying not to break down sobbing.

Anyway, the Liberators are no longer in last place. They've eked out their first win, beating Phillips Andover behind a 14-point performance by the blooming Kosoko.

Presto's sleeping fitfully.

None of them suspects anything.

Neither does Mayor Frank Wright, though his feeling of unease and apprehension has grown more knife-like by the day.

Barbara Wright is too busy with work to suspect.

Elijah Hart, dining with his family, is oblivious. So is Hank Hart, so put him out of your mind.

Ditto Ms. De Bono. Totally without suspicion. Eating with her own family, i.e., herself, as a recent divorce had cut short a childless marriage. She's quite comfortable with this, knowing that when she's ready to get back out there she'll have plenty of eager prospects. Even in a small town like Newburyport, where she's something of an outsider. Even in a town of civil servants, commuters, fishermen, and school teachers. Oh, *fuck it!*

She puts the aluminum foil over her half-eaten dinner and shoves it back in the refrigerator. The whole kitchen smells like bleach. So what? She likes the smell of bleach!

She's tired of thinking about Dick, about whether she was right to leave him. Whether she had in fact left him, or whether he'd manipulated her into thinking she was the one doing the leaving. She was tired enough that even dick jokes didn't help. The man had been suitable in many ways. Handsome, if not tall. Good family (whatever that meant nowadays). Anyway, he claimed to be from a good family. They seemed like assholes to her. In her abdomen she felt a residual glow of love for him.

Why hadn't he been brilliant? Or had he been? In *Brave New World*, people are divided into two supersets: Alphas and Betas in the first set, everyone else in the other. This was confusing because it had no relationship to the primate hierarchies with their alpha males and beta males, etc. Totally different use of the same Greek letters. Not her idea.

Was she remembering correctly?

The thing about Alphas was that they were more intelligent than anyone else, but they were also kind of absentminded and distractible. Head in the clouds. Betas were the ones who could actually get things done. Consequently the Betas viewed the Alphas with a resentful condescension. Alphas would make messes, Betas would clean them up. The whole (brave, new) world would come to a damn stop if not for the Betas taking care of all the boring necessities, and the Alphas would starve without them. So why were the Betas the Betas? Why weren't they called the Alphas?

God, she'd hated having to read that book. Science fiction. God. But was Dick an Alpha or a Beta? He could be terribly irresponsible, but he was no philosopher. Maybe he was a Gamma. Jesus, was that possible? Had she married a Gamma? And what was she, anyway? Maybe both an Alpha and a Beta. She was a capable administrator like a Beta, but she was also a scholar, she was learned, she thought, like an Alpha. Do most people think? Really?

Why didn't she have any friends?

Was she thinking of *Logan's Run?*

That night, while the other students and faculty slept, an insomniac Naomi Echeveria rose to get a drink of water. She'd been in a fitful hypnagogic haze for hours, a haze broken up by terrible visions of violence. She thought of ISIS, the terror group then in fashion, and its cruel and creative methods of execution.

This happened sometimes to her, but she found that she was usually very thirsty when it did. Getting a drink could help. Returning from the ladies' room, she thought of all these young kids asleep all around her. They were so exposed, so vulnerable, so inchoate. She wanted to protect them from the brutality of the world, from the Mr. Addamses with their pistols. She put her hand to the window, just to feel the cold.

In the morning, eating breakfast with Birdie in the cafeteria, Naomi asked Birdie whether she ever feared for her own safety.

"Yeah, I do," said Birdie. "Like lots of times when I see a cop or whatever, and like I got my hair back and I'm just wearing a hoodie or whatever and I could look like a boy. And I look at the cop's gun, and I think about how easy the cop could shoot me."

Naomi said it was a fucked-up world, and sometimes she couldn't stop thinking about all the troubles in it.

"Seems like...you ever feel like...we were born in this world, but like, the world wasn't made for us? Like the world doesn't know we're here at all? Or doesn't care? And all this stuff, like violence, 9/11, cops shooting people, gangs, falling out of windows, even car accidents, all of it is a constant threat just because we're kind of here on earth by accident, almost. Like there's nobody to protect us. Or like there's no guarantee. Nobody we can sue if it all turns bad. One minute you're here, next minute you could be torn up to pieces."

"You just got to keep your head low and your eyes up," said Birdie with a faraway smile. "Just stay under the radar. Like Nathan Hale."

"Nathan Hale wound up at the end of a rope, Birdie."

A very serious problem with which coastal defenses are concerned is the fact that a continent cannot be protected on a maximum basis from assault by rockets containing atomic bombs. Such rockets must be intercepted far from their targets in a very small amount of time over vast spaces. It cannot be assumed that every rocket contains an important bomb—a large proportion of them are likely to be bluffs. To mobilize full resources to destroy every one of them would be likely to cost more than the damage inflicted. Hence, again, an optimum would have to be achieved; an optimum system of detection and an optimum amount of interception, making it too costly for the enemy to chance the onslaught. War is chance and minimax must be its modern philosophy.

The theory of games may sometime have practical applications in many social fields. And yet even now, as theory, it has performed an important service in illuminating the meanings of strategy.

—John von Neumann, Theory of Games and Economic Behavior

Late autumn was turning out a bit crazy, as everybody got ready to head home for Christmas vacation.

The school was broke.

A teacher had waved a pistol around on the football field.

Inside his classroom, Dr. Professor Coach Harriman was losing his mind.

Everybody's familiar with the I-observing-I loop, in which one observes himself and thinks of the I that is observing and the I that is observed, and the fact that the observing I is itself being observed by yet another I, etc. You know about this, right?

Harriman had been trying all afternoon to break out of that loop, to change the subject and distract his mind.

But then another thought occurred to him, in the form of a mental image.

He imagined himself sitting there at his desk, as he was, looking out into the class, etc., but then blinking his eyes and being somewhere else entirely, say standing on a beach in a rainstorm.

And it came to him to imagine how in such a circumstance, where one reality replaced another in the blink of his eyes, a person would know his location hadn't actually changed,

But

would

not

know

whether

The classroom

Or the beach

Or both

Had been the delusion.

"Oh oh oh oh oh oh *oh!*" he moaned, contemplating this vision of madness. He swooned, tipped sideways, and fell from his chair with a crash. His students stared at him, saying nothing.

Jackie sat in his dorm room playing riffs on his guitar. Jackie was a guitar hero, 20 years too late in history. Guitar had rescued him. Whatever craziness had surrounded him in his young life, at home, at school, nevertheless he'd had his guitar. He would pose with it before the mirror, his face twisted into a grimace he called his "rock 'n roll face." There were kids in the early grades at Garrison who had never heard of rock 'n roll.

Two rooms down, Bent Sanger sat Indian-style on a rug. He also had a guitar, but an acoustic one. He was a slightly heavy kid. Wore glasses. Also, always wore a Yankee cap his father had given him. His father had died not long afterwards. If you tried to touch or even talk about the Yankee cap, Brent Sanger would punch you and then explain why he'd punched you.

He wasn't alone in his dorm room. Andrew Tangent and Milo Potter sat with him on the rug.

"This is one I wrote," said Brent Sanger. "It's called *Tiny Dick,* because I have a fucking tiny dick."

He began strumming violent, NYHC style, and snarled, "When I take my fucking pants off, all she does is laugh! Tiny dick! Tiny dick!"

Tangent and Potter interrupted him by laughing.

"It's not a joke," said Brent Sanger.

"It's funny," said Andy.

"Fuck you."

"Do you really have a tiny dick?" said Potter.

"Look," said Sanger, setting his guitar aside. "Listen." He looked at them very seriously. "Have you ever felt a girl's fucking tits?"

They both said no.

"Well, I have! So shut the fuck up!"

Chapter 18
A Pipe at the North Pole

Hank Hart

Is it necessary to mention that Newburyport High School had, under the captaincy of Hank Hart, dominated the Cape Anne league?

The top standings were as follows:

	W	L	T
Newburyport*	14	2	0
Mascomet*	12	4	0
Pentucket*	10	5	1
Triton	4	8	1
North Reading	3	11	0

* Qualified for state tournament

Other players on the Newburyport High School Clippers were either black, or affected in their speech and attire to be so. Not Hank Hart, their star, who instead affected to be indifferent to race, as to everything else. His blond hair was not quite shoulder length, and could be fairly described as "shaggy." He had blue eyes. One thing you noticed about him right away was his jaw. It was a bit too strong, too masculine, to be really attractive. But it was formidable.

Leadership came easy to Hank. His father was a leader. So was his mother, in a different way. Hank never thought about it. He just suggested that people around him do this or that, and they generally did it. Teachers, fellow students, his coach, his team.

School came easily, too. He never worried about his grades, or needed to. Likewise, his social life was automatic. It wasn't clear whether people liked him, but he was on top, so it didn't matter.

Everyone has secrets. And Hank Hart's biggest secret was that he hated all these things that came so easy to him. It wasn't just contempt. It was a loathing that hurt him in his stomach.

He hated basketball. He hated his studies, his social life, his natural leadership. And most of all, by far, he hated Garrison Academy. Because he couldn't go there.

It would have been impolitic.

His father was a local politician with his eyes on the mayor's office.

Sure, Mayor Wright could send his boys to Garrison, because it was a good thing for his black sons to go to an elite school. But being white meant Hank's attendance there would have been less a stirring story of overcoming than a simple case of privilege to the privileged. And there wasn't a soul in the world that he could talk to about it.

So Hank used every bit of his influence to push for a second scrimmage with Garrison. They were in different leagues, so this could be his only chance to play them again. It would again have no official standing, and it would again humiliate Garrison in the only way he knew how.

True, Garrison was playing better than they had when starting out, but Hank chalked that up to regression toward the mean. The team he'd scrimmaged with in September had barely been a team at all—more a pack of untrained spastics, other than the older black guy, who'd been athletic but unskilled.

Hank had easily browbeaten his coach into going to the principal, Mr. Faulken. Faulken had in turn been easy to impress into Hank's service. The great surprise was when the principal went to the disconcertingly elegant headmaster of Garrison with the request. Not only did she welcome the idea, she claimed to have had it herself. She even claimed she'd been planning to broach the subject when they'd beaten her to the punch.

This piqued the curiosity of young Hank. It gilded his pleasure with a sweetening hint of anxiety. Was it possible the Liberators could make this a game?

Hank went all in—he wanted a big crowd for his triumph. He rallied his adoring fans on the cheerleading squad (they had no idea he was gay) and he rallied the diffident but equally star struck student activists.

This would be more than a scrimmage.

It would be a huge pep rally and a gala fundraiser for some important cause or other.

Hank even asked some kids at Garrison to pick a cause of their own and use the game as a platform for it. They picked something to do with a pipe at the North Pole. Something like that. A river?

And so it came about that the #metoo Keystone Pipeline Benefit Scrimmage was scheduled and quickly acknowledged to be the social event of the season for the whole of Newburyport, for a game that would make history.

Chapter 19
The Roster

Dr. George Kistiakowski, PhD
Captain Kim Il Sung
Eun, his adjutant
His Highness the Reza Shah of Iran

George Kistiakowski could barely feel his hands, it was so cold.

But he had the vodka to warm him—a small flask he'd filled up before stumbling out of Oppenheimer's party and trudging up the hill.

Oppenheimer had been dressed up as a wild Indian, showing off for the girls, but there had been real Indians there, too, which George Kistiakowski found thrilling.

As a kid in the Ukraine, he'd played Cowboys and Indians with his brother Alexander and his uncle Ihor. George had always played an Indian. He'd practiced walking silently through the forest, taking the whole thing terribly seriously. Later, fighting the Reds in Russia, he'd often thought he might be using the skills he'd learned playing those games. He never dreamed he'd make it to America, to the Wild West, to see real American Indians.

But he'd escaped from Russia in a commandeered French steamer. He'd found his way to Berlin, and received his doctorate in physical chemistry. He'd subsequently left Germany for America, not, as so many at Los Alamos had, to escape the Communists or the Nazis, but simply to take a position at Harvard.

He stopped at the top of the hill.

The sun had set, but the night was clear and the moonlight cast a glow over the snowy mesa. He paused to catch his breath and take it all in.

Then he dropped his pack and extracted the first charge.

Somehow balancing a cigarette, his flask, and the high-yield daisy-chain, he wrapped it tightly around a cottonwood tree's trunk, very near to the ground. A half-necklace of high explosives. He moved on to the next tree.

George Kistiakowski was the Michelangelo of blowing things up.

His understanding of explosives went far deeper than any expertise or study of physical science.

He grasped their nature intuitively, artistically. He saw how to make explosives into lenses, and shape their blasts into simple, geometric, fluid processes. It was he who'd convinced Johnny the implosion was possible. Johnny Von Neumann was the smartest man in the world, so when Johnny told the bosses to trust in Kistiakowski's plan, they listened. And it was going to work. He was going to synchronize the inward-facing detonations so precisely, and focus them so exquisitely, that there would be no turbulence, no chaos, in the pressure wave.

Tonight, though, would allow for a far cruder approach. Kistiakowski tied the last necklace off to the last tree and began to pace out a safe distance, unspooling the fuse, walking backwards through deep snow down a steep grade. Inevitably, he fell and tumbled, but the fuse stayed quiet.

When he was well to the side of the hill, he fired the blasts, felling more than a dozen trees at once.

The next morning, the engineers cleared the trees away and began setting up a rope tow. And just in time for the weekend, the Los Alamos labs had themselves a very respectable ski slope.

At about the same time that Kistiakowski had blown up the trees, a small detachment of his old rivals the Red Army were busy in their camp on the banks of the Amur River. The indefatigable Captain Kim of the Soviet Army ran through the pine forest.

There was snow here, too.

Captain Kim could feel the breath burning in his lungs, and see it jetting from his mouth with every step he took. He'd trained himself to breath in rhythm with his stride. The others behind him, fellow Korean nationals he was turning into soldiers, were ragged, loose, undisciplined in their formation and their physicality.

Kim ran with perfect form.

He knew the Japs were losing, and losing badly. His time had almost come. He barked at the others to keep it up, to keep to the trail. Kim's control of his body would extend outside of it, to the unit, to the army, to the Korean peninsula and its starving, oppressed people.

It occurred to him then that he truly didn't believe in God. He'd formally renounced such beliefs years before, but he'd never seriously considered whether the beliefs were true. It was irrelevant, or had seemed so. Now, out here in the country, where life abounded even in the bitter Russian winter, he looked down from the hilltop and knew that God hadn't made this world.

He stopped, and the whole company stopped behind him. Some of them, even knowing the likely consequences, were unable to help grabbing their knees as they labored for breath. Kim turned to face his adjutant.

"Eun," he said, "do you believe in God?"

Eun said that he did. Eun was skeletal under his fatigues. Food was very scarce in the Red Army, even here, a thousand miles from the front.

"You want to know why I lead, and you must follow. You wonder why the will of the Korean race is channeled through me. It is very simple. The people are my God."

And in Johannesburg, in the warm air, surrounded by his family, with the smell of wild cosmos flowers in his nostrils, His Highness the Reza Shah of Iran died in exile. It was 1944.

Chapter 20
Almost Everyone's Favorite Thing in the Whole World

David Muratskian
The referee
Kosoko Wright, and his Liberators
Hank Hart, and his Clippers

A submarine is no place for an introvert.

This was unfortunate for Weapons Officer David Muratskian, who was much more inclined toward private contemplation than toward the society of his fellow officers and crew.

This evening, Muratskian had earned his privacy by leading his team through an exhaustive set of drills. His time, barring an emergency, should now be his own. Even alone in the officers' berth, in repose, he wore his usual expression of irritation; his eyebrows were arched, his mouth pinched.

Muratskian was reading Proust, but found his mind wandering, so that he kept having to return to the same sentence.

> He recognized that all the period of Odette's life which had elapsed before she first met him, a period of which he had never sought to form any picture in his mind, was not the featureless abstraction which he could vaguely see, but had consisted of so many definite, dated years, each crowded with concrete incidents.

He smoked as he read, leaving the cigarette in his lips, letting the smoke float up past his eyes until they burned. He thought of his family in Los Angeles, his wife whom he missed consistently but not to an unmanageable degree.

"Shit!" said Muratskian, sitting up hard and brushing off his chest. He'd dropped burning ashes from his cigarette right onto his shirt. "Fuck. God-damn it!" He examined the shirt and found a small hole burned through it. Stupid! He took his shirt off and ran it under the sink a little. The scorched area around the whole didn't fade at all. He balled up the shirt and threw it in the trash.

He'd been careless this way, careless of his appearance, since he was a little kid. He remembered the dissonance between his own self-confidence (he was the smartest kid in the school, he could play four musical instruments, he could write well and draw, etc.) and the reactions people had to him. His friends called him the "brown beggar," which he hated about as much as anyone has ever hated anything in the long annals of the human race. This was very early in life, third or fourth grade, but still. It had given him a permanent hatred of being underestimated. Unfortunately, it hadn't made him much more fastidious about his outer person.

This characteristic, in a Navy man of his high rating, was doubly problematic.

First, because being a Weapons Officer allowed absolutely zero in the way of fucking around and being sloppy. Second, because this was the Navy, for Christ's sake. Every cramped inch of that submarine sparkled and shone. If you spilled a drop of coffee on the floor, it would be cleaned up before you could bend over with your napkin. Every man and woman aboard spent at least 20 minutes each morning checking his or her gig lines, hair, shave, and shoe shine.

Muratskian tried to follow suit, always had tried, but when he focused his mind on stimulating subjects like whether his buttons lined up just so, his mind tended to drift into deeper waters. He'd have a thought, for example, and he'd need to write it down, and before he knew it he'd have forgotten to tuck in his shirt tails or straighten his cap.

All perfectly acceptable, even charming, in civilian life. But aboard the USS Nebraska it raised eyebrows.

"Okay!" he said, climbing back into his bunk.

He was determined to focus on his book.

While his conscious mind read the sentence again, his subconscious registered the sense-data of the submarine: the smell of his cigarette, the sound of the Pacific ocean rushing around him, the cold air of the ventilation fan. His thoughts mingled with his words as he read them.

"...but had consisted of so many definite, dated years, each crowded with concrete incidents."

As any reader must do, Muratskian related the story to himself. And without intending to, he began to contrast his own role, and the philosophical position it represented, against Proust's.

Proust's was a world of small things, fragile details suspended in memory as raindrops on a spider web, so that when a single memory was stirred it caused the whole web to shudder.

It was a private world of persons and objects of profound sentimental value, where a sigh or a gesture could unfold a universe.

On the other hand, there was the mathematical world of the Weapons Officer. This was the world of Mutual Assured Destruction and the theory of games. A world where his personality and feelings could play no part, where it was necessary for him to think like a machine and in fact to be part of a machine. A U.S. Navy Weapons Officer called upon to launch his missile can't ask whether his wife had ever dunked a madeleine into her coffee and savored it, or whether she would ever again walk a path through the woods to a neighbor's house, or whether she really loved him or only some idea of him that she'd had long before they'd ever met, when she was a little girl. Mutual Assured Destruction had to be assured. If the enemy were to sense any trace of hesitancy in him to strike, it would be given an opportunity itself to strike without facing retaliation. It would be an opportunity that the enemy, for its own safety, would have almost no choice but to use.

Yet Muratskian thought of how strange it was that the little world of Proust and of his wife should so absolutely depend on his readiness to burn it to cinders at any time and under any circumstances.

In the Greek dark ages, hundreds of years before Socrates and Aristotle, it was thought very unwise to treat a stranger rudely. This was mainly because the Greeks were a seafaring people who depended on shoreline hospitality for their survival. But the reason as *they* understood it was that the gods, unlike those of other contemporary civilizations, were of human shape. Any wanderer could be a divine person in disguise.

But this was nearly 2017, almost the Trump era (he had recently won election to the U.S. Presidency). It was in this and many ways a very sinister hour. It was a time of fake news, election interference, Birkenstocks, Tevas, street violence, and foreign wars. The rappers had begun to sing. *Star Wars* was now *A New Hope*. Newspapers were now content aggregators. It was the age of the woke, the alt right, the Antifa and the neo-fascist, the age of auto-tune, when sex became gender and race remained explosive. Gone were the days of Captain Sir Richard Francis Burton, the days of Harriet Tubman, the days of De Gualle, of King and X, the days when a dog could not write *Lord Jim*. It was the age of "lol" and antibiotic-resistant tuberculosis, the days of the Islamic State, of "tweets" and "hashtags" and such baby-talk.

But it was also a time of basketball, of young love, of philosophical investigations, scientific discovery, and the cool derangements of snowy late autumn.

And into the center circle at the center of all this strode our heroes, those nutty old Liberators, those young windows on the world. The referee blew his whistle for tip-off and tossed the basketball straight into the air.

Kosoko and Hank went up for it. Kosoko won. He batted the ball back to his kid brother Mazi. Mazi began a slow dribble up the court, one finger raised in the air.

"Five-five!" Mazi called the play. The old "Uni," the only play they'd ever practiced.

Mazi dribbled to the left wing and switched directions with the dribble. As soon as he reached the wing, Lefty stepped out to the 3-point line to set the screen, and Zero popped to the wing.

Timing was crucial. If Kosoko had missed his cue, he would have blown the play. But Kosoko followed almost immediately to set a second screen for Mazi near the top of the key. As Mazi dribbled around the second screen set by Kosoko, Jackie set a back screen for Lefty.

(Everybody clear on what a "screen" is, by the way? It's the same thing as a "pick," and it simply means coming to a dead stop in front of somebody so that he has no choice but to go around you. So for example, when the guy on offense who doesn't have the ball moves between his teammate and the opponent player who's guarding his teammate, and then stops. The guy guarding his teammate now has to go around the guy setting the screen, which gives the teammate for whom the screen was set about a half-second of freedom with nobody guarding him. Unless the defense switches, but even that can mean an advantage for the team with the ball. If the reader is saying, "That didn't help at all," well, sorry.)

As soon as Lefty cleared the screen set by Jackie, Kosoko in turn set a down screen for Zero.

Zero was experiencing a panic that was not unusual for him except that it was unusually apt.

He had no idea what was going on. He vaguely remembered having Kosoko try to teach the team to run the Uni, but he'd given it none of his attention then, and it had seemed like nobody else was paying attention either, and then he'd forgotten about it.

Since Kosoko had set a screen for him, Zero knew he must act out his role in this tragedy. But what that role might be, he had no idea. He ran out to the three-point line, where Mazi passed him the ball. Mazi expected him to fake a shot and then make a brisk pass to Lefty, who was cutting to the basket. But the terrified Zero knew only one thing to do when he touched a basketball: He shot it. It was a brick, high and long, nowhere near the basket. Zero closed his eyes—he couldn't look. But a moment later he opened them to cheers. Kosoko, weary of trying to get his team going, had snatched the rebound and laid it in. Two points, MOTHERFUCKERS.

Humperdink inbounded the ball with gusto—he threw a baseball pass up to half court. The Liberators gave chase, too stunned from almost having run a play to be ready for a fast break. They hauled ass, but in vain. The Clipper point guard Driskill had an open lane, but at the last moment tossed the ball back over his head to the top of the key, where Hank Hart did a stop-and-pop that hit nothing but nylon.

Zero inbounded, but before the pass could reach Mazi it was picked off by a streak of crimson called Bobby Driskill. Hank Hart cut back viciously to the goal, with Kosoko hot on his heels. Hank caught the ball in midair and put it up to the glass, but before it could fall it was pinned back by Kosoko, who collided with Hank in the air. Kosoko went down hard as Hart managed to keep his footing.

For a moment Hank Hart stood over Kosoko, staring down at him. The whole gym was silent, waiting to see if Kosoko was okay. Then Hank reached his hand down and helped Kosoko to his feet. Without releasing Kosoko's hand, Hank pulled him to his chest and whispered in his ear.

In the second period, Hank Hart was driving for a layup when Kosoko intentionally fouled him—hard. Hart fell on his side and slid for about three meters; before he'd come to a stop he was scrambling to his feet to retaliate. He charged full-speed at Kosoko, and then the two were brawling with their fists.

What a sight, and the Garrison Academy of all places, a black boy and a white boy come to blows! The referee, who was a senior citizen, heroically inserted himself between them and caught a couple punches to the head for his trouble.

"That's *enough!*" he yelled. "Knock it off!"

He gave them both technical fouls, which sent them to the bench, cursing each other as they went. Both coaches addressed their players.

"What the devil are you *about*, Wright?" said Harriman. "That boy's half again your size! Do you want that pretty face all rearranged?"

"It's between me and him," Kosoko said. "It's a question of honor."

Harriman had to admit he was a little bit impressed. A question of honor, indeed. Well, why not? But he sat the lad down and said, "What's honor? A word. And what's a word. Air!"

This tidbit of nonsense had a surprising effect on Kosoko, not because of its content but because this was the first bit of actual coaching Harriman had ever done.

"Now, I want you to get out there, son. Remember that if honor's to be won or lost, it will be won or lost in just competition."

In the last minutes of the first half, as the Newburyport Clippers started to really pull away, something clicked in Lefty's head. It was kind of like a cross between an out-of-body experience and a thing where time stops for everybody but you. He watched Driskill, the sturdy point guard, threw a bounce pass to Hart. Two points. But suddenly Lefty saw, almost ocularly saw, the object that was Driskill, and its properties. Driskill.passing = 16; Driskill.shooting = 14; Driskill.speed = 12. He looked at Hart and it was the same deal. Objects and properties and dot syntax. Humperdink, everybody on the Clippers, and his own team, too. Probability based on statistics. He paused a moment, even losing his man on the break, but what no one could see was that he was running the program in his head.

"Come *on*, Lefty!" said Mazi, already way downcourt on offense.

Lefty snapped out of it. "Hey!" he shouted. And he called time out.

The team came together in a huddle.

"Listen up," said Lefty. And he told them how Hart's leaping and blocking were shutting Kosoko down as a scorer, but how if they could force a switch, especially to Driskill, so that at the last second Driskill rather than Hart would be guarding Kosoko, then Kosoko would be able to score at will using his speed and height and quick first step.

"We need to set screens on Hart at the next possession. Right at the top of the key. Make Driskill come help. Like this..."

It was zero hour minus 26 minutes.

All across Newburyport, across Massachusetts and New England and the U.S.A. and the world, an era had come to a close and almost no one had the slightest idea. Every individual human mind was fixed on its own point of focus. For most, that point was agreeably, even delightfully banal.

Almost everyone's favorite thing in the whole world was to eat in front of the TV with a sweetheart, friends, or a loving family. Indeed, the phrase "TV dinner," though no longer current, remained a crystalline summation of the purest form of joy ever discovered, the apex and achievement of mankind's search for happiness.

But for uncountable millions, the dinner was over, and the TV screen would shine no more.

Chapter 21
Darkness Falls Across the Land

Kosoko Wright, and his Liberators
Hank Hart, and his Clippers
Ms. De Bono
His Honor Mayor Frank Wright
Peter Graff

We make a big deal about them, but coincidences are trivial. We marvel at them only because we attach meanings to the ones we happen to notice. A thing happens here, and at the same moment another thing happens there, and this is simply an ordinary function of time. With so much damned nonsense happening in the world, how could some of it fail to happen simultaneously? But if those two things happening at a given time are in some way related, then we startle at it as at something supernatural.

And so it is with the first coincidence of our story.

Vivid, cinematic, much wondered at, but ultimately of no consequence and quite ordinary.

That tall drink of water Kosoko Wright faced off against Hank Hart. Many heroes and villains of the coming storm are there, on the court or in the stands, and all their eyes are on the adversaries.

Hank, as Lefty has observed, is getting the better of the matchup. Blocking shots, bringing the hot hand. Kosoko is dragging himself down the court as the second half winds down, waving off Coach Harriman. Mazi sets that crafty screen that Lefty was talking about. As Kosoko rolls to the basket, Lefty feeds Mazi, and Mazi throws the ball up for an alley-oop.

This is Kosoko's first dunk in a game. Later he'll swear it was his first dunk ever. The move's degree of difficulty casts this into doubt. The way he seized Mazi's floating pass out of the air at its eleven-plus foot zenith and jammed it through the hoop suggests hundreds of hours of practice.

Mazi and Kosoko had a basket in their driveway (where, admittedly, they didn't live, but they visited at least once a week), and a public court two blocks from school, and daily access to the Filibuster Gym on campus. It would have been difficult, but not impossible, for them to practice this alley-oop without detection.

At any rate, the dunk was monstrous. And even if nothing notable had coincided with it, it would have made a powerful impression on everyone present.

It was good. It was magnificent. It was a thing in itself.

It's too bad it happened exactly when it did, because it deserved to stand alone.

Instead, it happened, to the split second, at the same time the lights went out. When he caught the pass in the air, it was still a golden age. An age of sunlit progress and achievement, a watershed in the history of a world which had never before seen so much prosperity, health, and knowledge.

And it's here that I enter the story.

You can call me Pete. I was there in the gym last night. That was strange, because I was really a baseball fan.

An army buddy of mine, Terry Driskill, had a son who played point guard for Newburyport High. And although Terry was still serving in Afghanistan, he'd gotten in touch with me and suggested I check out a game. I lived in Boston at that time, maybe 45 minutes away, so I figured why the hell not. I'd driven up to Newburyport and taken a seat in the bleachers. I could do this because I was between jobs (I was a reporter) and between wives. Pretty much between everything. These were tough times for reporters, especially for a throwback like me who'd actually hung onto his typewriter well into the late '90s.

Like everybody else there, I figured this was some kind of gimmick. Kid dunks the ball, the lights go out. Boom.

The gym was pitch black for a few seconds while our eyes adjusted to the darkness. Then people started clapping, cheering, for the slam dunk. I didn't know. We thought the thing was planned, like the curtains coming down at the climax of a show. The applause died out, though, and it was still dark. And you could just make out the players on the floor, most of them milling around like confused ants, and I figured this was a legit outage.

And it started to sink in that this was weird. Like, the next guess would be it was a blown fuse, but even the exit signs were dark, and those should have had backup power. And now there was a kind of moan building up in the bleachers.

I looked around in the darkness, and I could make out that people were taking out their phones, but nobody was actually turning his or her phone on. So I took my phone out, and the damn thing was out of batteries. Wouldn't light up.

The gym's windows were frosted and grated, and it was night, and it was really extremely dark.

I followed the crowd out of the stands, out onto the football field. I remember it smelled like new-mown grass. And out there in the cold night air we could see that this hadn't been no blown fuse. It was a big blackout. Really big. Not only was every window in Newburyport dark, but the sky was black and starry. No glow on the horizon from any neighboring town.

Somebody said something about something being broken.

Then we heard the roar of like a tornado or a freight train. Something big was moving, fast, overhead, but we couldn't make it out.

And then the impact, maybe five blocks away: One of the loudest sounds I've ever heard, and a brilliant flash.

People were screaming now, some of them.

I had the reporter's instinct, which could have been mistaken for a heroic instinct, to start running toward the fire. Some of the people were running with me. I almost ate shit when we reached a fence I couldn't see until the last second. We hopped it. I wished I were a taller man. I wish all parts of me had multiplied in proportion. It was a wooden rail fence at the edge of the football field. Then we were crossing the street. It couldn't have been nine o'clock, even, but there was no traffic. It was a moonless night. All the light that could be seen came from the impact site, which lay on the other side of several blocks of houses and small buildings. It was cold. My legs were tight and springy.

I didn't want to die.

We reached ground zero. It was a trail of fire and junk that had been some kind of commercial jet plane, plus a few row houses. No way anyone had survived inside that plane, but there might have been injured survivors in the buildings.

The air smelled like kerosene.

Some woman from the basketball game was taking charge. She was yelling at everyone to keep back, giving some instructions I couldn't make out.

I took out my phone to snap some pictures, but of course my phone was still dead. I wanted to know where the hell were the firemen, and the cops. It had been a good ten minutes since the crash.

The turbines in the jet engines were still spinning out their moments of inertia. There was an extraordinary quantity of glass all over the place. You have to understand that the flames were so brilliant, the smoke so thick, and the night so dark that all we could see was a refracting yellow glare, a diffuse, kaleidoscopic specularity, like the world reflected in a shattered fun-house mirror.

I'd served in Iraq and Afghanistan, first as a soldier, then as a reporter. I'd seen crashed planes, crashed helicopters, blown up buses and trucks and personnel carriers, hotels on fire, airstrikes, artillery strikes. I'd fought fires. But the difference in context was stark. It had been terrible overseas, nightmarish, absurd, but I'd had a definite role to play, a set of procedures to execute. I'd never had to wonder what to do.

A crowd had encircled the jet. Some people were tentatively probing toward it, but nobody could get in close with all that jet fuel burning.

It really looked like the end of the world, which at the time it was.

I turned away from the heat, and at that point I saw the other fires. Whole neighborhoods were going up now, far away, too far to have been sparked by the jet crash.

Probably every adult there was thinking about 9/11. What I felt specifically was like at that moment when the first tower collapsed, the hyperreality of it, that we were watching real people die.

Somebody asked what the hell was happening. I turned, and it was an old guy with a white beard. I don't know if I noticed it then, but there was something weird about this old man. He stood out from the others by the intensity of his face, his eyes. What was happening?

Not realizing the answer until it came out of my mouth, I said, "We're under attack."

A black guy was there, standing out. Well-dressed, handsome guy. He was shouting, waving his arms, making like "remain calm" gestures with his hands, like he was patting down a bedspread. Everybody knew who he was but me. I was a stranger.

He was Mayor Frank Wright, also come from the game.

I could make out a few words above the noise.

"Good people!" I think he said.

I looked away again. This was pointless, the commotion. The jet fuel burned too hot. Even if the fire trucks had come they couldn't have done much.

I'd seen another plane crash some years back. Not a civilian plane. A C-130 transport carrying heavy armor. This was in Basra. It was bad, but nothing like this. That C-130 had done a crash landing. The crew had survived. This airliner here hadn't crash landed, it had just crashed. Fallen out of the sky like a cannonball. Disintegrated.

Some people were crying. I walked toward the mayor. He was telling people to fetch water, that kind of thing. He had a bullhorn, but it wasn't working. Nothing was working.

I introduced myself to the mayor. "Pete Graff, sir." He tried to wave me off, but I told him I was ex-military and after that he wouldn't let me leave his side.

"What do I do?" I think he shouted in my ear. I gave him the thumbs-up, like he was already doing it. He started going around consoling people. Somebody had brought blankets, and he was giving them out. It was freezing.

"Hey!" a guy grabbed my arm. Black kid, looked familiar. "You know where my father's at?"

I realized this was the kid, the one who'd thrown the alley-oop pass so his brother could dunk it the ball.

"Yeah," I said. "He's, he's right down there, down the sidewalk." I stuttered a little, even back then.

Mayor Wright saw his son. "Mazi," he said, and he grabbed the kid. Looked like the mayor was comforting himself as much as his son. Then he looked up, afraid, and said, "Where's Kosoko?"

"Dad, he broke his leg. He's still in the gym with mom. He looks really bad."

"Jesus Christ," said the mayor. "I'll be right there."

I stopped him and told him I'd look after Kosoko. The mayor needed to be here.

"Graff," said the mayor. There was a terrible intensity in his face. He seemed like the only one there. "Have you heard anything?"

"Not as a far as you know," I said.

Weapons Officer David Muratskian stared into his instruments, which flashed in the same arcane patterns as ever.

His skin gratefully shed its heat to the cool of the ventilation fan. His eyes stung, and his lips tasted of salt, but Muratskian didn't know he was sweating.

His focus narrowed more and more tightly on a single pixel of his screen, as his mind floated somewhere beyond the submarine's alloy skin. The alloy was HY-90, a blend of nickel, molybdenum, and chromium. Like David Muratskian, the alloy had been crafted to withstand incredible pressure, and still the submarine creaked as it climbed to the surface. Muratskian's heart was all he could hear, and it beat fast, like the roll of a drum.

"DEFCON 2," said the radioman. It sounded to Weapons Officer David Muratskian like a cry from the ocean's deepest trench. The alarm began to sound.

Muratskian pulled a cigarette from a pack in his shirt pocket. Somehow he lit it without once looking away from that pixel. Somebody behind him kept saying, "Jesus, Jesus, Jesus" like a Baptist at a funeral.

Book II: Nulli Expugnabilis Hosti

Chapter 1
Critical

Kosoko Wright
Lefty Davis
Peter Graff
Barbara Wright
Mazi Wright
The staff of Anna Jaques Hospital

In America, nothing is ever as bad as it seems. And in America, nothing is ever as good as it seems.

Fast-forward 30 minutes, and we're carrying Kosoko down the street in a jury-rigged stretcher—really just a couple sheets he's already sweated and bled through. It's me, Barbara Wright, Mazi, and Lefty carrying him. Kosoko is semi-delirious, possibly feverish, possibly bleeding internally.

His right femur had snapped when he landed from the dunk. I'd set his leg as best I could and field-dressed it with some kiddie supplies from the school infirmary, but my medical knowhow extended just far enough for me to know that he was in very bad shape. Life-threatening shape. I'm yelling at civilians to get out of the way.

We're just getting to the hospital. Lefty stumbles and almost falls, jostling Kosoko, who lets out a scream and passes out. We run him into the emergency room.

It's surprisingly empty. Surprisingly, until you consider that the ambulances, like all motor vehicles, are toast. It's also pitch black. Some people have flashlights which for whatever reason are still working. Two nurses, man and woman, rush over to greet us. They listen to our story and then disappear, telling us it shouldn't be more than an hour.

"An hour" I said. "There's like five patients waiting here!"

"Sir," said the woman, "we have no lights, no computers, no diagnostic machines, no phones. No cars means nobody coming in for the night shift."

"Okay," I said, watching them hurry off. "Just know that this kid is in critical condition!"

Fucking unbelievable. And then, yeah, I sat there for an hour with these folks. I got to know them a little bit.

Barbara, the mother, was of course scared shitless. No surprise there. She loved her kid. She's holding his hand and whispering to him as he goes in and out of consciousness. She was extremely polite to me, polite enough to keep me at arm's length. I respected that. I'm from New York, all right? We don't get in each other's business.

Mazi was no less worried, but he was pretty stoic about it. He seemed real focused on the situation. "Mindful" is the pop psych word for it. He told me he "knew for sure" his brother would be okay. He looked like he meant it, too. The expression on his face, that sick worry, didn't belong there. That face was made to smile.

Lefty was weird. Obviously an only child. Kept trying to engage me on the topic of reusable objects and their properties. What fucking objects? Not uninteresting, but bizarre, timing-wise. He was a nice-looking boy, clean cut, black hair gold-rimmed spectacles, and of course, like Mazi and Kosoko, was still in his basketball uniform.

Funny thing: In all this time, they didn't really ask who I was or what I was doing there. I'd told them my name and that the mayor had sent me, and I guess that was good enough for them. Just as well, under the circumstances. They really wouldn't have understood if I'd told them.

They all wanted to know what the hell was going on, and for whatever reason seemed to think I was the one who could tell them. Something about my demeanor, or what? Strange thing was they were right. I knew what was going on. I knew why the lights had gone out.

"Coco Wright?" a nurse called.

Barbara didn't even correct him. We were helping them rush Kosoko inside.

Five minutes later we're in an operating theater, and Kosoko's full of tubes. I'm giving them info on what went down, rapid fire so I don't slow their progress. The doctor, a surgeon, loudly regrets that it's been over two hours since the accident. Well, who the fuck kept us waiting an hour? I mean, unbelievable! Barbara's chewing the guy out, and I'm nodding my head with seriously affirmative emphasis.

Chapter 2
Encircled

Barbara Wright
Frank Wright Davis
Chief Cruz

Barbara Wright had started planning her life early. She was in the 9th grade when she realized she wanted to be a lawyer; she'd read a book about Thurgood Marshall and that had been that. Her whole life had unfurled before her: college in Cambridge, law school in New Haven, career in Boston. No husband, no kids, just a dedicated service to justice and civil rights.

Now she stood in the kitchen of the house she'd bought for her husband and her kids, looking out into the faces of hundreds of strangers in the failing light of dusk.

"Get away from the window," said Frank Wright.

She turned around to see him, but it was too dark. The power and the heat were still out, though they still had running water. She wanted to laugh at him for his concern, for thinking he needed to protect her, but it wasn't funny this time.

Their house was surrounded.

Frank and Barbara were there alone; their kids Kosoko and Mazi were still living on the Garrison campus. It seemed safer for them to be there. Anyway, Frank had insisted. Garrison had put in all kinds of security features after the Addams gun incident. Frank had assigned some cops to patrol campus round the clock.

"We can't stay here anymore, Frank," said Barbara. "We have to join the boys."

Frank didn't move. Had he heard her?

It was so dark, so cold in the house. At least the crowd outside had stopped chanting and yelling. It was simply incredible that they had latched on to her husband as the bad guy.

There was no phone service, no power, no TV. How was Frank supposed to know what had happened, how long it would take to restore electricity? How was he supposed to know anything? What was he supposed to do?

"I'll get you to the school," Frank said. "But I can't stay there. It will look like I'm running away."

How long had it been since he'd slept more than an hour or two at a time? He'd set up a command station there at the house when the people had practically torn City Hall apart. Cops and staffers and doctors came and went at all hours. But now they were alone in there.

"I want you to stay with us at Garrison," she told him. "It's not safe for you here alone. I know you want to protect the city, but you have to protect yourself to do that."

He stepped toward her, and the last light of the evening sky fell across his face. He was transformed. His beard was rough. His face was drawn and hungry.

"Baby," he said.

But then they heard the bang, and she saw him jump.

"Jesus!" she said.

Two more bangs. It was something hitting the house, a metallic rapping.

Frank went to the front door, swearing under his breath.

"What do you want?" he called through the door.

"Sir, it's us," It was the voice of Cruz, his chief of police. "We're here to get you out."

Frank opened the door to let in Cruz and two officers. The people outside didn't try to rush the door. They just stood there.

Frank talked to Cruz. Barbara hadn't been able to persuade Frank to move to the Garrison campus with her, but Cruz was. They spent a hot ten minutes packing up and then assembled back in the foyer.

"Okay," Cruz said. "It's only about 15 blocks, and we're gonna want to cover the ground quickly. Sir, ma'am, I don't care what happens, what anybody says to you. Don't engage. Don't even look at them. Just keep moving fast and we're going to be okay. You got it?"

Frank thanked him. Barbara just held tight to the handles of her suitcases and closed her eyes.

"Let's go," said Cruz.

Chapter 3
Settle In

Naomi Echeveria
Birdie Love
Dr. John Harriman, PhD
Ms. De Bono
Mr. Landreneau
Rebekah Marigold
Fannie Romero
Tanya Roberts
Brett Sanger
Willie Maricino

The town of Newburyport, Massachusetts was dark, apart from the fires.

It had been two weeks since the blackout began, and there'd been no word about when the lights would be back on. No word, in fact, on any subject whatsoever. The mayor was here on campus, residing here with his family. And he had no idea what was going on. Like the power and the vehicles and everything else, communications were dark.

The fires were everywhere. Mostly campfires, arrayed across the hills like yellow stars.

But there were also house fires, building fires, burning gas stations and convenience stores. Mostly the fires just burned. With their trucks not starting, the firemen couldn't get to most of the fires to fight them.

It was sublime watching those flames reach into the night sky, haloed by the falling snow. But the air was never quite clean. Everything smelled like cinders. Probably that's what people missed the most—the deep lungful of fresh air.

Naomi and Birdie were walking that evening hand in hand. Naomi was crying. She feared for the safety of her parents and her little brother. She feared they might be dead. Birdie said nobody could know that—there was no evidence for it.

Naomi's family lived in Chicago. They probably had power there. They were probably right as rain. Naomi's expression was of startled pain, as though somebody had just surprised her with a punch in the nose. It was hard for Birdie to look at.

Birdie was one of those who has a very hard time being around people who are depressed or upset. She wanted to be a comfort to Naomi and was doing her best, but what was she supposed to say? She didn't even know how her own mother was doing, even though she lived right there in Newburyport. It was too dangerous to walk the streets, and there was no other way to get home to find out.

Anyway, Birdie knew Naomi's family was okay. Even if they'd lost power in Chicago, as we had here. Naomi was the kind of person to whom no harm every really comes.

"Bottom line," said Birdie, "we need to worry about ourselves. We got problems enough here. We need to stay warm and fed. We need to watch out for crazies."

They walked along the edge of campus, but inside the edge, on the grass, not on the sidewalks. The darkness without was deeper than the darkness within.

From that darkness had come many refugees. Parents of local students, families of teachers. People from the town, too, who'd fled their homes. With the cops unable to remotely communicate and traveling only on foot, they were close to helpless. The crazies were guys in black hooded sweatshirts and animal masks who ran through the streets beating people up, stealing, starting new fires. Word was there were other safe areas in Newburyport where people had gathered. Schools and hospitals, mostly.

There were god-damn flies all over the place.

One thing Ms. De Bono had never expected was to ask the advice of Dr. John Harriman. Especially a Dr. Harriman who was drunk. And crying. But there she was, standing outside her office in the cold, in the darkness, sharing a cigarette with the old fool and asking him what she should do.

From an administrative standpoint, it was a nightmare scenario.

Hundreds of students under her protection, no electricity, no phones, no way to contact parents. Most these parents living out of state, many out of the country, with no way to get themselves there to collect their children.

The gas pumps weren't working. The school might have had enough food to last another two weeks, but without refrigeration it was mostly going bad. The vending machines had all been smashed and emptied. At least half a dozen kids had the flu, incidentally, which was an outrageous number even for winter.

One bright side was that a lot of police had come with him when the mayor had moved onto campus. They were far luckier than most in this respect, having that protection.

For a man sobbing through a whiskey haze, Harriman looked rather shrewd, rather superior. He plainly enjoyed being asked for help, especially by her.

"Look to the classics, my dear," said he, blowing his nose and composing himself. "Look to Plutarch, and Thucydides. Ah! Let Themistocles be not far from your mind. And Cyrus the Great! And Alexander! For we find ourselves, you'll agree, knocked back a few civilizational stages. We must live as men did in the antique world."

De Bono nodded, and exhaled a jet of smoke. She looked at him for a second, and then said, "Yes. Right. But seriously, Dr. Harriman. You've got nothing for me? I need your help."

Harriman said, "I'm perfectly serious, Ms. De Bono. The habits of modern life won't answer in this hour. Look around at these brats, these young weenies. My God. If you want to find a violinist, you need only throw a stone. If you want the verb *etre* conjugated in the past perfect tense, you'll find these youngsters expertly equipped. But to stay alive is quite a different matter. Their every need, like ours, has been catered to. Our every desire has been at hand. No more. The buttons we've pushed will not reply. The lights that guided us are dark now."

So they were.

And it was a new world through which our heroes stumbled and searched. Turning the light switch on when entering a room, checking their phones, staring at their computer screens, all habits ingrained since birth and now totally pointless.

At the same time, sweating in his dorm room, lay a stoical Kosoko Wright. Half the school had offered to sit by his bedside, to read to him, to wet his lips with damp cotton balls. But he'd banished all the world. Even his mother.

Kosoko had suffered a broken femur. The pain in his right leg shone right through the cast. He was, he knew, extremely fortunate to have made it this far.

The night of the blackout, when they'd brought him to the dark emergency room, had been bedlam. On top of the plane crash, there'd been something like 20 car crashes just in the area of Anna Jaques Hospital, not to mention all the fire victims (mostly smoke inhalation, but also nightmare-inducing burns).

Kosoko had sat waiting with his leg elevated for what had seemed like hours. In the dark. All of this, remember, was in the dark. He'd been stoned out of his mind on whatever endorphins and other neurotransmitters his body could generate to mask the anguish. Everything had seemed to be reaching him from far off, whether his mother's words of reassurance or the crash of gurneys through the corridors.

He'd thought about the game, about the pick that had been set for him so that he could go up for the alley-oop. About the weird certainty in Lefty's face as he'd called the play. And of course, over and over, the way the lights had gone out as he dunked the ball, and then how he'd fallen through the blackness. When he'd hit the hard wood he'd thought at first that he was punching right through it, but it was his leg snapping under him.

What he remembered less clearly was the small team that had scrubbed down and tended to him at last. It had been, thank God, what's called a closed reduction—no surgery, but a setting of the bone through the skin. But the pain was almost cosmic—it became the entirety of his consciousness at the moment that the femur reconnected. Later they'd told him that they didn't dare give him anesthesia without being able to monitor him on the machines.

He wouldn't be doing pirouettes in the near future, or for that matter helping out in this emergency, but they said he'd be walking in about six weeks and playing ball not long after that. But six weeks is a long time when you're fifteen years old and in pain and lying in the dark by yourself.

So he lay in his soaked bedsheets and listened to the silence of an unplugged world. He had a view of the tennis courts from his window, but it was too dark to see them.

I'd love to be able to tell you that Kosoko Wright, a young man I greatly admired, was quite free of self-pity. He was not. He was fairly drowning in it. But if you've never been a promising athlete suffering a disabling injury, maybe you should suck it. Yes, the whole world seemed to be in pain. People were hungry, half out of their minds. But our young man here was all of fifteen years old, remember, and the world had just clipped his wings.

People in those days spent a lot of time outdoors, especially at night, despite the cold. If you've never been in a blackout, you'd be surprised by how many candles you need just to read a book. And such resources as candles had to be jealously husbanded.

Have I mentioned that school was still, sort of, in session? It had been Ms. De Bono's idea, and it had impressed me quite a bit. What other way did she have to keep the students occupied than to continue to hold classes? In fact, they were now held seven days a week. It was kind of understood that none of what was happening right now was going to leave much of a dent in anyone's transcript, but everyone carried on as though it were any other semester.

Anyway, yes, outdoors, despite the snow and the bitter chill. Tonight some of the teachers and students had gathered in the middle of the football field. Everyone was lying down on blankets and sleeping bags in the snow. Everyone looking up at the stars, except Brett Sanger, who sat Indian style with that funny little pucker in his mouth, with his acoustic guitar in his lap.

The cherubic Fannie Romero spoke up and broke the silence. "I think it was the earth that did it."

Rebekah Marigold punched her in the arm.

Sanger strummed out a chord in emphasis.

Mr. Landreneau, the Newburyport High chemistry teacher who'd somehow wound up bivouacked at Garrison, quieted everyone down.

"Fannie," he said. "Tell us what you mean."

"Because," said Fannie, making this up as she went along, "the earth needed a rest. From pollution, global warming, that stuff."

The kids were giggling about this, but Landreneau said it was interesting. He was half participating in the discussion and half keeping an eye out for Presto. Presto roamed the campus freely, and Harriman was not to be reasoned with on the matter.

"The earth. Very interesting. You're certainly right about one thing, Fannie, in saying that the earth is getting a break from this blackout."

"It's not the earth!" said Rebekah. "The earth doesn't like *do* things. With *agency*. It's not a *person*."

"That's true, Rebekah," said Landreneau. "But right now, we're just throwing out thoughts, okay? No bad ideas, no dumb questions. We've heard some of you say it was a cyberattack, or a solar flare, or some new military weapon, but we really don't know. Nothing seems to fully explain why the cars don't work or the plane crashed. Even an EMP— anyway, I really think Fannie's brought up a good point. We know that climate change is already happening, but we're approaching a tipping point. There's a certain amount of CO_2 in the atmosphere, a certain temperature the earth can reach, and after that we'll get a kind of snowball effect and we'll see some really bad things happen."

Sanger strummed the same chord several more times. He didn't know too many chords.

"Like the cities getting covered with water?" said Tanya Roberts.

"Yes, and like hunger, and mass extinctions of all kinds of wildlife. Maybe viruses and diseases could be released by the melting permafrost. Have you all learned about permafrost? It's very serious business. And now, kind of whether we like it or not, we're taking a little pause here in Essex County (and who knows where else). And the planet has a chance to catch its breath a little."

Senior Willie Maricino smiled up at the falling snow. "Yeah, because the politicians are too stupid to do anything about climate change."

"And the corporations," said Rebekah. "Too greedy."

"Well, that's true," said Landreneau. "We've had a lot of people doing the wrong thing for a very long time. But it's a very tricky problem, trying to solve it, because you see *everything* we do adds to the CO_2 in the atmosphere. Every factory and every car, certainly, but also every person walking down the street, every dog or cat, even when they're asleep. We're contributing CO_2 right now, just lying here talking. Anything that burns or breathes makes the problem worse."

Fannie punched Rebekah in the arm. "So maybe it was the earth!" she said.

Landreneau sat up on his elbows and looked around. No sign of Presto, but who knew what was out there in that blackness? "Well, I'll tell you this, Fannie. There's an idea called the Gaia hypothesis that's not so very different from what you're talking about. Maybe in a complex set of reactions, the planet's ecosystem could lash out in a way that would be almost like anger, but—" he squinted his eyes. "Shit."

"All...she...does...is...laugh," Brent Sanger sang, softly strumming away.

A few meters away, in the gym, I was standing before those Liberators who could still stand: Jackie, Lefty, Zero, and Mazi. They were at attention, or a lazy slovenly weak approximation of it.

Birdie and Naomi were there, too, observing.

There was so much anxiety among them that none could stand still or keep from glancing around and whispering. They worried about the food running out. They worried about the crazies in the streets, the fires, and about Kosoko's leg.

"You were a team. You still are," I said. "But the name of the game right now ain't basketball. It's survival. Do you dig me?"

"Okay, but sir? We can still play basketball, right?" Jackie was gripping a Wilson Evolution indoor ball, holding its cool dimples against his cheek.

"Kid, I saw your game against Newburyport. You couldn't play basketball before. But seriously, folks. You're the closest things to athletes we've got, and that means you're the fastest and the fittest. And that's what we need. You know I was in the army. I'm going to train you."

I was pacing like General Patton. Actually, I was kind of talking like him, too, in that stentorian growl. Or, I guess, I was talking like George C. Scott as Patton. In *Patton*.

"Mr. Graff," said Mazi. "It seems like you're worrying too much, right? Blackouts happen sometimes. They come and go."

A thrill rose in my lungs. These kids had little more insight into what had happened than their teachers. I didn't like being the one to spoil their illusions.

"I don't like being the one to spoil your illusions," I said, "but this is no ordinary blackout. You've got to know this. You're smart. Blackouts don't destroy battery operated radios. Blackouts don't fry laptops or turn cell phones off while they still got juice left."

"What do you think is going on?" said Zero. He looked even more gloomy than the others. His eyes were gleaming. Even the famine that was settling in couldn't account for how hollow his face looked. "We hear all sorts of stuff, but it all sounds like bullshit."

"I don't know for sure either," I said. "But I'll tell you what I do know. About 18 months ago, a group called the EMP Commission presented a paper before Congress. It said that the country was at serious risk. Like, existential-threat type risk. Because all North Korea or Russia or China had to do was detonate a nuke in our upper atmosphere to fry every circuit in the contiguous 48. They said it could take years to restore power if such an attack took place. It said that a lot of people could starve to death, because we wouldn't be able to use powered vehicles to sow, harvest, and ship food."

"How many people?" said Lefty.

You've got all kinds of schools of thought about how to handle this kind of situation, and up until that moment I really wasn't sure what the right approach was. But looking into their faces, I felt pretty sure they should get it straight, no chaser. What do I know, right? I was doing my best.

"A hundred million," I said.

I let that sink in.

"So with that out of the way," I said, "You think the rations you're getting at the moment are stingy, but I'm going to go to Mayor Wright and Ms. De Bono this very night and recommend cutting them in half, and then maybe in half again. Garrison is our base of operations. We got cops here, six of them, and here they'll stay because we've got to protect our people. These kids. Okay? But while they're here standing watch, we have to keep everybody healthy. You lot are going to be our first line of defense in the event of a violent incident. I'm going to teach you how to stop bleeding, how to apply a tourniquet, how to treat a burn or even a bullet wound.

"Out there," I said, pointing through the gym window, "are a lot of good people. And a lot of them are hurting. We're trying our best to help as many people as we can. But not everybody out there is good. And without the rule of law, things can go south in a hurry, believe me. Some people will do things they never thought themselves capable of. Without the rule of law, you've got what they call 'might makes right.'

"I'm going to teach you how to handle emergencies, how to keep cool, how to know when to stay and help and when to take off and regroup. And a ton of other stuff. Don't worry. I'm telling you, you'll be good."

"Yeah," said Mazi. "We'll be good. Me and Kosoko got this."

"Well," I said, "I hope by the time he's up on his feet this will all be over. But yeah, your help is going to be invaluable."

"I can learn this shit as good as anybody," said Birdie. "My moms is a nurse."

Fuck. I couldn't send these little girls out there to deal with active shooters. It was an unacceptable risk. But the looks on their faces. Damn it. Okay.

"Fine. I'll train you, too. But you're going to follow orders and no god-damn back-talk."

And that was it.

The Liberators were, for the moment, no longer just a basketball team but a squad of first-responders. I knew they weren't ready for it, but hell, kids not much older than them had fought and died for this country.

I was going to say something else, but there was a commotion outside. Shouting. Really loud.

We ran out into the snow, and I could just make out some figures in the dark a short way off. Definitely a fight brewing. Hollering, curses, shoving. We were running over, and then we heard a shot.

And then a second shot.

We reached them, and saw two men on the ground, and a third man, Mr. Landreneau, standing there shaking.

"Jesus fucking *Christ*," said Landreneau, staring at me. "This guy came out of nowhere. He said he was a parent."

The guy was dead, and the other guy, one of the cops, was wounded. Fatally, I guessed. Gut shot.

"He said his *kid* went here, but he couldn't—he couldn't—didn't know—his kid's name! Guy didn't know his own kid's name!"

The officer lasted until morning. A lot of valuable medical supplies got spent trying to save him. But he died just the same. These kids had never seen a man die before.

Chapter 4
Tiger Style

Jackie Polish
Dr. Harriman, PhD

The next morning found Jackie in bed with covers over his head, not sleeping but composing in a spiral-bound notebook.

Something you should understand about Jackie is that even though he grew up in a well-to-do household, he'd had his share of troubles. And getting out of the house, out of Manhattan, to boarding school at Garrison, had been good for him, but he'd retained some habits of his childhood. He lived in his head a little bit. He'd focused all those brains and all that imagination for which he'd later be famous on banal totems, bringing them to life and color. One of those totems was cereal.

He loved cereal.

He loved the characters on the boxes, the sugary crunch, the childish motifs. He regarded them the way he regarded his elderly relatives in Brooklyn: ridiculous, weird, but adorable and dearly loved.

He collected the boxes and put them on his wall; his favorite boxes were from obscure brands he'd picked up on his travels. Local supermarket off-brand offerings, regional favorites not available in his native New York. King Vitamin was a favorite box. Instead of a cartoon drawing, it showed a photograph of a grinning older man in a plastic crown and ermine robe. "Look at that! It's *insane*," he'd tell his friends, showing old King Vitamin off to them.

Now they were about out of food at Garrison.

Crazies were starting to surround the campus. The world was coming to an end. I, Peter Graff, was training him to be some kind of medic, and all Jackie could think about was the taste and texture and coldness of a heaping bowl of Cap'n Crunch or Cocoa Pebbles. It would float before his eyes as he went about his day. Against his will, he fantasized continuously about the innocent days when he'd sat at the breakfast table and retreated into the dulcet milky flakes and the campy charm of those cereal boxes.

Now, in his composition book, he wrote,

Tiger, Tiger, burning bright

From the rich expressive blue

What immortal hand or eye

Could loose him from that kerchief, guy?

Sworn from first to ever chew

Your flakes of gold

My heart to warm, but aching cold

And each particular flake

Embossed

Laced with the touch

Of morning's frost

Incisors mine to set on edge

And greet each day as newly fledged

From bottom dredged, each golden thing

The chill white rivers through your gaps

Another Lactaid gush I taps

And sweetness from the vex't Bermooths

Grand fleetness, shocks for each my tooths

Love's great thirst is undiminished

Proving worth of every crown

And when at last

The whole is finished

    Set aside thy spoon, great tiger!

    Tip the bowl

        And slurp it down.

God-*damn* it, he was so hungry.

The next morning he ran into Harriman and Presto. The old man looked like he'd been crying. That made two of them.
"Coach?" said Jackie, "can I maybe ask you something?"
"Hmm? Yes. Yes, of course, my boy."
"Do you think—my parents, my sister, they live in New York. Upper West Side. Do you figure they lost their electricity and such, too?"
"I won't soft-soak you, Lefty," said Harriman.
"Jackie."

"Yes. I'm afraid my head hasn't cleared up quite yet. That's why Presto and I are taking our constitutional. Jackie, I won't soft-soak you. I have no way of knowing for sure, but my instinct tells me this blackout extends far beyond here, far beyond New York, even. But I wouldn't lose hope if I were you. Why, do you know, boy, in my time I've seen four wars? Yes, and fought in one of them. I've seen violence and terror, collapsing towers, the side knocked out of the Pentagon.

"I've seen good things, too, of great moment. I almost cried the day the Berlin Wall came down. Because it showed me what I've always felt. That we could take it. This country's been through one hell of a lot, but we're still here. We've survived it all. And I think we're going to survive this, too."

Jackie was really crying now. His eye patch was flooding. Harriman's words had struck a very lovely note at that moment, a note that resounded through Jackie's mind and heart. "I hope so, sir. I sure do. Because if anything was to happen to my mom and dad, or my sister, shit. I'd want to lay down and die right here."

"Lie," said Harriman.

"What?"

"Lie. Lie down and die."

"What?"

"You said you'd want to *lay* down and die. The correct usage would be *lie down*."

Chapter 5
How the Leopard Got His Spots

Dr. John Harriman, PhD

Twice-born Dionysus, that epicene superstar, the dying-and-rising god, the lord of ritual madness, tragedy, the root and the vine, transcended Greek antiquity.

He was Thracian, Minoan, Asiatic. The god that came.

He drove the ladies insane.

He elevated them to divinity and reduced them to the state of red-toothed nature and made them more dangerous than lions.

In this way, Dionysus separated himself from the rest of the twelve Olympians. While they stood gorgeous and aloof, inscrutable and apart from human life, Dionysus became a precursor to Yahweh and Allah. He was a personal god, with whom human beings had a direct, gnostic connection. His cult was mystical, inspirational, in a way that was alien to the sunlit world of the Ancient Greeks.

Dionysus was a god of firelight.

Harriman, brooding and autocratic, stood before a fire and thought about Dionysus.

Dionysus who sets us free, who makes us wild, who gives us courage. Harriman had spent his life, in a way, at this god's altar.

So where was his courage? Drunk or sober, he walked around all day knotted up in terror. And it wasn't just the fact that the world was ending. He'd been this way for years, for decades. He was responsible for the safety of these kids. He should be a rock for them. But he wasn't a rock. He was a stuffed cloak-bag of guts.

"Dionysus," he said to the fire. But he couldn't go on. It was too absurd, too pathetic. He wanted strength, power to be himself. But he had no power.

The power was still out, of course. Two weeks and counting. And it had been power that had caused the trouble: a power surge almost certainly resulting, as I had told him, from an EMP attack.

Harriman knew about power surges well enough.

He'd been baptized by one in 1967, off the coast of Vietnam.

Aviation Support Equipment Technician Harriman, young, strapping, tall, and handsome, standing on the deck of the USS *Forrestal*, helping his crew perform a preflight check on a Phantom II fighter-bomber in the South China Sea.

Harriman had been drafted, of course.

He hadn't anticipated the massive escalation of the U.S. military presence in Vietnam. He'd thought it was safe to take time off between college and grad school. He'd been hitchhiking across Ohio when he'd called his parents and discovered they'd received the dread telegram.

But now, he didn't mind the navy. It was an interesting situation to be stuck in.

He'd found to everyone's amazement that he had a knack for working with heavy equipment. And the whole business lined up nicely with a romantic vision he had for his life. Ploughing the wine-dark sea, defying the elements, damning the torpedoes.

He liked serving aboard the carrier.

So much power, with the full strength of the nuclear reactors driving her big screws. So much power, too, in the full strength of her carrier group's arsenal. Jove himself couldn't have hurled such terror as they could. Fighters, bombers, Gatling guns, depth charges, all this in a group of ships of which the *Forrestal* was the center.

The submarines alone, with their warhead-tipped missiles, could with a single shot deliver more, far more destructive force than all the weapons used in World War II, including the two atomic bombs. In the whole world there were only a few countries that the *Forrestal* and her group couldn't easily sterilize.

Harriman was hung over that day. Just lightly hung over, though, from social drinking with the boys the night before. He was a drinker even back then, but not yet a drunk. Anyway, he had overdone it last night. Now he focused his bleary gaze on the bomber's underwing pod. It was hard going. The heat was intense.

He grabbed his second in command, a mechanic named Bill Sicangu. Grabbed him by his coveralls to get his attention. He shouted above the whine of the engines.

"Hey! Cover for me! Five minutes! Getting coffee!"

Sicangu gave the affirmative and got back to work as Harriman made his way below deck. There he found a coffee vending machine. He slumped against the wall, dazzled and giddy, as the coffee maker went to work.

That was when the power surged.

The pilot of the F-4 phantom Harriman had been working on threw the power cutover switch, believing that the standard safety pin was in place. The power surged into the LAU-10 underwing rocket pod that Harriman had been about to check.

They say alcoholic beverages launched the agricultural revolution some 10,000 years ago, and so launched human civilization.

The hunter-gatherers would leave their baskets of wild barley out for days. Rainwater would mix with the barley and ferment it into beer. The people figured out what was happening, and they began mixing in the water on purpose to make more beer.

From then on, they paid a lot more attention to barley. They began to cultivate it, domesticate it. With their new crops to attend to, they could no longer rove around as they had before. They founded settlements. Settlements became villages, villages towns, towns cities, cities city-states, city-states nations, nations empires. Hence history.

Whatever humanity may owe to alcohol, it has paid back.

The power surge into the rocket pod launched a Zuni rocket from the parked Phantom II. As the rocket screamed across the deck, it severed the arm of a crewman before striking another parked plane, an A-4 Skyhawk, whose pilot was Lieutenant John McCain. The rocket exploded on impact, starting a fire on the Skyhawk. McCain managed to exit the plane and was headed away from the fire 90 seconds later when the plane's payload, wing-mounted, 1000 pound B-Bomb, detonated.

Thirty men died in that blast, though McCain escaped with minor shrapnel injuries.

This bomb's explosion was the trigger of a chain reaction; eight more B-Bombs would explode over the next 30 minutes.

Harriman puked up his breakfast. He collapsed in terror against the coffee machine, halfway fainted. He couldn't think, couldn't move. For a moment he felt all the power and all the noise of every jet plane in the United States Navy screaming through his head.

And then a kind of peace came over him. He gave himself ten seconds to do nothing. He closed his eyes.

And then, god-damn him, he was on his feet. And more than that, he was rushing onto the flight deck, deftly stepping through debris and over writhing fire hoses, running right into the flames. He knew at a glance that another surge was likely. Another power surge, another rocket firing, and redoubled destruction and horror.

In such situations, we always hear, the hero denies he's a hero because it all happened so fast, he didn't have time to think or be scared, and he did what everyone would have done.

But Harriman thought, and he was afraid.

He picked up a big hammer and got in as close as the flames would allow him, and then he smashed the hammer into the rocket pod. It was loose, softened by the fire's heat, and it came unfixed and fell into the flames. Another smash sent it off the deck into the ocean.

Then he looked around.

The fire was completely out of control. Crews moved with maximum urgency, removing external fuel tanks from the planes, fighting the fire, falling by the dozens.

The smoke, the heat, the screams overcame Harriman by now. He collapsed to the deck. Then the plane sagged. One of its landing struts buckled and smashed into Harriman's leg.

Harriman lay in the direct sunlight, staring into the cloudless blue. He felt nothing, not even the heat, not even the pain from his shattered leg. Here was the world in all its weight, clamping down to the flight deck, paralyzing him. The world, real life, as others lived it. Before the navy, Harriman had lived in books, in fantasies, adventures, all his life. Now the world had taken its turn.

One hundred thirty-four sailors would lose their lives in that conflagration. It was the deadliest post-World War II U.S. aircraft carrier fire.

Chapter 6
Hunger

Peter Graff
Dr. John Harriman, PhD
Birdie Love
Mayor Wright
Barbara Wright
Naomi Echeveria
Some crazies
Officer Rosewood
Officer Taggart
Elijah Hart

SITUATION REPORT
Week four of the blackout. The Garrisons are slowly
coming together. Mayor Wright and his wife Barbara still
living on campus to be near their sons; it's also a good place
from which to lead, near the center of town and with lots of
accommodations.

Ms. De Bono, still responsible for the children, shares
leadership with the Mayor. Ironically not the best with kids,
De Bono relies a great deal on Naomi Echeveria to keep them
calm. Naomi reads to the younger ones, talks to them listens to
them, tucks them in at night.

There ain't hardly any food left. Most of the households in
town have bare cupboards. No power means no vehicles, no
vehicles means no food distribution.

All of the stores had been smashed open and looted. The
looters hadn't had cars, either. It was kind of impressive that
they'd been able to carry so much off.

They'd carried everything off.

Bathroom sinks, four-poster beds, rivers of melted ice cream, bread, peanut butter, beer, wine, and liquor, produce, meats, sour milk, handguns, rifles, shotguns, ammunition, tents, sleeping bags, tampons, bug spray, windshield wiper blades, big TVs, computers, hard drives, mice and wireless keyboards, lumber, nails, tools, lamps, cement mixers, window panes, motor oil, dog food, cat food, baby food, diapers, shirts, pants, socks, shoes, underwear, hats, winter coats, summer jackets, bathing suits, suitcases, books, candles, kerosene lamps, battery-operated flashlights (some batteries still worked, others didn't. No way to know except to try them), batteries, sex toys, ladders, tires, pharmaceuticals, Blu-Ray discs, trucks, antiques, industrial supplies, vaccines, and jet skis.

Who, me? I'm informally looking out for everyone.

Not in command—that role belongs to the cops and the mayor. Cops mostly living on campus too, by the way. But I'm giving them advice, giving the mayor and Ms. De Bono advice, too.

Bottom line is the interests of the people of greater Newburyport no longer correspond to the interests of those of us on the Garrison campus. The people out there in the darkness, mostly folks with families, are precious and filled with love. But where the rubber meets the road, we've still got a little food, and they don't. And that's a very serious matter.

And sure enough, there have been incidents.

Nothing organized, nothing major. Just outsiders, some of them the anarchist-type crazies, some members of the occult societies that were rising up, some regular civilians, find themselves drifting onto the grounds. Seldom overtly hostile, they nevertheless tend to ask a lot of pointed questions.

Like for example, this evening. Guy in a black hoody. He's not wearing a bandana on his face or one of those stupid Halloween masks that scare the shit out of the kids. Just a guy, mid-20s, in a hoody. Anyway, cops call me over there right away. It's dusk.

"Campus is closed, man," I tell him. "Private property."

Guy says, yeah, but he's not doing anything.

I tell him it don't matter he's not doing anything. He can't be here. Private property. Nobody wants any trouble. Standard script.

"I got stuff I can trade for food," he says. "Guns, whatever you need."

I tell him we're all set re: guns. We've got a whole shitload of guns.

"Don't you worry about that."

He says sure, all right, only he hasn't had anything to eat but a few peanuts in two days. Maybe we can help him out.

And I'm telling him we've got just enough to keep the kids fed, and I look up and there are four of them, not just one. And these others *are* wearing masks. Officers Rosewood and Taggart start getting in the crazies' faces. I motion for them to stay back.

"Now, you gentlemen (yes, I'm calling guys in animal masks "gentlemen"), wouldn't be armed this evening, would you?"

"Come on, man," one of the masks says. "We know you're eating here. We're just asking you to share. You know, there are kids all over town, not just the rich ones you're protecting."

By now there are five or six cops behind me. We've got guns, they don't. They put their hands up, like, "Okay, man, okay," and they back away into the settling darkness.

And it's going to get a lot worse.

It's a miracle the great powers aren't at war now (I know they're not because we'd have noticed if Boston had been blasted off the face of the planet). But the war could start, and the world could end, for real, at any time.

So now it's time for me to step up. Which, thanks very much, I'd actually much prefer not to be the one who has to. I've spent a long time wrestling with the decision, and now I have to commit.

I go to Harriman and tell him I need to borrow Presto. Old man is pretty freaked out these days, but he seems to understand. Presto sure does. He's game as can be. And then we leave. No time for goodbyes. We'll be back, but we gotta go.

Somehow, Elijah Hart had made it to campus. He'd arrived with his son Hank about three hours after I'd left with Presto. He'd come to see the mayor.

Mayor Wright had an office set up on the third floor of the science building, and there he received Hart father and son.

Hart settled into his chair and stared at Wright for a long time before speaking.

"When I was a young man coming up in Quincy, I worked in a fishery. Ever work in a fishery, Wright? Don't answer that. I know you haven't. You're an educated man, Wright. Something—one of those things I admire about you. Me, I didn't go to college. Not an option. So I worked at the fishery.

"Learned three things there. First, I learned to set aside any ideas I might have had about the honorability of an honest day's work. Oh, I'm perfectly serious. An honest day's work, the nobility of working with your hands and your back, to hell with that. Drudgery and wasted time's all it was. Doing work a trained monkey could have done, work not fit for a human being who could think. Wasting the best years of my life in that stinking factory, up to my knees in blood and guts, freezing to death in summer. I could have been learning, like you, eh, Wright? Maybe not at Harvard. Maybe just in a public library. But I could have been developing my mind instead of rotting my feet in that damned slurry."

Wright didn't smile. "Okay," he said. "What's the second?"

"Second?" said Hart.

Hank Hart leaned in and whispered to his father.

"Oh, yeah," said Elijah Hart. "The second thing. The second thing I learned in that fishery was to set aside any ideas about the nobility of the working man."

Wright was surprised to hear it. He'd always thought of Elijah Hart as a great friend of the working man, and he said so.

"Hell, Frank," said Elijah Hart. "I'm everybody's friend. That's what it takes to be a leader. But being in that union in that fishery, I learned soon enough that the organizers were just as crooked as the management. More crooked, in fact. Do you know why I say more crooked, Frank?"

Frank thought a moment. "Because of the hypocrisy?"

"Because of the hypocrisy!" Elijah jabbed his finger toward the mayor. "That's exactly right. Now Mr. Mayor, that's why I admire you. You're free of that kind of cant. You are what you say you are.

"Take this now, this situation here, this end of the world. You could have wasted a lot of resources making a show of saving the whole town. You could have spread your people thin, maybe gotten a lot of cops hurt. But you didn't, Frank. You picked a side and fought for it. You staked your ground right here on this campus, at the school where your kids go, and you secured it against the rest of us. You said, 'To hell with the rest of town. Let them fend for themselves. I'm going to look after my family, my kids' school, my cops, my staff.'"

Mayor Wright felt a stab in the small of his back, right between the shoulder blades. GERD. The digestive acid in his stomach was boiling up into his esophagus and leaking out into his trunk. More stabs, now. His stomach, his sides. His head starting to ring.

"We send out foot patrols every day," he said. "We offer help to all who apply."

"Sure!" said Elijah. "Sure, I know that. Hell, I hope I don't sound like I'm criticizing you. Not at all. Only those of us on the outside, we could use a little bit more than your patrols and your kind offers to help. We could use a bite to eat."

Mayor Wright felt very tired. He hadn't been sleeping, and he hadn't exactly been hanging out at banquets himself. He was subsisting with the others on jelly packets, chocolate milk powder, a little stale Wonder bread.

"What's the third thing?" said the mayor.

Elijah Hart smiled and relaxed in his chair. "Third thing is you can't get the stink out. You can shower five times a day, you can wash your clothes until they fall apart. But that stink, that reek of fish guts, ain't going nowhere."

Harriman threw his Virgil at the gym wall.

"God-damn you puppies!" he cried. "Not one of you is going to bed tonight until we master this play. Not you, Mazi, any more than the others."

"Shit, coach. I got this down a month ago! How it's my fault Zero can't remember to cut to the damn basket?"

"You watch your language," Harriman said. "This is a basketball gym, not a bordello. Mark my words, Mazi Wright: This damned profanity is a defect of your race. Amend your life!"

"Coach, I wouldn't bring race into this if I were you," said Mazi. "We've got enough problems as it is."

"Zero," said the coach. "Zero!"

"What?" said Zero, who had been standing to the side, staring into space.

Harriman told Zero that if he couldn't muster enough enthusiasm to actually pay attention, he should really consider whether he wanted to be on the team. He also pointed out that Zero was the one responsible for the great inconvenience everyone was suffering in having to be here at all on such a miserable freezing gray twilit noon.

Zero, who usually endured such lectures in bewildered silence, surprised everyone by speaking up.

"Well, what the hell are we doing here? The world has come to an end, we've got a total of four lousy players left, you're drunk, Kosoko's in traction practically, and you want to put all this on me?"

It was a damn good point.

Zero could also have added that it was nutty to spend hours in voluntary hard exercise when everyone was on a tightly rationed diet. Or that there was no particular reason to believe the basketball season would ever start back up, or that his was only the most obvious nervous breakdown in progress on the Garrison Liberators.

"All of you guys shut the hell up!" said Jackie. "Jesus Christ. I never heard so much crying outside of a kindergarten. Coach, you want to lead this team? Lead it. Zero, quit making excuses. Mazi, quit blaming Zero. Lefty, take off those stupid glasses and try to look like an athlete."

"Stupid glasses?" said Lefty. "That's pretty funny, Jackie, from somebody wearing an eye patch when he's got two good eyes!"

Jackie threw the basketball at Lefty, that curly haired kid. Lefty, no slouch at dodge-ball, dodged the ball, which soared out of bounds and would have struck the gym doors if Birdie Love hadn't opened them at the last second to enter. She also ducked, and the ball skidded to a stop halfway across the snowy football field.

"I'll get it," said Jackie.

What can I say? The kid was disgusted with himself and everything else. He shook his head in silence as he walked out into the cold air wearing only his sweaty basketball uniform.

And you know how sometimes your heart can just about break when you walk outdoors into the darkness of a winter noon? Yeah. Jackie got to the basketball, which was soaking wet and already starting to freeze over. And Jackie sagged to his knees, and then let himself fall over a little so now he was sitting in that wet snow. Was there ever going to be power and heat again? Would there ever be Frosted Flakes and cold Lactaid? Was he ever again going to see his sister?

That night, Lefty—whose preoccupation with the heavens had not been relaxed by the perfect viewing of the blackout, wandered off of the campus.

He was staring up at the planets as he somehow navigated the bollards and fences that protected the school.

What meaning lay in the positions of those worlds above him? He almost reached up to snatch Jupiter out of the sky. Some answer lay in the firmament, he felt sure, and with that certainty came a rising feeling that blended with the darkness and the cold in his lungs.

"This way," he heard.

Turning, he saw the dark figure of a teenager who was pointing down the trapdoors of a sidewalk into a basement.

Somewhere in Lefty's brain pulsed a synaptic bunch that represented, in the abstract, his rationality and his good judgment. But the rays of dim, sparkling light that had shone down into his eyes from the wandering stars above had, for the moment, silenced the hum of sensibility and caused a sleep of reason. And Lefty thought following this figure into the cellar of this unidentified building seemed a perfectly reasonable idea.

And so he went.

Down into the darkness, into what may have been a kitchen or a storage place for food before it was looted. Down a damp corridor, through a steel door, and now he was in a candlelit ballroom full of people he could barely see. There was a stage at the far side of the ballroom which was itself somehow illuminated.

Lefty felt hands on his back, first just one or two but more and more, moving him through the crowd toward that stage. The stage was bare except for a symbol that hung from the darkness overhead, and the symbol was one he'd never seen: three disks in a triangular formation, with rays of light extending from the whole. The largest disk was yellow, and the smaller ones were blue.

And now, as he reached the lip of the stage, onto it stepped a woman.

She moved to the center, standing before the symbol. It was very seductive, yet somehow not odd, to Lefty that this woman was entirely nude. She was shapely, with full hips and bosom; her hair was long and black, and her skin was almost blue in the limelight. She raised her arms forward toward him, and he saw that crawling up each of her arms was a large live snake. Another snake coiled around her scalp, and yet another was coiled around her waist as a belt.

And now Lefty had the most absurd sensation of rising into the air toward this woman, and so he was, as the gathered people were lifting him off his feet.

Chapter 7
Callithyia

Peter Graff
Presto

So! Presto and I had set out on our mission just before sundown, resolved to cover as much ground in the darkness as we could. We wanted as little human interaction as we could manage on our journey.

Our destination was the Artichoke Dairy, on the outskirts of Newburyport, out on Rogers Street on the other side of the reservoir.

Presto was in high spirits, fascinated to be outside of his usual territory, sniffing everything, wagging his tail, bounding through the snow. We saw a couple guys walking along Ferry Road and he just about broke loose from his leash. He was growling and snarling to beat the band.

I didn't share his enthusiasm.

It was dangerous to be out on these roads, even on a moonless night. Hell, everything about this situation was dangerous.

I had my rifle slung across my back, my parka hood cinched tight. The townspeople were hurting, and that meant pissed off. Far as I could tell, the whole world was pissed off.

"Seems like the whole world is pissed off right now, boy," I told Presto. The air smelled clean the way it does when it's cold. My boots crunched in the snow's crust.

Presto turned and looked at me for a moment.

"How should I know?" I said. "Maybe it will work, maybe not. Damned if it's ever been tried before."

The likelihood of failure, which would have discouraged a sane man, exhilarated this crazy mutt.

We walked for a long time in silence. It was too dark to read the street signs until we were right up to them, but Presto moved forward with confidence. Maybe he could smell the dairy farm.

We began to walk along the edge of the Artichoke Reservoir now. It was safer there, more hidden. But it was rough ground with heavy greenery, so fatiguing. We'd been walking for almost two hours.

"She's been planning this since the early 19th Century," I said. "Did you know that, boy? And it's finally happening. Frankly, I don't know if anything can be done. The wheels are already in motion. Nato forces are on a hair trigger. They're just looking for someone to retaliate against, and when they find one, it will all be over."

Presto agreed that the situation had passed the point of no return.

The Americans would soon have proof that the cause of the blackout was a North Korean warhead. The power loss had prevented their investigating properly, but it was a matter of time. Once they had their culprit, they'd have no strategic choice but to cleanse DPRK with nuclear fire. That would bring in China, which would bring in Russia, and global thermonuclear war.

The unthinkable, they'd always called it.

"So how come we're even doing this? What's the damn point?" I said.

Presto was a sun-dog, an avatar of Helios, as sanguine as they came. As far as he was concerned, it was never too late even when it was too late. If the Americans were going to discover that the EMP had been caused by a North Korean missile, it was our job to make sure that the EMP wasn't caused by a North Korean missile.

I told Presto that made no sense at all. He just looked up from sniffing the ground and barked. We'd reached the dairy farm.

Naturally, we damn near got our heads shot off when we stole the cow. We would have been Swiss cheese if there had been a moon overhead, but it was too dark. Still, it had been very close. God knows how many of their cows had already been stolen, or how many people they'd had to run off.

So what had happened was that about four billion years ago ripples had naturally formed in the cooling surface of the earth. The ripples shaped the clay into patterns that repeated themselves, promoting further similar shaping, and then we had crystallization and self-replicating crystals, which led to evolving patterns that became the medium for the advent of genes and then life. Right? We've been over this. Keep up.

But the thing was, only some of those crystals had evolved into a quasicellular substrate and biogenesis.

Other ripples crystals had kept evolving on their own, and inevitably, that evolving crystalized clay began to take on cellular automata/computational structures. In other words, the clay had evolved in two directions, after a fork.

Some clay had become the birthplace of life, which billions of years later reached consciousness. But other clay skipped the whole biogenesis phase and went directly to becoming itself conscious. As in information processing, as in energy flowing through gates that could be opened or closed. As in the very matter of the planet became a mind, a computer, that was the entire planet.

And this didn't just happen here.

It happened throughout the solar system as the earth, via complex light signals, seeded the matter of the other planets. They had the requisite physical characteristics for computation, including large mass, stable orbit, and some kind of disruptive energetic flows like wind or liquid currents.

And so, long before the human race joined the party, the planets themselves had awoken. They were computers on a titanic scale, slowly grinding out their thoughts, communicating through photons. Are you following me? The planets weren't just named for the gods. The planets were and are the gods. And the Earth seethed with a righteous fury.

Presto and I were avatars of these planet gods. Servants of the gods incarnate So really, if you want to get technical, I was a symbol or messenger of Uranus, while still for complex technical reasons remaining Peter Graff. So yeah, nice to meet you. I represent Uranus. And that's YOUR-i-nus, not your-ANUS, tough guy.

We named the cow Callithyia.

Chapter 8
Apprehension

Birdie Love
Zero Bardoff
Dr. John Harriman, PhD
Presto
Some crazies

Nobody paid much attention to the little things now. Zero could drop by Birdie's room (both day students, they'd been allowed to stay on campus during the emergency) at any time, even at night, and nobody said a word. The administration was just happy to get a complete head count for the students each morning.

Birdie lay on a cot opposite Zero's.

Birdie had been crying.

She cried every day now. She couldn't stop thinking about all the people out there, the desperate conditions they faced. At Garrison they had a small detachment of cops to protect them, but out there? How were mothers supposed to protect their kids? Garrison had a cafeteria with many weeks' food supply (now almost exhausted, but still). Where were parents elsewhere supposed to find food?

She cried for Kosoko, too. She liked Zero, liked him something awful, but Kosoko needed attention. There was just so much the school nurse could do. Sometimes Birdie would help out, tending to Kosoko's leg. It was rough work, seeing all that pain. And Kosoko was in no shape to say thank you.

But this afternoon she was with Zero, and Zero could make her feel just a little bit okay.

"You know what's weird?" she asked him.

"What?"

"You seem happy."

Zero rolled onto his back and looked up at the ceiling. He said, "I guess that is weird."

"I don't know if I've ever seen you like this," she smiled. Her face was puffy from crying, but of course her smile was the sun through the clouds. "You seem relaxed, even. Plus, what's that you're reading? I never seen you read a book before."

Zero showed her the book. "*The Great Gatsby*," he said. "It's good."

"A book for school! Are you actually studying, Zero Bardoff?"

"I guess. Sort of."

Birdie started to talk about how good it was, and how funny it was that he could be so nervous and sad all the time until the world basically ended and then be all cool, etc. But for Zero there was only her face, her voice (it sounded to him like a stream in the forest), her smile. He couldn't see the toll this was taking on her, the sleeplessness, the hunger. None of it registered. Instead, there was a single frightful, exhilarating thought: He had to tell her.

"...bet I know what it is, too, Zero," she went on. "All the stuff you worry about all the time? School, getting kicked out, all that? It's all gone. At least for now. Every weight you been carrying around is off you now. It makes me—"

"I love you," said Zero.

She laughed and jumped on him. "You do not!" she said. She was pouring little kisses all over his face. "You do not! You do not!" She laughed and laughed.

"Yeah, I do!" laughed Zero.

Everything she'd said had been true.

The end of the world was like a vacation for him. Let other people worry about malnutrition. The threat of random violence excited him. This whole thing was like a movie, and he was a hero, one of the Liberators. The name sounded like a superhero group, like the Defenders or the Avengers. How bad could life be? He was freezing and hungry, but he was getting kissed by the prettiest girl in Massachusetts, and his grades had probably been erased by the EMP.

And yes, he was reading *The Great Gatsby*, and he'd even asked Lefty to help him with his algebra. Lefty thought it was nuts, but he didn't mind. It felt normal, at least, to be doing schoolwork instead of learning to apply a tourniquet or do CPR.

"Teach us," said Harriman to Birdie that afternoon. "Teach me, teach my boys. The team is what we have, now. It's our thing to strive for."

Birdie's eyes were big and her face serious, like, "Oh, really?" "You want me to teach the Garrison Liberators how to play basketball? What makes you think I can do it, old man?"

"Everybody says you're the best player in the school," said Harriman. He'd never spoken directly to Birdie before.

"Yeah, okay," Birdie was looking at her fingernails. "Okay, 'cause that's just the thing, Coach Harriman. I *am* the best player in the school. And if you want my help, you need to sign me. That's *my* stipulation."

"Sign you?" Harriman was honestly confused as they stood there in the cold afternoon.

"You need to put me on the team. Let me play. Then I'll teach your boys to play basketball, and teach you how to coach, too."

"But—" Harriman's heart was in his shoes. "—but how can I...it's the *boys* basketball team."

"Not no more it ain't."

So that was that.

They shook on it, and Harriman's head mind was far away as he decided to walk home, to his real house. He thought of leading his team to a winning season, and the idea of what that would mean for him.

A sports hero! No longer a figure of fun.

No longer laughed at by students and faculty alike! Could it even happen? Would they let him sign a girl to the Boys Varsity team? What if she got hurt? Whom would they sue?

He didn't notice the crazies until they were right upon him. Now they beat the shit out of him. He, a silver-haired reverend institutional figure. He, who in the Gulf of Tonkin had given life with his right hand and taken it with his left.

And now he's lying here while these two dicks in animal masks rifle through his pockets, hoping, one supposes, to find a candy bar or some shit, and he's not even thinking about them or his possibly broken nose or the scant protection his fat had offered against their kicks and blows. He doesn't notice the symbols on their coats. He's thinking instead of what he really hates in this old world.

Because Harriman is a man who hates.

He hates everybody, for starters. Bitter, self-important, moralistic liberals: mean, bigoted self-congratulatory conservatives: young impudent imbeciles with their internet slang and their smiley faces: old broken down unburied doddering seniors: self-pitying, droning, preaching women: stupid, bullying, chickenshit men: postmodern quasi-Marxist literary studies philosophers: unregenerate brutal quasi-Nazi thugs: this god-damned and blasted fucking whoreson blackout and whoever had caused it: every goose-stepping robot in North Korea: every dirty stinking Russian commie rat: every sneaky devious Chinese son of a bitch.

He hated winners with their superiority and their excellence. He hated losers with their down-in-the-mouth miserable grit. He hated the tyranny of sex and the dreadful paucity of sex. He hated violence, and could have killed anyone who said differently. He hated sports, that beef-brained diversion, that oily sweaty buffoonish sideshow. He hated art, which was a circus of phonies and damn blowhards. He hated science, which forever proved him both wrong and irrelevant. He hated anyone who held him in contempt. He would have hated anyone who admired him, if anyone did.

Except maybe Presto.

Speaking of whom, *here came Presto* like a bullet from a gun, his eyes narrowed and his ears pressed flat against his head, and knocking one of the crazies flat on his ass and scaring both of them off into the night with his grievous white fangs and his "ugly face." And now Presto's licking the twitchy old man's cheeks, and the old man is obliged to admit he could never hate Presto.

After climbing to his feet and brushing the snow off of himself, Harriman walked, not to the infirmary, but to Douglass Library. There he found no sign of Mrs. Vite or anyone else, but the door was unlocked and soon he was working his way through every humanistic section, all the essays and novels and philosophies.

He didn't know what he was looking for, though it had something to do with finding a reason not to hate everyone and himself.

Why does one need a reason to love?

Harriman needed one badly.

It was tough to find. There were very ample arguments against the human race, arguments for he depopulation of the planet, a voluntary extinction society. But when he tried to find opposing arguments, they were mostly question-begging. Man is worthwhile because God loves man. (Okay, but why does God love man?) There were arguments about whether man was inherently good or evil. But few existential proofs.

Why was it better that human beings exist than that they should not? Carl Sagan and a few others defended human beings based on their intelligence and sentience.

"We are the universe's way of knowing itself." Possibly so. Dumb animals could perceive the world, but not know it, not explain it.

"In apprehension," said Hamlet, "how like a god."

Chapter 9
War & Peace

Presto
Peter Graff
Lefty Davis
Naomi Echeveria
Dr. John Harriman, PhD
Callithyia
The killers

The morning Presto and I got back with our cow, after Presto saved Harriman from the ambush, the first person I met was Lefty, the basketball player. And what's funny is he didn't ask where we'd been, and didn't even ask why we've come back leading a skinny Holstein cow.

Instead, he asked me, "Graff, where are you from?"

"What?"

I wasn't fully attending to this kid, as you might imagine. I was trying to lead this cow up the hill to the quad, while keeping an eye on Presto. Presto was a rough dog. He was great on the road, heading out to the dairy farm and back, scaring the shit out of anybody who got too close to us, but now that there were little kids around it was a bit worrisome, how high strung and mouthy he was.

"Where are you from?"

"New York," I say. I've got a strained smile on my face. Come to think of it, I almost always wear a strained smile.

"Where are you from, really?" said Lefty.

I looked at him. He had my attention now. "The fuck are you talking about? I'm from New York. Briareos Manor, New York."

"Okay. Okay," said Lefty. "Let me ask you this. Do you think the planet earth can think?"

My return was starting to get a lot of attention. Kids were coming up to us, teachers, even the mayor. Lefty was fading a little into the background. Everybody was asking me what the hell was going on.

"We're having a barbecue tonight." I told them.

An hour later, with the cow secured to the Garrison statute, I was making the rounds, letting people know what I needed from them.

I started with Naomi.

She'd shown an amazing faculty for taking care of the younger kids. I told her I needed her to get them out of sight after the feast.

"Why?"

"Trust me, you'll be glad you did. Get them into a big basement or somewhere they can't be found. They're gonna need to stay quiet. How do you get them to settle down?"

Naomi said, "I read to them. We're reading *War & Peace*."

I was a bit surprised. "Little bit bleak, isn't it?"

"They're smart kids," she said. "And I'll tell you what else. They need to know what's going on."

"Tell them this: We're going to flip the script."

Next, I was off to see Harriman. The old fool was in the library, standing by the window with an upside-down book in his hands. He looked pretty out of it.

"I need a favor, pops," I said.

After a productive talk with Harriman, I felt like I needed to be alone for a little while. Alone, which is a funny word for somebody who's never alone anymore. Being the avatar of a sky god doesn't mean you can't have your own thoughts anymore. But it means they're no longer private. I stood outside the Douglass Library and looked up at the sky where Uranus would be visible if it were nighttime. All I could see was the white glare of an overcast firmament, but I knew he was there. We were bound together by the mystic chords of a signal that was never broken.

"Easy for you, huh?" I said.

But I didn't know. Was it easy for him?

The gods have such a fetish for sacrifice. It's the only damn thing that propitiates them. But when do they sacrifice themselves? Never. Because it makes no sense to sacrifice yourself.

That night we started at sundown. Everybody at the school was gathered in the quad. There were people watching, too, from across the street. Most of them probably looking at the cow. Regular people along with the crazies. None of them saying a word.

The cow's wearing her ribbons, dolled up, you know, supposedly an equal in the proceedings. Supposedly playing her role voluntarily.

I told Harriman to kick things off.

He looked perfect, by the way. Face painted white, with black ashes around his eyes. Had on some kind of robe, some improvised thing. He raised his hands and began to chant in that crazy bass voice. He swayed back and forth, reciting the hexameter verse in Ancient Greek, calling on the sun, the earth, the sky for mercy. Kids threw their barley seeds on the heifer. Beautiful animal. Real prize-winner. Then I poured water on the cow's head, making it bow in agreement.

When Harriman reached his peroration, I took out a machete and cut the heifer's throat. Little kids were screaming by now, scared out of their wits, but I needed them to see this. The cow keened forward onto her forelegs, and then dropped to her side, still trying to breathe. I took her head in my arms, my hand closing her beautiful eyes. I whispered to her to shush.

I ordered them to light the bonfire. It was a big one several of us had spent the afternoon building. It went up like a matchstick.

What you've got to understand was how bad it had gotten, and how bad it was going to get.

The power grid was shot, winter had begun, starvation stalked the land.

And that wasn't the worst of it.

Most of the U.S. nuclear capability was out of commission, but nowhere near all of it. There were hundreds of silos hardened against EMPs, and the oceans were swimming with nuclear missile submarines that hadn't been affected at all.

The only reason the U.S. hadn't launched its attack on North Korea was that there was so much confusion and breakage in the chain of command. But sooner or later one of those silo commanders or sub captains was going to go off on his or her own. How long could we expect them to keep sending unanswered signals home before they started to fiddle with the trigger?

The deal with the Fates is that they weave their nets and we're all caught in them, and that's it. When your thread is cut, you're done. No different for the king of the gods or the lowest bum on earth. But you have to remember that these folks *know* each other. They're family. And if a few strings get twisted around, it's not the end of the world.

I was in a strange frame of mind. People talking about a feeling of oneness with everything, that kind of crap. But it was like I could have extended my arms and risen with the gathering wind. I felt the thrumming engine of the world.

We threw the cow on the bonfire and let her cook. We'd separated the fatty parts from the long bones, which we burned for the sun. A lot of the kids lined up to dip their hands in the blood, and they rubbed it onto their faces and chests. It looked a little spooky, not funny.

And then it was time to eat.

The teachers and students and cops and everybody lined up to take meat. And as they did, the wind carried that fragrant smoke out over Newburyport and beyond, down to Boston, out to sea. And everybody who smelled that smoke knew where it was coming from.

"Okay," I said. "You, Naomi, listen up."

Naomi came up to me.

"It's time to take these kids where they'll be safe. Don't tell anybody exactly where you're going, okay? Don't even tell me. When you get there, keep them quiet. The younger ones are going to want to cry, maybe to yell. Naomi, don't let them. Read to them, like you do."

Some of the crazies were heading into the quad. Some of them had firearms. The cops lined up between them and the kids. They yelled at the crazies to fuck off or else.

The sky had been threatening to storm all day, and now it started to rain in a cloudburst.

Ever take a cold shower with your clothes on? It was that kind of rain.

The wind was rising. It was so dark and so bitter. Some of the cops had flashlights that worked. Some of the crazies had torches or lamps.

Now nobody was saying anything. Just hard looks across a gulf of maybe ten meters, there in that quad under the stern gaze of William Lloyd Garrison's statue. You know what? Deep down, I was still hoping one sacrifice would be enough.

"Take this," I said, handing my cup of wine to Lefty.

"Hi!" I said to the crazies, striding toward them with my right hand extended to shake. "My name's Pete Graff, man of many devices, stringer for Reuter's, avatar of Uranus, ex-U.S. Army, Columbia U. graduate, son of the sky and the earth. They call me the guy with 100 heads and 50 hands. Long story. It's actually possible you've seen me before; I did TV commercials when I was a kid. Prince's spaghetti sauce, stuff like that. What do they say? Every Jewish man's dream is to be mistaken for an Italian? That was me. Played a lot of Italians in a lot of TV commercials. Stella D'Oro fudge cookies. So, yeah! I was saying, what was it, Lefty?"

"I asked you if the earth could think," said he.

The rain had slowed down now enough that you could talk without shouting.

"Kid wants to know if the earth can think," I told the crazies. "You believe that? What an imagination, this kid. But I'm gonna humor him a minute, okay?"

"We want some of that beef," said one of the crazies.

He didn't sound crazy, actually. Looked crazy, in that bunny rabbit mask. Didn't really sound crazy. Intimidating, though, at the head of that growing crowd. Much bigger than me. But I like to remind myself that I'm every bit as tall as Tom Cruise, and he's constantly kicking everybody's ass.

"In a minute," I said. Gave him a big smile. "So let's say the Earth can think. And the sun, and the other planets, whatever. To me the question is *how* they would think."

"Tell us later," said another one of them. "Right now we want to eat."

"We're *going* to eat," said a third. This one was a bear.

"Would you hold on? Now, just a minute, okay? Listen, this is interesting. You ask, *how* would a planet, or a sun, whatever, *think*? And I'll tell you the answer. Very slowly. All right? I mean look at the human brain: Loaded with synapses, each about ten microns across, and the whole thing is maybe ten centimeters across. Pretty quick, pretty efficient, right? And then, and then look at a microchip." I paused here, because the bunny rabbit man had pulled out a 9 mm pistol and had it pointed at me from about two meters away.

The cops all drew, real slowly. It was unclear whether the crazies could see the cops now, as the rain was picking up again.

It was strange to look down the barrel of that 9 mm pistol. But I had a sense of calm that came as a surprise.

Because I knew. I knew that at that moment the whole of the cosmos was a wheel, and that I was the hub of that wheel as it turned. The barrel of that pistol was an opening, a door in time.

"Come on, man!" I told the bunny, moving slowly towards him. "Just listen, this is good!" I was talking, but as I talked, I was planning my next move. I knew three ways to disarm this guy before—

—and it's here that I exit the story.

Chapter 10
Full Fathom Five

Kim Jigu
Ryu Gun
Subordinates

Major Kim Jigu's guilt, known to everyone, obviated any trial.

Her execution was highly informal.

She was forced to her knees by one of her subordinates, and another subordinate shot her behind the temple. So much for her. Several soldiers carried her to the surface, dragged her out beyond the razor wire fence, and left her on the cold flat ground. And there she would have remained, if not for Ryu Gun, a corporal in the Rocket Force who was in love with Jigu.

He put her in a jeep and drove her to Heaven Lake, which turned out to be frozen. He spent about ten minutes trying to hack through the ice with his entrenching tool, but he and his nerve failed (he was absent without leave). So he left her on the ice, stripped to the nude so that she'd be more difficult for a passing tourist to identify.

As it turned out, Ryu had weakened the ice enough that she broke through the next day.

Down into the lake she sank, then bobbed up to the surface, up against the bottom of the ice. She floated in the current. The rains had been heavy that month, and there was a strong pull in the Erdaobai River, which over the next weeks carried her into China, then to a series of other rivers and back to North Korea, where at last she was washed ashore at the top of a steep bluff by the Sea of Japan.

There she lay in a depression in the high bluff, her body preserved by the near-frozen waters.

And when the rain came, the depression became a pool, and from a pool to a lake, and then a river that became a waterfall. Jigu drifted with it over the high cliff and plunged deep into the sea.

And there, below the eddies and the sparkling waves, Kim Jigu floated upright, as though standing, with her head up and her eyes wide open. The sunshine stabbed through the surface to illuminate her still-lovely nudity.

One by one, tiny red and orange fish swam to her and kissed her body, remaining there with their little mouths locked to her skin.

One by one they schooled around and attached themselves, each taking its place where there was still bare skin, until no room remained, and Kim Jigu suffered a sea-change, and became a white incandescent spirit glowing with the kisses of red and orange fish.

Chapter 11
You Know I'm a Dreamer

Peter Graff
The killers
Many crazies
Ms. De Bono
Lefty Davis
Naomi Echeveria
Birdie Love
Kosoko Wright
Mazi Wright
Mayor Frank Wright
Barbara Wright
Dr. John Harriman, PhD

The man in the bunny rabbit mask fired one shot right into my face, killing me instantly. There was no pain.

The cops showed highly uncharacteristic restraint in only shooting the rabbit man, who was dead before he hit the ground, and winging the bear.

Now the cops shot it out with about a half-dozen crazies, and, behind them, there were more crazies—a lot more— running up to join them. The cops fell back under cover of darkness and rain, which was coming down now as hard as before.

Ms. De Bono shouted something aggressive at the crazies and took off running. One of them fired at her.

Leave a half-eaten peach on the ground sometime, and watch the ants pour over it in a liquid flow, each moving at random but as a group forming a perfect network of driving mandibles. So now did the crazies, dozens strong, rush into the quad through the downpour. They were hollering something awful and they spread out to search the buildings.

Lefty was running away at full gallop, exploiting all those wind sprints Harriman had made him do, and exploiting the poor visibility and his own knowledge of the ground. He ran out onto the football field toward the gym.

An alarm bell was sounding in the distance; somebody was whacking it with a hammer. There were sounds of breaking glass, doors getting kicked in.

The crazies found the cafeteria. It was locked, of course, but also barricaded pretty well from inside, which they hadn't counted on.

In the basement of Filibuster Gym, Naomi read to nearly 300 kids.

The kids were as old as 15, as young as nine. They listened carefully to every word she read them, barely blinking at the sound of gunfire overhead.

Naomi had that rarest of qualities, grace, in this least gracious of ages, and it transfixed the children. Some of them started to cry at the sound of the thunder and the shouting outside, but she just raised a finger to her lips and kept reading, and they fell quiet again.

She read,

> A few of them stir feebly, trying to lift themselves, fly indolently and settle on the hostile hand without strength left to sting it ere they die—the rest that are dead shower down like fish-scales.

The bee-master shuts up the compartment, puts a chalk mark on the stand, and, when the time comes, knocks it down and drains out the honey.

In the same way, Moscow was deserted, when Napoleon, weary, uneasy, and in a bad humor, walked back and forth at the Kammerkolezhsky ramparts, waiting for a deputation—a ceremony which, although one of mere show, he nevertheless affected to consider absolutely indispensable.

Lefty had found Birdie and Zero in the gym. They were huddled together, whispering to each other.

"Come on," said Lefty," we've got to tell the mayor."

Mazi was there, too. He and Jackie had been shooting baskets in the dark. Now all five of them busted out into the night full of rain.

There was madness everywhere.

The crazies were running wild on the grounds, getting into fights, firing off their pistols into the sky. Some of them were breaking into the buildings, looking for trouble. Some others had got hold of a dead pickup truck. They started pushing it across the football field, through that wet slush, toward the cafeteria.

They weren't stupid. They knew the food was in there.

When they got close enough, they released the truck and let it keep rolling on its own, setting fire to it. They must have soaked the damn thing in gasoline, because it lit right up. It crashed through the glass front of the cafeteria and plowed right into the tables and chairs inside.

Zero, Lefty, Birdie, Mazi, and Jackie had made it across the field to the science building. In they went, out of the rain and into the chilly darkness. They raced up the staircase (why the hell had Mayor Wright chosen the top floor for his office?). As they reached the top of the stairs, they could hear crazies busting into the building behind them, hooting and smashing tiles and gaining on our heroes.

As his teammates banged on the door to Mayor Frank Wright's office, Kosoko Wright stood in his dorm room on his crutches, peering down at the chaos below. He could see torches flaring in the rain, the fire spreading through the cafeteria. It looked like a rock concert or something.

It seemed to him that at that moment there was nothing in this world quite as useless as he was, balanced on those crutches, trying not to ding his cast against the floor.

The leg hurt, he knew, more than it was supposed to. It hurt like nothing he'd felt before—like nothing anybody there had ever felt before, not even old Harriman when he was pinned to the deck of the *Forrestal*. There was something terribly wrong with his leg. Kosoko, who never cried, felt tears running down off his chin and soaking the front of his Celtics t-shirt.

Inside his office on the top floor of the science building, Mayor Wright lay crumpled on the floor, clinging to his softly weeping wife Barbara. They hadn't seen everything that had gone down, but they knew enough. They knew I was dead. They knew we were under attack.

Ms. De Bono stood at the rear of the office, her back to the wall, bolt upright, eyes wide.

Acid reflux had crippled the mayor, now of all god-damned times. This particular episode was so severe—a chainsaw-in-the-guts anguish—he could barely focus on the danger at hand. He'd been vomiting for hours, which had brought no relief, only further abdominal strain. His forehead glowed with pain and sweat.

Barbara Wright, his long-suffering bride, had seen the worst the world could throw at her without despairing.

But now she despaired.

Her children, the tender loci of her fierce love, were doomed with her.

In burst the Liberators, Mazi first, then Lefty, Jackie, Zero, and Birdie.

"Come on, Dad!" said Mazi. "We got to get out of here!"

"We can go through the basement," said Jackie.

Mayor Wright, now somehow on his feet, hollered, "You god-damn kids. GET OUT OF HERE, NOW, ALL OF YOU." He grabbed a yardstick from a desk and hefted it in the air as though it weighed a ton. "GET OUT, or I'll bust all your fucking heads."

"No, Dad!" Mazi was crying.

The Mayor took a lurching step toward the boy. "You want a chance to survive? *Get these kids out of here.*"

Mazi was frozen in place; he couldn't speak.

Jackie spoke up. "C'mon, guys. We got to *move, now.*"

But it was too late.

A crowd of crazies had followed them up the staircase and were pounding the office door practically off its hinges.

"They might take my head tonight," said the dreadnought mayor through flashing teeth, "but I'm going to *kill* some motherfuckers first."

He doubled over in agony, and the yardstick clattered to the floor.

"No, honey," said Barbara to Frank. Her voice was soft, a mother's cool breath on a child's burning forehead. She looked into his face. "You've done your fighting. It's time to rest."

As the mayor slumped back down, Ms. De Bono disappeared behind the curtain of a closet. Inside, she whispered, "Universe, help me out of this. Help me. I know I haven't been good. I know I don't believe in you. But—well, of course I *believe* in the *universe,* but you know what I mean. I don't believe in a personal universe or God or anything like that that could help me out. Anyway! If you're listening, whoever is, *please.* I want to live. I can't die here. And the kids—they can't. They *can't* die here tonight."

She closed her eyes, and she knew that every innocent person who'd ever lost her life in every disaster, every war, every slaughter of the innocents throughout history, had prayed the same prayer .

The door broke down, and there were dozens of them flooding in from the hallway. Dozens of animal masks and inscrutable bandit scarves. Weird symbols.

For a moment, some instinct of civilization held them there, staring at these kids, this father and mother. It may have struck one or two of the crazies that just weeks before there'd been a town called Newburyport in a state called Massachusetts, and that there had been the law.

But now they shoved the kids aside and took hold of the mayor.

They dragged him out into the hallway by the stairwell, with its huge picture windows overlooking the campus. They forced the mayor to his knees. Somebody'd gotten hold of a blindfold, and they were tying it around the mayor's head when Birdie shouted, "Look."

They turned, and where a moment before all had been darkness, they could see the windows of the buildings across the football field. They could see the streets, and the buildings beyond, and the smoky mist and rain were all visible.

The lights were back on.

It took about three minutes for the last of the crazies to high-tail it out of there. Some of them turned and yelled something before they disappeared into the night.

The Wrights and the Liberators and Ms. De Bono made their way down to the field and stood in the rain, absorbing every ray of electric light. They could hear some kind of music, and they turned to see Naomi. She was leading the children out of the bright fluorescents of the gym, and they were all singing, every last one of them, a song Naomi had learned from her mother.

"I'm on my way," they sang. "Just set me free. Home, sweet home."

Book III: Apparent rari nates in gurgite vasto

Chapter 1
I Am Aware that Many Object to the Severity of My Language

Ms. De Bono
U.S. President Barak Obama
U.S. President Donald Trump
Dr. John Harriman, PhD
Birdie Love
Zero Bardoff
Lefty Davis
Jackie Polish
A construction worker, and his fellow crew
A foreman of construction

America is the land where resentment can find no home.

And America was coming back, piece by piece.

The power in Newburyport was restored on 18 January, the day I was shot and killed.

The entire Eastern Interconnection, which had been rebuilt, in parts, virtually from scratch, had been lighting up one county, one town, one neighborhood at a time for over a week, and the last of its sectors would be dark for another five days.

The next day, as Birdie and Zero kicked around in the slush of the quad, a squadron of airplanes flew overhead, and as they did the sky began to bloom with parachutes. The first food had arrived, in the form of USAID airdrops.

One of them landed right on the roof of the admissions building, which was a small, house-like structure with a gabled roof that sent the crate barreling down to the ground, smashing it. Zero, at least, had never thought his heart could be warmed by the sight of dried lentils and flour.

No one was in the mood for more rationing. The cooks in the burned-out cafeteria set straightaway to preparing a feast of starchy beans and legumes, using even more of the crate's contents than all the students, faculty, and others on campus could eat.

Harriman ate enough hard biscuits so that he could have slept standing up. Presto ate himself sick and then immediately went back for seconds. Jackie and Lefty got into a food fight after stuffing themselves.

Almost as exciting as the food was the return of TV. The phones and internet were still out, so TV became the sole conduit for desperately needed information. The stations themselves, though, were largely in the process of coming back online.

So it was the next day, January 19, that President Obama and the national weather service broke the news.

Contrary to all rumors, the United States had not come under attack by North Korea or any other earthly power.

"My fellow Americans," he said, in his last official address as President. "What at first appeared to be an act of war is now known to have been an act of nature. Four weeks ago, the outer sun erupted in what is called an X-class solar flare. This is an astronomical-scale explosion that happens only about once every two centuries, and it had the force of roughly a billion hydrogen bombs.

The flare sent a huge wave of particles, an electromagnetic pulse, toward the earth. Later that day, as the sun was setting over the Atlantic, this pulse grazed the surface of our atmosphere, causing the tremendous disruption we in the northern western hemisphere endured.

"Folks, this was a natural disaster of boggling proportions. It has cost our economy, and the economy of the world, a sum of money that's still being calculated, but which is certainly in the trillions of dollars. The cost in lives, which we're also still measuring, was more than any of us will be able to bear.

"As we mourn the dead, let us also celebrate the human spirit.

"The peoples of the world, from nations great and small, who were spared the blackout, did not abandon us in our hour of need.

"In vast numbers and at huge expense, they came here to help us. They did so at great sacrifice and with the greatest urgency. It was the largest voluntary transfer of wealth since the Marshall Plan. Not only traditionally close allies like the European Union, Great Britain, and the Nato powers, but even rivals like China and Russia came to our aid.

"They journeyed here by the hundreds of thousands. They came as computer experts, engineers, medical teams, organizers, ordinary working people, specialists of every kind, men and women, young and old. They came from Africa and South America, from Australia and Asia, from every corner of every continent.

And they're still here, working around the clock with their American partners to bring power back to the Western Exchange and to Texas and to northern Mexico and southern Canada.

The world will little note nor long remember what I say here, but it will never forget, we, the people of the United States of America, will never forget, the courage and generosity of those who ended the period of our darkness and saved countless of our lives."

Job one had been the nuclear power plants.

Brilliant innovations were conceived and executed to prevent core meltdowns and eventually to bring them back online. Traditional power plants, largely reduced to scrap, had been rebuilt with extraordinary dispatch.

Nearly inconceivable quantities of food had come across the seas. No one, after all, had known how long the blackout would last. With power restored in the East, the priority there became the distribution of food.

And now it was, in Newburyport and the United States, a period of reconstruction.

The quantities of data that must be restored were so huge that they have no names. Many, many machines had broken and needed to be individually repaired. The same was true with state and local governments, the army, the whole economy. It all needed to be put back together again.

Were I still alive, I'd have had some tough questions to answer from my friends at Garrison. I'd promoted the North Korea story, which had been exactly true at the time but now was mostly false.

The next morning was January 20, 2017. Inauguration Day.

President Obama had offered to stay on in any capacity whatsoever to help out with the ongoing crisis, but had been rebuffed.

Shortly afterwards, the new president had addressed a sparse, half-starved crowd on the Washington Mall, and in broadcasts, those of his people who could be reached by television and radio.

Trump made many remarks that seemed immaterial to the circumstances, but also one statement which stirred the hearts of everyone who heard him: "The American carnage stops right here, and it stops right now."

Despite the perfect suitability of this call to arms, former president George W. Bush was afterward heard to describe the address as "some weird shit."

As the country was being rebuilt, Garrison must now be too.

She'd seen her cafeteria reduced to cinders, her furniture piled up as barricades, her fields torn to shreds by fighting.

First, though, the vehicles must be fixed.

This was now possible because power had been restored to the automotive service stations. It was a slow process. The stations' computers had to be restored from backups, and then these computers in turn had to boot up and repair the computers in the tow trucks' engines, and then these tow trucks had to haul basically every car or truck in the town so that they themselves could be fixed.

It took weeks, and so it was nearly March before the first construction crews could make their way to the Garrison Academy. Meanwhile, classes had been back underway, for real this time, and not only as a morale-boosting exercise.

The healing of the students and staff was approached, here as everywhere, in a systematic way. There was a severe shortage of trained counselors, with the demand extending virtually to the entire country.

At Garrison the solution was to hold mass therapy sessions at mealtimes in the auditorium. Students were, according to the fashion of the times, invited to say how they felt about what topic happened to come up. They were told how natural their feelings were, and their willingness to cry, etc., was duly celebrated.

Ms. De Bono, despite having had her prayers answered, was in a deep funk. All this work to rebuild the school might be quite necessary, but it was probably futile.

The institution, already on the shakiest of financial grounds, was now almost certainly ruined. It wasn't just the cost of physical repairs. It was the urgent need to fix her reputation and her pocketbook. Fully one-third of the students had been pulled out by their parents within a week of power restoration. Their tuition had been nonrefundable, but would these students be replaced by new ones in the fall?

De Bono watched the workmen as she took her morning run. One of them, on this chilly morning in early February, called out to her. He paid her the gentlemanly compliment of saying that he wanted to "tap her ass."

Ms. De Bono got the message. But she really didn't know exactly what "tap your ass" meant. Like, why those specific words. She jogged about another four paces, then stopped and turned back.

"What did you say?" she said to the worker. She got right up in his mug. She had no fear.

The worker replied that he wasn't sure.

"Yes, you are," she insisted. "Please repeat what you said."

He was unable to recall. She helped him.

"You said you wanted to 'tap my ass.' I'm afraid I don't understand what that means. I'd like you to explain it to me."

The worker turned to his fellow hardhats in appeal. "Just— like—"

"Please explain it to me as though you were speaking to a child. Just what is meant by the phrase, 'I want to tap your ass?' What am I, a beer keg?"

"No."

"No, what?"

"No, you're—you're not."

"Not what?"

"Not a beer keg, ma'am."

"Well," she said, seeming to grow in height. "You *are* a beer keg, buddy. A great big, fat, fucking....beer keg. And you know what?"

"No."

"You're *floated*. Do you know what that means?"

"No."

"It means you're tapped out," said Ms. De Bono. She was making this up as she went along, of course, but she was rolling now. "You're empty. Done. Worthless. It means you're going out with the trash. Get your stuff and beat it. You're fired."

"You can't fire me," said the man.

"She can," said a different worker. All the workers were standing and watching. Their faces didn't show how much they were enjoying this. "She's the headmaster of the whole school, man."

A foreman ran out at full sprint from inside the cafeteria. "Miss De Bono, Miss De Bono!" He stopped for breath. "Miss De Bono, I'm so sorry. I would have cut my throat before I let this happen. Cut my throat!" He grabbed the offender. "You get your ass out of here! Collect your pay and get lost. I don't want to see you again."

Ms. De Bono started to walk away, but then turned back to the foreman. She'd thought of a real zinger. "I don't want this man around children, foreman!"

"Yes, Miss De Bono! No way, Miss De Bono!"

She began to run again. She was exhilarated. Fuck that guy! She hadn't worked her whole god-damn life—fucking *animal!* Who did he think he was dealing with?

She smiled. Me, that's who. You don't fuck with the headmaster if you don't want a damn ruler across the knuckles.

But that word, headmaster, killed her smile in its crib. Now she resumed thinking about the work to be done, the damage they'd suffered. Six kids hospitalized. No student fatalities, thank God. They'd had just enough time left in the spring to get the semester in, so classes were running fine. But the numbers involved, the dollar amounts! And every dollar of debt was a lead weight pushing her down. Something like a trillion dollars had vanished in the blackout, which meant nobody had money to donate. And if they did, it would be for a charity that was saving lives, not an ivy-covered fucking prep school for rich kids.

William Lloyd Garrison stared at her from his pedestal. On the plaque below the statue was his most famous quotation.

I am aware that many object to the severity of my language; but is there not cause for severity? I will be as harsh as Truth, and as uncompromising as Justice. On this subject I do not wish to think, or speak, or write, with moderation. No! No! Tell a man whose house is on fire to give a moderate alarm; tell him to moderately rescue his wife from the hands of the ravisher; tell the mother to gradually extricate her babe from the fire into which it has fallen–but urge me not to use moderation in a cause like the present. I am in earnest–I will not equivocate–I will not excuse–I will not retreat a single inch–and I will be heard.

She'd read it a hundred times, but today it had a particular force for Ms. De Bono.

A force that set her jaw and narrowed her eyes.

Chapter 2
Big Blue

Ms. Hercule
Zero Bardoff
Liz Marquart
Birdie Love
Jackie Polish
Lefty Davis
Dr. John Harriman, PhD

Ms. Hercule, the ninth grade English teacher, called Zero to her desk as class was letting out.

Classes had been in session for a few weeks now, following a rebuilding period after the restoration of power. So now it was early March, well into the second trimester.

"Zero," said Ms. Hercule, "I don't think it's too inappropriate to share with you some information that I received from the headmaster herself. You've been placed on academic probation."

"Academic probation?" the phrase settled into Zero's stomach like—what? Like a bag of wet cement.

"If you can't improve your grades to at least a C average by the summer, you'll be expelled," she said. "This can't be too great a surprise, right?"

"No," he said.

"No. Yes. Because attending Garrison isn't a right, it's a privilege. Do you understand?"

"So, yeah," said Zero. "Actually, I was going to talk to Ms. De Bono about a scholarship, on account of my old man got sacked and my parents are getting divorced and we're a little bit strapped for cash. But it sounds like the scholarship's probably not on the table at this point."

"No. No, it isn't. Zero, I'm very sorry for your troubles at home. You seem like a nice young man. But standards are standards, and we have to uphold them. We have to. Now, I've noticed you have some...eccentric study habits."

"Eccentric?"

"You don't do your homework," she said, "and you don't study."

"I do!" he said. The lie made his eyes tear up.

"I'm going to give you an assignment. It's for extra credit, but I hope it will also serve to get you on track to turning in your assignments generally."

"Oh, yes, that would be great! I really can't fail out, Ms. Hercule. I mean, it would be the end for me, I swear to God."

"Okay. Here's the thing, though: I'm not going to give you a chance to screw this up. I know you have a free period now, and you're going to sit right here in front of me and you're going to do the assignment and I'm going to collect it at the end of the period."

"Yeah? Because I was going to..." Zero stopped himself. *Going to have a beer and shoot a little pool* would have struck the wrong note.

"Do you want to stay at Garrison, or don't you?" said Ms. Hercule.

"What's the assignment?" said Zero.

The assignment was to write a short essay of not less than 250 words about his experiences during the blackout.

Everyone, she told him, had been traumatized by the disaster to one degree or another. She believed it was very important to express that pain in words.

Zero sat and chewed his pencil.

He searched his brain and found nothing there. He thought of his parents, how much they were both going through, and how much hope they'd pinned on him. He thought of returning to the public school system in disgrace. There were metal-heads at Newburyport High who did nothing all day but dream of another chance to slam Zero's head into the lockers. He thought of disappointing Ms. Hercule, who was giving him a god-damn *chance* here, trying to be *human*, by handing her a blank piece of paper. He thought of everything, in other words, except the topic of the assignment.

"Okay, Zero," she said after 40 minutes. "Let's have it."

"Hold on," said Zero, furiously scribbling. "One sec. Okay. Okay." He handed her the paper, which she read as he stood there.

Death

by Zero Bardoff, 9th grade English

Death, I hear you calling

And I can't resist you now

I've lost the path and I'm falling

To a depth no line could sound

Your seductive powers

Are drawing me to you

Eternity is calling

O, Death, what can I do?

My sepulcher yawns empty

In the frozen ground, my home

My final steps to nowhere

On a path I tread alone

Just a few more hours

And I'll face what must be true

I hear your dry voice calling

O, Death, what can I do?

Death, what can I do?

Death, your call is final

And you'll snuff the last strong light

Farewell to love, embrace me, long night

"A poem," said Ms. Hercule, her face and voice betraying no reaction, positive or negative. "Death."

"Yes," he said.

"Oh, Mr. Bardoff. This is very good. It moves me. You've taken a risk: You've looked into yourself and found something real, something that's uniquely your own." She took out her red pen. "I'm giving you an A."

Two minutes later, Zero was on the quad, literally bouncing on his feet.

An A.

He'd never gotten one, not a single one, in his whole academic career. He stopped a passerby called Liz Marquart, who had blonde hair. "An A!" he told her, and kissed her hand.

Then he raced to meet Jackie and Lefty in the cafeteria. As he ran he felt like Mercury on the wing—he never touched the ground. And he thought that this was his chance to turn his life around.

And then he ran headlong into a thought: that he was losing Birdie, if he hadn't lost her already.

Because, he realized, jealousy was a self-fulfilling prophecy, a feedback loop. The more jealous he became, the more he'd drive her away, and the more likely she would actually wind up in someone else's arms, and the more jealous he'd become.

And then another thought: He'd have to study like a champion if he was going to salvage his failing grades in all of his other classes. And studying like a champion would mean excelling at something he'd never been able to do even to minimal expectations in the past. He'd have to pass Latin, that parade of gibberish. He'd have to pass algebra and chemistry, both of which obviously included a lot of math, which his math skills were a good deal "delayed" in the current parlance.

And then he thought of the dark circumstances of his parents' divorce, and how his kid sisters had grown hard and cynical at their tender ages. He thought of the hunger and darkness and terror of the blackout. He thought of Kosoko, falling through the darkness, shattering his leg. He thought of my death at the hands of the gunman.

"Graff," he said.

He was just a kid, Zero was, and overawed with the idea that a person could be made null. And his legs turned to jelly, and he stopped running.

Everybody was surprised when Kosoko showed up for practice.

They'd known he was going to be getting out of his cast that week, but nobody thought he was going to be ready to get back on the floor.

But there he was.

A little huskier than before, except for his atrophied right leg, and a bit sullen, but there anyway, shooting free-throws.

"Kosoko Wright, as I live and breathe," said Harriman, limping briskly to shake the young man's hand. "How do you do, how do you do? Everything ship-shape?"

Kosoko looked around at the other players, still in their street clothes, staring at him.

"So you for real on the team now?" he said to Birdie.

"That's right," she said.

"Let's see you handle the ball," said Kosoko, throwing her a crisp chest pass.

Birdie had on a heavy winter coat and a knit watch cap and gloves. She threw the coat and gloves off with a flourish, picked up the ball, and drove straight at Kosoko.

Kosoko, underestimating her, went for the steal.

Bad idea. It left him unable to recover in time to block her shot as she pulled up and drained it.

"You reach, I teach," said Birdie.

Zero couldn't watch.

He ducked into the locker room to change. His mind was like a debate society. He was telling himself he had nothing to worry about, and then telling himself he damn well did, and telling himself that was the depression talking and his worries seldom came to anything, and telling himself that he was pathetically naive and kidding himself.

Back in the gym, Birdie took another drive to the basket. She and Kosoko were playing one-on-one while the others changed.

There's a thing you do sometimes in basketball: You intentionally foul a guy who has you beat to the basket to make sure he can't score. He gets two free throws, but that's better than a guaranteed two points.

Anyway, when you do that, you really have to tie the guy up. You can't just slap his arm or something like might happen with an unintentional foul. So you kind of grab him in a bear hug, and sometimes the guy will be in midair, so you're almost carrying him in your arms for a second.

So that happened now, as Birdie crossed Kosoko over and got around him. He was laughing, and he grabbed her from behind as she jumped for the lay-in. So, yeah. Nothing untoward about it, perfectly conventional deliberate foul, but yeah, he's holding her in her arms for just a second and she's giggling her head off, just as Zero returns from the locker room.

Kosoko gets the ball back, and he decides to create some space with a hard fake and then pull up and shoot. And he does. Only when he lands, he winces.

"You okay?" she says.

"Yeah," he says, hobbling forward fast, hopping on his good foot. "Yeah." He stops and leans against the bleachers. "Fuck," he says. He gingerly puts a little weight on the leg, and reflexively stops as pain shoots through from his foot up to the base of his skull.

"Lie down, son," said Harriman. "Let's take a look."

Outwardly Harriman and the whole team is solicitous as hell, giving him room to breathe, gently asking if he's okay. Inwardly, they're all thinking, "This is just fucking great."

The next night, the basketball season resumed without Kosoko.

All the schools in the Nine Schools Association were well within the boundaries of the Eastern Exchange, and so all had power. Internet was very spotty, mobile service was still down, but the elite prep schools had no difficulty kicking it old school. Basketball was a winter sport, but with so much of the winter having been snuffed out, they'd agreed to extend the season until the summer.

So anyway, this was a very big deal because it was Birdie Love's debut as a player (and unofficial player-coach) for the Garrison Academy Liberators.

It was an away game, at Phillips Academy at Andover. Harriman was too overwrought and too tipsy to make any real speech, and in any case even the impeccably progressive Andover administration wouldn't allow a girl to change in the boys' locker room.

Birdie, therefore, was alone in the girls' locker room in the last minutes before the game. Birdie had a lot on her mind: She was about to play her first officiated basketball game: The Andover Big Blue were in first place in the league: Birdie's teammates left a certain amount to be desired in the way of athleticism, skill, court vision, coaching, shooting, passing, defense, etc.: Her boyfriend Zero was not only also on the team, but was the worst player on the team and still couldn't touch the basketball without shooting it: Kosoko Wright, on whom she had a scorching crush, was their best player, but was still convalescing: Zero's jealousy was becoming intolerable: Zero was probably going to flunk out of Garrison, which would leave them where, exactly?

Mazi was the only other one on the team who could play, but he wasn't much bigger than her and was really not all that great: She was now the best player on the team, which brought with it all kinds of baggage, not least of which the male egos she would inevitably be stomping on: She could get hurt playing against boys who were, in sheer mass, literally twice her size: Her tits were too big for her jersey and they hurt like hell.

Out onto the court, in spite of everything.

Birdie was officially a shooting guard, but after five or six turnovers she started bringing the ball up herself. Mazi was not thrilled about this, but Harriman backed her up.

"For God's sake, boy, she's our best player! Let her do her thing!"

Birdie took over the game.

She synced with Mazi in a powerful offensive combination. She was slower than the guy guarding her, but way craftier and a better ball handler. She beat him to the rack, Isaiah-Thomas-style, again and again. She was careful never to pass to Zero. This was her chance to prove herself not only as a player but as a leader, and she wasn't going to lose the game just to make her boyfriend feel better about himself. Which, you know, he didn't. Feel better about himself.

With ten minutes left in the game, the score was Liberators: 15, Andover: 22. Birdie went up for a three-point jumper, and just before the ball swished through the basket, she got bumped on the way down and knocked on her ass.

The kid who'd knocked her down was mortified. He looked like he was going to cry. Was he ashamed of having maybe hurt her, or of failing to block her shot? Either way, he reached down to help her to her feet. The whole place was quiet—all those Andover brats holding their breath to see if she could even get stand, much less play. She got up, but was bent over, holding her knees. She waved Harriman over.

"Yes," he said. "Are you okay?"

"Did I make the shot?" she said.

As they got on the bus back to Newburyport, the defeated Liberators held their heads high, mostly. They'd lost by only eight points to the best team in the league.

Signing the girl was working.

It was of inestimable value to them all, including Harriman, to be so improved.

It had not been a year of triumphs.

On their short trip home, Jackie peered out the window in silence. There was still so much wreckage left from the blackout. Burned-out buildings, closed businesses, dark houses.

Mostly it was in people's faces. They still hadn't gotten back to full weight after having nearly starved. Hollow cheeks, sunken eyes, mournful looks flashed by in the headlights.

David Muratskian was still a little bit in shock, even all these months later.

Things had gotten so close, so much closer than the public realized. DEFCON 2, the last stage before a shooting war. If the order had come, it would have been he who launched their battery of thermonuclear-armed Trident-2 missiles against Pyongyang and various military bases across the DPRK. Long before his missiles had hit, though, North Korea would have released its entire arsenal against the South, particularly Seoul, wiping out the city entirely and devastating the rest of the peninsula.

The captain was making the rounds, and when he got to David Muratskian, he made a general inquiry.

"I won't tell you I'm not shaken up as hell," said Muratskian. "But I can hack it."

"Son," said the captain, "it's a terrifying thing for a man to wonder whether he could stand up to the moment and do his duty. But I know you, Weapons Officer Muratskian. And I want to tell you that I never doubted for a moment that you'd do what you had to."

"What's got me shaken up, Captain," Muratskian replied, "is that I never doubted it either."

"Mayor Wright!" a man shouted as Wright walked up to the steps of the town hall.

"Yes, sir!" said the Mayor, smiling.

"What do you have to say to your constituents who you left in the freezing cold to starve during the blackout?"

This kind of thing was growing more frequent, and more irritating; random people coming up to him with their accusations. Why did they all talk like newspaper reporters in a black and white movie? These were just regular people, not media.

Frank Wright was very strongly tempted to say, "No comment." He was tired of explaining himself over and over. Instead, he said, "I intend to address that very question at my press conference."

"What press conference?"

This guy—Frank recognized him, sort of. He was some kind of businessman or lawyer, a guy who commuted to Boston to work.

"The one this afternoon," said Frank.

Walking into the building, he shouted, "Somebody call the news people. I want a press conference this afternoon."

Stares, and the faint smell of panic.

Mayor Wright had never before called a press conference. Nobody could remember any Newburyport mayor ever having called one. The mayor had spoken to the press, of course, such as when there'd been a violent crime or a tree had fallen on somebody's house or something. But this was different. This was the mayor announcing he wanted an organized deal with the cluster of microphones and the semicircle of journalists with their exploding flashbulbs and their fedoras.

Nobody knew exactly what to do.

Presumably the reporters would bring their own microphones. They certainly didn't have any at the Town Hall. Were they supposed to put up a backdrop or something? No. It was quickly agreed that the hall itself, that gorgeous old (ca. 1910) blazing red pile. Yes, it would be absurd to hide it behind a backdrop, even if one could be found. The real problem was that nobody was really in charge of the press conference. The mayor was locked in his office, presumably getting some kind of statement together.

Anyway, the staff did their best.

At four p.m., correspondents from the Daily News, Channels 2, 5, 6, 7 and 8, and local radio arrived at the appointed time.

Frank Hart got up from the chair where they'd done his hair and makeup to walk out into the open air before the building. He wore his best blue suit, a real beauty he'd had made for himself when he'd first taken office. He was a handsome son of a bitch, and he knew it.

He commended the people of the town for their courage and fortitude during the blackout. He thanked the police, medical workers and emergency technicians for their efforts under extremely adverse circumstances. He reminded the reporters that this was a crisis for Newburyport. To make sure he was clearly understood, he chose to define the word "crisis," reminding his audience that the word implied a moment not only of danger but of important decision.

Would the town continue to show its great resolve in the aftermath of the disaster? Would it apply the lessons learned in its hour of darkness to the great work of rebuilding?

He was confident that it would.

He pointed to the long and proud history of Newburyport, from its settlement in 1635, its incorporation as a town (1764) and as a city (1851), its construction of the first clipper ship, its being home to the first U.S. Coast Guard station, the first Tea Party of the Revolutionary period, first state mint and treasury building, and oldest superior courthouse in Massachusetts.

Very obviously, this was a town worth saving.

But it had not yet been saved.

The mayor had done what he could during the blackout, organizing police foot patrols and the distribution of food and the administration of the town, such as it was, throughout the period, for which he gave all credit to his staff and the city workers and the people of Newburyport.

But almost one in four of the town's permanent structures had burned down, and many had suffered, and a police officer and three other men had been shot down like dogs, and as-yet unidentified persons had run riot over the grounds of a local school.

It was time for Newburyport to roll up its sleeves, and do what the mayor could not do alone.

As the good people reconstructed houses and assisted in the distribution of food rations and medical supplies, the mayor would be grappling with FEMA for the funds needed to pay for it all. As the people came together to heal, he would be overseeing the criminal investigations to ensure that no one who'd exploited the emergency for personal gain got away with it.

"The people of Newburyport can take it. They can take anything. They've been proving it for more than 380 years, and they aren't going to stop now."

The reporters, who had generally shown him appropriate deference in the past, had their knives out today. Their questions were impertinent in the extreme. Why had the mayor chosen Garrison Academy as his headquarters instead of City Hall? Was it perhaps because he'd placed a maximum priority on the safety of his own children, who went there, to the exclusion of the rest of the town? Was that why he'd had a personal bodyguard of half a dozen police officers with him? Had Garrison served as a kind of enemy fortress in an occupied territory? What did he think of the accusations leveled against his administration by Elijah Hart?

"Hart's a good man," said the mayor, wincing. "He and I...worked together during the blackout to negotiate... logistics."

"Hart says there was a failure of leadership, a power vacuum, during the crisis!" shouted somebody. It was impossible to see anything with these god-damned lights in his face!

Chapter 3
Thanks for the Cornbread

Kosoko Wright
Birdie Love
Barbara Wright
Frank Wright
Ms. De Bono
U.S. President Donald Trump

Kosoko lived now almost exclusively with his parents.

He didn't come in for classes anymore, either.

The modern capacity for telecommuting to school was so advanced that Ms. De Bono really wanted to downplay it; she made frequent reference to the importance of community and togetherness and the shared experience of learning, because of course the ruination of Garrison would only be accelerated by an uptick in "distance learning."

She had no choice in Kosoko's case. The kid was in bad shape. Somehow during the weeks of his convalescence, his leg had become saturated with staphylococcus bacteria.

This was no joke.

Even now under his aggressive new antibiotic regimen, it was expected to take many weeks for him to get back on his feet.

There was still time; it was April, and the season didn't end until June. But it would be very close, and he'd only get to play if they made it to the sectionals.

His leg burned like it was in a furnace, or a Bene Gesserit pain box. The infection, excruciating on its own, also aggravated the fracture itself.

Mayor Wright, who had battalions of troubles in this blackout recovery phase, was grateful every hour for his wife's superior medical insurance, which paid not only for the antibiotics but for round-the-clock pain management, an at-home hospital bed (this one had also been made possible by his position at City Hall), daily nursing care, and frequent outpatient examinations at the hospital.

Birdie showed up that afternoon after classes, as she did most days. Sometimes she brought Zero, who was still her boyfriend. But not today. Today she brought cornbread that her mother had baked. Her mother was from Arkansas, and she knew from cornbread in a way that folks up here in Newburyport just couldn't grasp.

One of her secrets was jalapeños, chopped up so fine you couldn't quite tell what they were. Especially up in Newburyport, where folks don't know from jalapeños. Birdie had brought it in a metal baking tin wrapped up in a dish cloth to keep it hot. She sat by Kosoko's bed and balanced the tin in her lap, carefully buttering a slice for him.

She'd never really appreciated how sweet and lovely he was until his infection.

He was so appreciative, so flattering, so respectful of her romance with Zero. He'd never once tried to take her hand, or flirt, or pull her up onto the bed and start kissing her, putting his huge hands on her body.

But today he was low. He barely acknowledged her, and he waved off the cornbread without a word. He lay looking at the wall. He hadn't even bothered to turn on the TV.

"Hey, kid," she said, concern vibrating through her voice. "NBA season resumes tonight. Celtics/Cavs. I could stay and watch with you if you want."

Kosoko shook his head again. He was gaining weight somehow. He'd more than gained back what he'd lost during the blackout. Much more. It looked okay on him, but not necessarily that great.

He said, "I need to be alone, Birdie. Thanks for the cornbread, all right?"

On her way out, Birdie ran into Barbara Wright.

"Thank you for coming by to see Kosoko again," said Barbara. "I know it means so much to him."

Birdie said it was no problem.

"Birdie, does he seem to you like he's getting better?"

"Yeah," said Birdie, inching toward the door. "Sure he does. He's strong."

"I know he is," said Barbara. She was ashen, trembling. "You know how a mother worries. I know he's gonna be okay."

Birdie was horrified to have been thrust into this intimate situation with Kosoko's mother. Was the woman going to start crying? What was Birdie supposed to do, give her a hug? Jesus! And now Birdie started to cry herself.

"I think," Birdie said, pulling in the reins, "he just...he's sad he can't play basketball."

"I know," Barbara nodded, vigorously, sniffing. "Yes. But he'll play again soon! He's going to get through this and he'll be stronger than ever!"

Birdie said of course, and they all knew he'd get better, but that he was sad because he was missing the basketball season and probably couldn't play until the fall.

Five minutes after Birdie left, Frank Wright came home.

"Barbara," he said, not expecting to see her home so early.

"Hello, Frank," she said.

"Barbara, Elijah Hart just delivered a direct threat to me."

Barbara made no change in her aspect other than to raise her eyebrows. "Is that right?"

"He says he has proof."

"Proof of what, Frank?" she was going to make him say it.

"Shit," he said. "The union. You know damn well."

It was pouring rain outside, so the disconcertingly elegant Ms. De Bono was climbing a Tartaros Infinite Staircase machine at Planet Fitness over on Storey. The TV was on CNN. Everybody lately had wanted to watch nothing but the news all day. The blackout details were still only starting to crystalize.

Right now the news people were talking to a guy who was a CERN scientist, and he was talking about something to do with the solar flare that had toasted everything. Since it was a live show, the close captioning was semi-farcical and the sound was off, so it was hard to follow.

There was some kind of 3D animation showing lots of instances of the earth moving along, and some of them forking off to the left or right while the others stayed in the main stream.

Ms. De Bono was highly distractible just then. All of her troubles had been multiplied and multiplied again, and besides this she was just getting used to a normal diet, with food brought on trucks instead of dropped from airplanes.

It was basically impossible to follow what was happening on CNN under the circumstances, but she had nothing else to look at except the depressing posteriors of the stair climbers in the next row.

She was listening to some old song on her headphones, anyway. She focused on it a second: Yes, it was *In My Life* by the Beatles. Not to be confused with *A Day in the Life*. "There are places I remember," she half-sang as she chugged along. Then she remembered that there were people around, and she shut up.

"Damn," she thought.

The Beatles.

Kind of interesting, wasn't it? If we'd really gone to war with North Korea, and the other great powers had jumped in, then there would be no more Beatles. There were only two left, anyway. But there would be no one to listen to their records, and probably no records left either.

This got her meditating on all the big and little things that would have vanished for all times in a war. All the songs anybody had ever sung. All the pictures anybody had drawn, except for maybe the first ones, the ones in deep caves might have survived, maybe, down in that cool darkness. Yes, and no more kids, no more old men and women, no more socialists or people who believed in the theory of Atlantis, no more French people. No more France, no more French. Just nothing.

Cockroaches.

And then she remembered the spaceship, the one Carl Sagan had sent up with the golden record on it.

It was a literal phonograph record, and on it were a couple of songs. So the songs would survive the earth.

They were out there now, moving almost at the speed of light through intergalactic space. Voyager. It was the only human artifact ever to leave the solar system, and even that had taken over four decades. She thought of Voyager after a war, even more alone than ever, sending its little pings back to earth and hearing no reply.

President Trump was on the TV now. People were shutting up to hear him. The title on the screen read, "TRUMP ACCUSES NORTH KOREA: 'SOLAR FLARE WAS "COVER" FOR NUKE ATTACK.'"

Somebody turned up the volume, and Trump was suddenly audible: "...these are bad people, folks. Believe me. They knew there was gonna be this solar flare—astronomers all over the world had predicted it—and they figured this was their chance to hit us with an atmospheric attack, and folks, I'm gonna tell you, that's exactly what they did."

Ms. De Bono found that all of a sudden, she wasn't able to follow what Trump was saying, even though she was trying. She hated Trump, he disgusted her, but that wasn't it. It was like there was a tiny, very-high-pitched tone ringing through her ears and her brain. She felt dizzy, and she gripped the handrails of the stair-climber more tightly.

Chapter 4
Presto

Dr. John Harriman, PhD
Presto
David Muratskian

If a ray of light from the sun bounces off of Uranus, it will take about two and a half hours to reach earth. It will pass Saturn and Jupiter, then Mars, and each time it passes a world its vector will be modified slightly by gravity.

Tonight, our ray of light had travelled all these vast distances only to drop straight out of the sky and directly into the eye of our little buddy Presto. And if we could have seen Presto's eyes close up, we would have seen the tiny starlike scintilla reflected there.

Presto was, you might say, communing with the cosmos, or at least with the solar system. It was the only way he now had of learning what was going on with the gods, and he had no way to reply. If he had, he'd have sounded the alarm with all his might. As it was, he could only bark into the heavens, jumping up into the air as high as he could.

"Presto, god-damn you!"

Harriman was in his drawers and slippers. He'd been asleep on the sofa, and his beard was pressed flat on the left side. When Presto came over to him, it was from the sublime to the ridiculous. Presto could see his master getting still fatter, still older, even as he stood there.

"Knock off that confounded barking!" said Harriman. "Come and have your kibble, scamp! There, now. There's a good gentleman."

Presto slid past Harriman into the house.

Like his master, the hound had fallen onto evil times. He looked like one of those pitiful strays one sees on the news, scouring the rubble of some disaster site, tail down, ears depressed. The house was an ongoing catastrophe. Presto paused to sniff a plate of petrified spaghetti. He looked at Harriman accusingly, then curled up in a pile of books and magazines.

"There's a good boy," Harriman said.

Harriman lay down on the sofa, too drunk to find his way to bed, and with no motive to go anyway. It was all one. Bottles, newspapers, dirty plates, forgotten garments, dead houseplants.

Harriman could see the moon through the filthy glass. It was a filthy yellow moon, yellow and rotten. It looked like an old basketball left outdoors for too long.

He picked up his copy of the *Book of Basketball*, which he'd been rereading.

He loved the book, though its style was irritating—the author's syntax was so poor it actually shocked the old man. But it lifted his thoughts to the realm of giants. The names were exotic and sublime, and the stories were the stuff of epics. Bill Russell, Wilt Chamberlain, Kareem Abdul-Jabbar, Pete Maravich, Larry Bird, Magic Johnson, LeBron James.

These were men.

Kobe Bryant, the ruthless antihero. Bill Bradley, the Rhodes Scholar, Princeton Man, Senator and presidential candidate, with two championship rings. Alan Iverson, an undersized tough guy who faced down the world's elite. Tim Duncan, who had silently humiliated the best the league had to offer. And Michael Jordan, whom the world worshipped not because he was good but because he was great.

Presto ran to the window and started barking again, with terrifying volume. Harriman threw the book at his dog, missing by two meters and sending the venetian blinds clattering to the floor. Presto bared his teeth at the scholar.

Harriman was too fatigued to retrieve his *Book of Basketball*, but he had a whole stack of books at hand. They were books he'd been poring over to find a reason not to hate humanity. He picked up *Mankind's Search for Meaning* and read it until he fell asleep.

On the far side of the world, the *USS Nebraska* and her entire submarine group were in the Sea of Japan, some fifteen nautical miles off the coast of North Korea.

Weapons Officer David Muratskian had the officers' berth to himself, though he didn't know why. He lay in his bunk, still reading his Proust, still smoking in his white t-shirt.

They were at DEFCON 3. There was strong indirect evidence that a nuclear warhead had exploded over the continental U.S. just minutes before the solar flare hit. NORAD had detected a possible unannounced NorKor ICBM launch about 20 minutes beforehand. Antimissile systems had fired, and then gone dark in the EMP.

Now, as the *Nebraska* silently swam through the darkness, a rocket was being prepped for liftoff at Cape Canaveral. The rocket's mission was to capture gaseous samples from the upper atmosphere. The rocket's capsule would then return to earth, and its samples would be analyzed for the presence of plutonium, Uranium 235, strontium, or other indicators of a detonation months earlier.

While the world awaited this analysis, the war machines went into action. China, Russia, the United States, NATO, Pakistan and India, were on maximum alert.

Somehow, Muratskian, through all this, was able to concentrate on his book. It was a talent he'd had even in childhood; the whole world could be falling apart around him, but if he had something good to read he could tune it all out.

But now his eyelids were getting heavy.

The captain had been running drills continuously and at all hours; nobody was getting enough sleep. Muratskian stuck a bookmark in and leaned over to stow the book.

He saw a shape, like a white square in the darkness, out of the corner of his eye. He turned to look, and what he saw bent reality around him as a black hole bends space.

There, in the corridor just outside the officers' berth, stood a woman.

She was soaking wet, trailing puddles as she approached him. She wore a white towel. Her wet hair hung straight down. She said something to him as she reached his bunk. He couldn't understand what she was saying, but he knew it was Korean. He tried to sit up, but found himself trapped by a pressure like that around the submarine. The woman, who he could now see was herself Korean, put her finger to her lips.

Chapter 5
The Kid Was Like a God-Damn Cartoon Character

Barbara Wright
Mazi Wright
Frank Wright

Barbara Wright, normally the most unflappable of women, was coming in hot on her final approach to nervous breakdown.

She worried. She had been heard to utter the odd minor complaint. She had been seen fretting by credible eyewitnesses. She bounced her knee when she sat cross legged, which was always. She chewed threw forests of pencils. Pens tried to look inconspicuous when she entered a room. She was compulsive. She did ten sudokus and half a dozen crosswords per day. She flipped her hair in a way that was perfectly charming until you noticed that she was doing it eight times a minute. She hyperventilated, driving everyone nuts with her yawning, signing, and breath-holding.

"Breathe!" her husband Mayor Frank Wright would yell at her.

It was Frank who was really being driven nuts. Barbara let out little moans and put her face in her hands when at home. She was given to staring. Sometimes she'd stare right at you without realizing it.

Mazi came over that evening for family dinner. He was in a chipper enough mood.

What else was new? The kid was like a god-damn cartoon character, grinning all the time! What was he, an idiot? Jesus!

"Hey, mom!" he smiled, throwing his book bag in the middle of the floor.

He ran upstairs to see Kosoko, who was of course moping in his hospital bed. That hospital bed was a first-class ticket to the poorhouse, that much Barbara Wright could tell you, insurance or no insurance. A hospital bed in a private residence!

This was all, by the way, bullshit.

She wasn't nervous about the hospital bed, or Mazi's perpetual grin, or bags in the middle of the floor. She wasn't really even nervous about North Korea, or Frank's political troubles, or even, much, about the household budget. She was nervous—fixated, preoccupied, obsessed—over Kosoko.

You couldn't blame the kid for being down. He was in pain. His basketball thing might be over and done with for a long while. She tried to empathize, but it wasn't easy.

Basketball? Talk about a cliché. Talk about an intellectual dead zone.

She wasn't paying a fortune to have her son turned into some failed jock reminiscing in a bar. But, yes, she knew he loved to play and he was very good at it, and it hadn't really done him any harm in his grades.

He was in pain, and that was the heart of it.

Her son was suffering.

His leg hurt, but what hurt worse was his isolation, his failure to recover more quickly, even now that the infection had cleared up, his prospects for playing again.

Her baby. Her firstborn.

She knew she shouldn't let it affect her so strongly. She needed to stay on top of things Who else was going to do it? Frank?

Speak of the sun and up it comes.

Frank opened the front door and walked right in like he owned the place.

"Hey, babe," said he.

The great man! His Honor!

She just looked at him, waiting for him to step right over that backpack without picking it up—bingo. There he went. He stepped over the backpack and up to her to give her a kiss. She turned her head and gave him a cheek.

"Babe, everything okay?"

"Oh, fine, Frank," she said, "Thanks for asking."

He looked at her. Was he in trouble? She didn't know yet—not any more than he did. But she tended to think that he was. One more slip-up.

He went over and got out a bottle of wine from the fridge. He had a gloomy expression on his face, and he looked guiltily up at her as he poured himself a glass. Then he headed into the living room to sit on the sofa and drink it.

"Oh!" she said, moving slowly toward him. "Were you planning to pour me a glass?"

He sprung to his feet.

"Sorry, honey," he said.

Maximum sheepishness. Probably not an attitude he conveyed to his adoring staff down at city hall. Ha! He got a glass out for her.

"No thanks," she said. "I can get my own. That's what I do."

"You sure?" he held the glass and looked stupidly at her, like this was some kind of test.

That night in bed, Frank turned the light off while she was still reading. *He* was finished reading *his* article, so what possible reason would there be for leaving the light on?

"Okay," she said. "I guess I'll read the rest tomorrow."

"Shit, I'm sorry, Barb," he sat up in the dark and looked at her. "I can't seem to get anything right today. I got a hell of a lot on my mind."

"Do you want to talk about it?"

So Frank talked about it.

He told her about his latest chat with Elijah Hart, that snake. Jesus! What balls on this cocksucker. Presuming to *blackmail him?* Blackmail the mayor? Absolutely beyond the pale.

Anyway, the bastard had the goods on Frank, and that was that. As far as that went, it was settled. The cocksucker must have spread a few bucks around, was the only way Frank could figure it.

What kind of goods? Did he really need to get into it?

Fine. The business with the alleged malfeasance with the fucking union, for starters. Kickbacks, it was alleged. Proven, he guessed, since there were the goods in black and white.

Never mind that we were talking about a couple grand spread out over four years.

Never mind that this was simply how business was done in Massachusetts, since time immemorial, that it was expected of him and frankly he would have been crazy to get on the union's bad side by refusing to play ball.

And what was more, he'd like to see what Elijah Hart was going to do when it was his turn! The son of a bitch's ass wouldn't have hit the chair in that mayor's office before the same union was putting the screws to *him*. So fuck it! Bastard was welcome to it. Probably. He hadn't made up his mind how to respond, and he'd told Hart he'd get back to him in a day or two.

"What does he want?" Barbara asked.

"What do you think, babe?" Frank was talking at full volume now, not caring who could hear, i.e., Kosoko. "He wants me to take a dive, that's what. He wants me to give up the whole thing."

"Resign?" Barbara couldn't stand to think of it.

"Nah," Frank sank back into his pillow. He looked so handsome in this light, but it had no effect on her. She saw right through that. "He just wants me to stand down in the fall. Not run for reelection."

Two hours later, Frank was sleeping like a dead man and Barbara couldn't even close her eyes.

Every time she blinked she saw bank balances, old Hart's hoodlum face, Frank walking out of city hall with his head hanging. Frank maybe getting disbarred, so she really would be the only breadwinner instead of just the primary one.

The thought of this—of Frank becoming unemployed and unemployable—actually made her sit up and catch her breath. She looked down at his back and watched it rise and fall with his breathing.

She'd been at war with herself over this man almost since they met. And the part that hated him, wanted nothing to do with him, was getting stronger by the minute.

Could she really divorce him? Even with the kids, even with Kosoko doing so poorly?

Yes, she thought. Damn right she could.

And then she realized that it was really true. Not only was she ready and willing to divorce him if she had to, but that breaking point was almost here. As in, His Honor Frank Wright was exactly one more fuck up from forcing her hand.

Birdie Love was awake, too. Couldn't sleep. Thinking about all the things she needed to take care of.

Kosoko was out for at least another month, maybe more, maybe much more. The real hole left by Kosoko wasn't his strength or his speed.

It was his leadership.

Who would take that role now that it was sorely wanting? Zero? A neurotic who was probably going to flunk out before the season ended? Lefty was sharp, but his head was full of crazy shit and he seemed unable to concentrate. Jackie? No. If Jackie was going to lead anything it would be some crazy rock band. Mazi was smart and knew the game, but he was far too deferential. So that left Birdie.

The Liberators had their first game since the blackout the next morning. They were playing the Phillips Exeter Big Red. Kosoko showed up to sit behind the bench and watch. He looked so furious that everybody was scared to talk to him, including Harriman. They all just gave him a fist bump and then kept away from him.

Jackie had a good game.

He was developing into a pretty good defensive player, which the Liberators dearly needed.

Defense is special for a couple reasons. It's much less dependent on skill than offense, and somewhat less dependent on athleticism. On offense, you could play your heart out, leave everything on the floor, and still not make your shots. But on defense, effort always paid off, at least a little. All things being equal, the team that wanted it more was the team that won that battle.

Another crazy thing about defense: It had a unique pronunciation for sports. In any other usage, it was pronounced d'-FENSE. But in sports, it was pronounced DEE-fense. Why? How the hell should I know? Also, another weird thing: Normally, when you defend someone, you're trying to protect him or her. But in basketball, defending someone meant trying to stop the person.

Zero, however, seemed, out there on the court, like he was thinking about something other than basketball.

As indeed he was.

And Birdie knew all the troubles facing Zero, and she sympathized with him with all her heart, but this was getting ridiculous. She needed a strong man, not a weak one, both on the team and in her life. She felt that she was taking care of everyone--her mom, her team, Naomi with her worries, Kosoko with his leg.

She didn't need a boyfriend who needed coddling month after month.

Anyway! They won. The Liberators won without Kosoko.

Birdie had stepped up as she'd known she'd have to. She was the best point guard in the game. When the final buzzer sounded, she looked into the crowd and turned on the full wattage of her smile, which was something to see, until she turned and saw Kosoko. Then the smile went dark.

Observing the game with her usual passion and gusto was none other than the lovely Natasha Reinhardt. Jackie had never had the nerve to follow up after the time she'd waved to him. Now it occurred to Jackie at some point that her being here was strange. He'd seen her at games before, but only against her own school, Newburypoint High.

For some reason she was here at Garrison for the game tonight, when Newburyport wasn't even playing, cheering her head off as always. Jackie figured she just really loved basketball, which was evident to everyone. But then he caught a glimpse of her after the game, smiling and looking right at him just like before.

The next morning, Naomi Echeveria, with her very upscale luggage, was met by an Uber driver at the front gates of the school. She gave Birdie a hug and a kiss. Birdie told her to be careful, "Seriously."

Naomi was taking a leave of absence to head out west; the Western Exchange still hadn't come back online and millions remained in the dark.

Chapter 6

The Logical Structure of the World

Kosoko Wright

Mazi Wright

Zero Bardoff

Lefty Davis

Jackie Polish

Natasha Reinhardt

Two gentlemen of Newburyport

America was still getting to her feet.

Some major West Coast cities had restored electricity. They were acting as emergency havens for the tens of millions still without power west of the Rockies. Many others from the Western Exchange had made their way east, some as far as Essex County. You could spot the refugees right away. They were broke, carrying all they owned. Plus, they pronounced the R's at the end of words.

Everybody did what she or he could do.

People sent care packages they made at home or in church. The government shipped countless tons of food and fuel oil and water and supplies west in semis that often pulled two or even three trailers. Every train line in the country was closed to commercial travel; every train had to bring cargo.

People were still dying, dozens every day, from the blackout.

The government was in a state of advanced paranoia.

Half of the Navy now patrolled the coasts, especially the West coast, full time. Fighter-bombers roared over the vast deserts of Arizona and New Mexico, and the frozen wastes of Montana, British Columbia, and the Yukon. Bases and radar stations had been given first priority for power restoration, as they had here in the East.

The 24-hour news cycle was loaded with fuel for terror, some of it manufactured, most of it quite legitimate. World leaders convened and begged the U.S. not to rush to war, even as President Trump's blockade tightened its grip around North Korea. There were incidents at sea, none serious enough to escalate the conflict, but all serious enough to give half the country nightmares.

Through this sea of gloom and slow recovery, Harriman shone incandescent.

During the eastern blackout, in that dark hour, he'd determined to turn his team around, to coach the team for real. He'd set aside his Montaigne and his Frankl and his *Book of Basketball*, and picked up *Basketball Skills & Drills* by Krause, Meyer, and Meyer.

The book forced him to confront the fact that there were some subjects more difficult than Latin grammar. Nevertheless, he pored through it again and again, leaving the bottle alone and forcing himself into a comprehension. He owed it to his team, and especially to Birdie.

But practice that day didn't go well.

Kosoko was there, but didn't participate.

The grumbling began. Everyone understood that he wasn't fully ready to play, but his infection was gone and he was close.

Mentally, though, Jesus Christ. The kid barely spoke a word, even to his brother. When Zero asked him point-blank whether he was still a Liberator, he just said, "Yeah, for sure." But the look in his eyes was dead. Was it the fact that he'd been replaced by a talented girl who might be leading the team to a .500-plus win percentage?

Kosoko was done talking. He got up and walked out.

Next day, Zero ran into Birdie on his way to class. He gave her a smile that said, "We haven't talked in three days. What's going on?"

She gave him a no-smile that said, "The world ended a couple months ago, the country is in ruins, war with North Korea is imminent, the school is a disaster, my U.S. History term paper is due, Kosoko Wright is at home sulking, and now you're gonna get on me with some bullshit that I'm not paying enough attention to you? Zero, you need to stand down and sort yourself out. I'm 14 years old and I'm not looking to get married. If this thing here is gonna work out, I need some damn space right now. Got it?"

Zero replied with a nod and a shrug that said, "Okay."

Half an hour later, Zero was in Chemistry class, which was not his favorite class. He didn't have a favorite class, but if he had one it would not be chemistry. That was flat.

His head was a flurry of confusing and contradictory thoughts and feelings.

The Liberators, which he'd himself created as a joke, had shown signs of actually coming together as a team. But with Kosoko out, how were they going to stay competitive?

Birdie was just one player. She couldn't keep basically taking on whole teams by herself, especially if she kept getting fouled hard. The Exeter and Andover wins had been fun, but they couldn't count on anything. Frankly, Zero suspected that his being on the team was the only thing that had kept Garrison from expelling him. Take this class, Chemistry.

He hated to even think about it, but it was a real thing. He was really there, right then and there among the Bunsen burners, before a chalkboard crowded with equations.

He needed to concentrate. He knew that. That was the main thing.

If he could concentrate, he could listen. If he could listen, he'd have at least a chance of learning, of understanding.

How simple it was!

He needed to stop thinking about Birdie and failing out of school and basketball and start actually listening to what the teacher was saying. Take right now, for instance. The teacher was talking, lecturing on and on at the blackboard. And everyone around him was hearing every word she said! And he was spacing out, thinking about nonsense! Not anymore, he resolved one again. From now on he was going to hang on her every word.

"Zero? Hello?"

It was the teacher. She hadn't only been talking, she'd been talking to him.

"What? Yes!" said Zero.

"Do you care to take a stab at this question, please?"

Zero felt no more fear than he might have if he were being dragged to the gallows. Why hadn't he been listening? He'd been sitting there thinking that he needed to listen instead of listening. And now he was doing it again! She had just repeated the question for him, and he'd been thinking about how he should have been listening instead of thinking that he should be listening. It was absurd in the existential sense. It was his own private hell. What was wrong with him?

"Sorry," he said, his mouth as dry as dust. "Sorry, yeah. Could you please...repeat the question?"

She looked at him for a moment, and it was the same look Birdie had given him, except this time it simply said, "Is this kid for real?"

But she didn't say a word about it. Instead, she did as he'd asked. "Which of the following compounds," she said, pointing to the chalkboard, "has the most double bounds in its Lewis Structure?"

On the chalkboard was written,

BF_3 $\qquad$ H_2CO_3 $\qquad$ PCl_5 $\qquad$ CO_2

After class, he ran into Harriman. There was something so distracted and pitiful in the old man's appearance that Zero did, impulsively, something entirely uncharacteristic in him: He asked for help.

Harriman knew the young man's GPA. He knew he'd be giving up a lot of hours at the old Carousel Lounge. To you and me, that might sound a small sacrifice, but you and I are not Coach Dr. John Harriman, PhD.

He paused for a moment.

He was going to tell Zero that there was nothing he could do, that Zero should apply to the tutoring staff that had been set up exactly for cases like this and which was very reasonably priced. But he thought about Zero in that gym, worst player on the team, staying after practice night after night to work on his shooting.

The old man said, "Come to my office every school day before practice. We'll make a scholar of you, boy."

Jackie got on Facebook as soon as he could and found Natasha Reinhardt. Before waiting for his nerve to fail, he sent her a friend request. That night he got a notification that she'd accepted. And just like that Natasha was his friend. He went across the hall to Lefty's dorm room.

"Left-y!" he said, grinning, "You ready to be jealous?"

A glance told Jackie that Lefty was not ready to be jealous. He was a mess.

He wore nothing but boxer shorts and a white t-shirt and stood in the middle of the room.

Now that Jackie was looking, he noticed that the room was almost bare. There were pictures on the wall, mostly of the sun and the planets. There was also a picture of me, the late, great Peter Graff, and one of Presto. There was still a desk and dresser, but no bed--just some sheets and a pillow on the floor.

Lefty started talking to Jackie about data blocks with methods and properties. What separated two identical objects? The values of their variables? Not necessarily. They could have exactly the same values. Was it just an extrinsic factor like the object's memory address? What made objects reusable? What was the difference between reusing an object and making a copy of an object? He'd been writing pseudocode in his notebook.

When he'd been a kid, he'd gone to the family beach house every summer. He had a sand machine there. The sand machine was just a hollow piece of driftwood. He'd pour sand into one end with a bucket, and watch the sand pour out of the other end. A machine that turned sand into sand--sand into itself. What about the idea that the ancients had been right? What was the logical structure of the world?

"The logical structure of the world?" Jackie sat down on the floor. "How about I just got friended by Natasha Reinhardt, and you don't even care? How is that logical?"

"I'm telling you," said Lefty, "there's a ton of stuff about the blackout that doesn't add up. Thousands of eyewitnesses say they saw a brilliant flash in the sky at the moment the lights went out. A solar flare wouldn't look like that. It would be like an incredibly huge and bright aurora borealis that went on for hours. Do you remember seeing anything like that? Hell, no. It was pitch dark. What if Trump isn't talking out his ass? What if there really was a nuclear detonation in space?"

Jackie looked at him seriously. "Lefty, man, we need you here, okay? If you go nuts, what chance to I have? And the team? We've already got one crazy friend, but at least with Zero it's more like emotional, not like some conspiracy--"

"All right, all right," Lefty shooed Jackie to his feet and out the door. "I should have known you wouldn't get it." He shut the door.

Jackie stood there for a moment, nonplussed. Then he turned around and walked back to his room. He sat at his desk and just stared for a minute. "So bizarre."

He got up and started to leave again, but thought better of it. He sat back down. "I just...I can't believe I'm friends with Natasha Reinhardt."

It was Natasha who, a few days after accepting Jackie's friend request, initiated the deepening of that friendship through an online direct message.

They "chatted" through several conversational topics, e.g. what each had done, and in particular had eaten, during the blackout, favorite subjects in school, smoking (neither smoked), drinking (both, a bit), age (both 14), what it was like being a basketball player (Jackie made it sound more fun and less stressful than it was, generally, for him), what it was like being an opera singer in training (Natasha was the daughter of a famous violinist and she aspired that her voice should be her instrument), what Coach Harriman was like, what Newburyport High School was like, what Garrison was like, pet peeves (Natasha hated "bad music" so much it made her depressed, Jackie hated religious people and guns (Natasha, being from the Northeast, was neither religious nor a gun owner)). And of course they talked about the fact that the U.S. Navy had initiated a blockade against North Korea, which was technically an act of war.

The efficiency with which they worked through these topics was remarkable. They managed it in about 30 lines of text. Then Natasha got down to business, as Jackie seemed unable to.

Natasha: so, yeah, you looked pretty cute in that game the other night.

Jackie: really?

Natasha: Totally

Jackie: I guess a man in uniform can't look too bad.

Natasha: Unbearably cute. I love your eye patch.

Jackie: Are you messing with me?

Natasha: Ha ha, no!

Jackie: You're mad cute too. Beautiful

Natasha: I know! Isn't it great? My father says, "You should never complain when you're young, rich, and beautiful."

Jackie: Have you ever been to Carousel Lounge?

Less than 24 hours later, they sat in that wretched hive. Natasha had a French 75, Jackie had a Schlitz. The lame Harriman was there, naturally, his limp exaggerated by his drunkenness. Zero and Birdie and Lefty were there too.

All the gang descended on Jackie and Natasha as soon as spotting them. Birdie introduced herself with a little curtsy. Zero made bold to kiss Natasha's hand. Lefty, as usual lately, seemed distracted. Harriman scolded Natasha for even being seen in such an establishment, but he smiled with pleasure.

Through all of this, Natasha delightedly met each of them in turn, and for each had a particular word or two of praise, as though she were giving out little bouquets to guests at a wedding.

Jackie, on the other hand, was scarcely aware that the coach and his friends or indeed anyone at the bar was present but he and she. And each time there was a pause in Natasha's introductions, she would steal a glance at him, and her eyes said that every aspect of the evening was a silly joke except that they were together.

Newburyport, Massachusetts is not a high-crime city.

The Carousel Lounge, however, was its own little slum, and its baleful influence radiated for a few blocks in every direction, especially now in the depths of the post-blackout recession. And this was to have consequences tonight, as they stumbled tipsily out onto the sidewalk.

"Can I walk you home?" asked the gallant Jackie, offering his arm.

"Why, that would be so kind of you, Jackie," she said, placing special emphasis on his name.

It sounded in her mouth like the ring of a bell. Jackie's eyes were not so much drinking her in as sipping at her in tiny glances, first her long, upright figure, then the dark brown hair that reached down her back, then the arch mischief of her eyebrows, the fullness of her mouth, the intensity of life in her eyes.

They had walked only half a block when she began to sing *Si Un Jour* from Verdi's *La Forza del Destino*:

Mon père me dit en remets donc ton jupon

Ne touche pas à ce ballon ça c'est pour les garçons

Cesse de gémir tu as des occupations

Des fils et des aiguilles des perles et des boutons

Jackie was so alarmed he was unable to speak, and simply motioned with his hands that she must either stop or greatly reduce the volume of her singing. Your true diva must have the faculty to sing high notes in "full voice," which meant maintaining her pitch while singing loudly enough to fill a large theater without amplification. Natasha, at 14, was well on her way to achieving this mature skill.

All around them were the denizens of the night. Men who went unnoticed most of the time, but who were now extraordinarily conspicuous in Jackie's sight. Men who slept under bridges, men who carried small blades, men of evil appearance. All of them, from behind every dumpster or doorway, from behind every lamppost, now stared at Natasha, and at him.

"Natasha, you can't sing here," Jackie managed to say. "You're a great singer, but this ain't the time, okay?"

To which Natasha brightly replied,

Mais moi j'aimerais vraiment pouvoir abandonner mon Moulinex

Devenir unisexe

Pour savoir cracher

Two young gentlemen had taken a particular interest in her singing. They were crossing the street to meet our lovebirds.

"Natasha, seriously! Please don't!"

Fumer toute la journée

Marcher tout en sifflant

Porter—

Now the two gentlemen had placed themselves directly in their path, and they could go no further.

The gentlemen were short, shorter and smaller than Jackie. He felt that he could probably beat either one of them up. This is a superstition wrongly arrived at by many a civilian when confronted by a street person. Street persons, however slight of build, do not lose fights. They do what's necessary to win, and win quickly.

"My friend don't like you singing like that," said the first.

"And why not?" said Natasha, who seemed authentically surprised.

"His father just died. He thinks you're making fun of him." These were young guys, maybe early 20s.

Jackie stared at them for a moment, then looked around. Was any of his crew around for backup? No, damn them.

"Sorry," said Jackie. "She didn't know about your father."

"Okay," said the first gentleman, motioning for Jackie to hush and relax, as though he had the situation well in hand and Jackie were in hysterics or something.

"So we're gonna punch you in the face," said the gentleman to Jackie. "So my friend feels better."

Jackie said, "Oh, that's--" and the second gentleman, the bereaved, hauled off and socked Jackie right on the end of his nose.

"Fuck!" said Jackie. "You fuckin' punched me!"

But he had only just straightened up his body when the first gentleman, whose father was presumably alive and well, followed up with his own punch, which also landed squarely on Jackie's nose.

Jackie was sure he'd heard a snap or a crackle or a pop or something.

"FUCK. That's *two* you got me, you fuckers!"

The two gentlemen, laughing at their grief avenged, went on their way.

Jackie turned to Natasha.

Here's a good rule for those who like to hike. Don't bring a dog with you when you walk in the woods. The reason is that the dog, if it sees a bear, will first run up and antagonize it, and then run back to you, luring the bear with it.

The gorgeous, infinitely charming Natasha Reinhardt was nothing at all like a dog, but she had here played the dog's role. But Jackie made no mention of this, now or ever. He said nothing about the fact that he'd implored her not to sing the beauteous aria, repeatedly. He made no mention of the fact that she had, without his approval, created a consequence that affected him and not her. He forbore from saying any of this, but he was thinking of it.

"I think they broke my nose!" said Jackie.

He was bending forward with the pain, then straightening up to see her, then bending forward again, bobbing up and down.

"Fuck, it hurts!"

He would never have admitted it, but he was gently exaggerating the level of his discomfort, hoping to provoke some reaction in her. But each time he bobbed up to see her, waiting for her to weep for him and beg his pardon, he saw that she was not saying a word, but rather screwing up her face to control herself.

Her obvious mirth inflamed Jackie's rage. Not ordinary rage, but a rage of frustration at her failure to grasp the situation, or indeed to listen to what he was telling her.

He'd been assaulted. The bastards had probably broken his nose.

And she stood there, trying not to laugh. He had an unconscious compulsion to become increasingly demonstrative, so that she'd have to face up to what she'd done.

Still holding his nose, he began to leap up and down in an odd way. With each leap, he would kick back his forelegs almost to his backside in emphasis. "Fuck, it hurts! It hurts so bad!" he cried.

At this point, Natasha, who contrary to appearances was extremely sorry at what had happened to poor Jackie, was no longer able to restrain her laughter. It burst forth in gales, no less loud than her boldest singing. "I'm sorry!" she said between laughs. "I'm so sorry, Jackie! Ha ha ha ha ha ha ha!"

That same night, as Jackie and Natasha departed the scene of the crime, Birdie and Zero had a chat.

Mostly her chatting, he listening.

The situation, romantically, was not good. It had developed not necessarily to Zero's advantage. She was nice about it, and she even cried. She didn't get into his many faults and deficiencies, or how his long suffering had exhausted her to her very core. She just told a kind of truth: They were way, way too young to be this serious. That kind of thing.

"So you don't love me," said Zero.

Chapter 7
Emergency Action Message

Good old Lefty Davis
Zero Bardoff
Ms. Hercule
Weapons Officer David Muratskian
The captain of and officers the USS Nebraska

Good old Lefty had got himself a bicycle.

Riding a bicycle wasn't Lefty's style. Not at all. Riding it wasn't bad. It was even fun. But wearing that bicycle helmet made him look like a dick, and he knew it.

"I look like an asshole," he mumbled to himself when he caught his reflection in some store window, "or a dick."

But he didn't care, as he had before.

Bottom line was he needed to get around, and only your true weirdo rode the bus.

Why this sudden need for speed? He was building a model of the solar system. It was based on the Sagan Planet Walk in Ithaca, New York.

Even though he was mainly interested in two celestial objects, the sun and the earth, he figured he should model the whole shebang to account for gravity.

The deal with the solar system is that things are very far apart. Like, when we see a picture of the solar system, with all the planets next to each other, that's not what it really looks like. In fact, it was impossible to draw a picture of the solar system on an ordinary piece of paper because to account for the vast distances you'd have to make the planets too small to see. So for his research, Lefty needed a very big model.

He started with the sun.

That was logical enough.

And it happened, by sheer coincidence (if you believe in coincidences), that the sun at the scale he was using (1:5,000,000,000) was almost exactly the size of a basketball. So he put one in the bushes on the edge of the Garrison campus, very near to where Harriman had gotten his ass kicked during the blackout.

Next came the terrestrial planets.

Mercury at this scale was a few dozen meters from the sun, just up Ferry Street. It had to be just one millimeter across, so Lefty had brought a sharp pencil and now broke off the tip of the graphite. He carefully set it down in the grass beside the sidewalk, and built a circle of stones around it to mark the spot.

About a quarter of a block up he put Venus, a shining BB. A little ways further up was Earth, another BB (the two planets are pretty much the same size), and at the end of the block he put Mars. Mars was a very smooth, round, smaller-than-a-BB pebble Lefty had put in an Altoids tin and brought just for the occasion. So far, he'd been walking his bike, so no need to wear the damn helmet.

So those were your terrestrial planets, all within a block of campus.

Now he turned right onto Elmira Avenue and went another half-block.

Here was the asteroid belt.

The real asteroids of the belt would be microscopic at this scale, so he just put a regular belt, which he figured was comparable in width, at least, to the actual asteroid belt. He hid the belt up against a chain link fence that edged somebody's lawn. This is all residential around here, by the way.

At the end of the block he put mighty Jupiter, largest of the planets. This had been a hard one. It had to be 2.6 centimeters across, and there just weren't many household objects that size. He'd been about to give up when he came across a well-stocked set of gumball machines. He stuck the gumball right in the grass by the corner.

Now he had a choice to make.

He could ride about eight blocks out of his way, or he could cut through some family's property to get over to Merrimack Street. Cutting through meant walking, and walking meant no helmet. Easy choice. It was a pain in the ass sneaking through the trees, and he got a bunch of cobwebs in his face, which he hated more than anything. But he got to Merrimack, and there he turned right and got on his Huffy.

Saturn's orbit lay another block and a half up Merrimack Street, near the corner of Cushing. Saturn was another gumball, but he put a loose rubber band around it to represent its rings. Close enough.

Now he got on his bike for his longest stretch so far. Uranus was up another three-plus blocks, right where Merrimack met Jefferson Street. There was a bright red fireplug right there in the middle of the sidewalk, and there Lefty placed a perfect, clear blue marble, so signifying the garden spot of the whole galaxy.

In a minute, he'd go on a much longer stretch to place Neptune, and for the hell of it would drop a fleck of dried paint that would be Pluto, but not yet. Right now, he knelt down beside that Uranus marble. He picked it up again, staring right through it, staring all the way down to the end of Merrimack, and over, in his mind's eye, to where he'd placed the earth, and just a bit farther to that solar basketball hidden in the bushes.

"What do I know?" he whispered. "What do I know so far? I know what was done was undone. I know that what was the truth was made a lie. I know that a planet can have a mind, and think. Was the end made a beginning, only to end again? Is the world a garden of forking paths?"

A thought came into his mind: There was me, Pete Graff, and there was Presto, but there must be a third. A woman. The angriest woman in the world.

He looked up into the blue sky of springtime, through the stretched cotton ball clouds and into the glare of the sun, the real sun. He started to cry. He knew now what everyone who'd ever discovered a conspiracy knew: first, that he was being lied to. And second, that no one would ever believe him.

Zero had but one consolation as the days grew longer. The agony of his tutelage under Coach Harriman was paying off. He was getting passing grades, by the skin of his teeth, in all his classes.

It was a remarkable feeling.

If not for the once and future end of the world, my death, his congenital depression, his failure to improve at basketball, and the loss of his darling Birdie, he would have been lighter than air. Even now, in his weakened state, some part of him was buoyed with just enough force to carry the rest.

Now he sat in English class, watching Ms. Hercule scratch away at the chalkboard. There was something quite marvelous, quite unfamiliar and wonderful, in the fact that, having done the reading, he was able to follow her lecture. It was as though his teachers had actually wanted him to succeed all along, as though effort was rewarded and there was logic, not chaos, to the entire academic structure.

Ms. Hercule! Most noble of women.

It had been she who'd lifted him from the morass into this new clear light. He smiled at her. She didn't smile back.

The bell rang. Zero was rising to gather his iPad and his backpack, when she called his name. The other students filed out, and he went to her desk.

"Hi!" he said. He was actually smiling, the poor sucker.

"I'd like to talk to you about this." She held up, as though it were a filthy rag, the extra credit essay/poem he'd written for her, *Death*.

Zero, for the first time in his life, experienced tunnel vision. Ms. Hercule seemed to be at a great distance, radiating heat.

"Would you care to tell me about this poem?" she said.

"I'm sorry?"

"Okay," she said, her face as stern as any Roman frieze. She paused, and then said, "This poem is *Beth*."

"*Beth*," said Zero, who was simultaneously pretending not to comprehend and, at some higher level, actually not comprehending.

"*Beth*. Peter Criss, Stan Penridge, Bob Ezrin, 1976, from the A-side of Detroit Rock City by Kiss."

"It's...not," the round-shouldered Zero said softly.

"I've seen some pretty sad plagiarism come across my desk," she was shaking her head. "But Kiss? Jesus Christ."

She directed his attention to a row in her grade book. It read, "Extra credit essay: F."

Weapons Officer David Muratskian left his station and walked up the stairs onto the command center of the submarine.

"Gentlemen!" said the captain. "What I'm about to tell you is classified top secret and it should not be repeated to anyone, sailor or officer, not here present. Is that understood?"

"Aye, captain," said Muratskian with the others.

Muratskian felt a little like he'd just woken up. Or more than that, like he was in the process of waking up, trapped between dreams and the new day. His shirt was soaked with sweat, but it was cool in the command center.

"We have received an Emergency Action Message," said the captain. There was something strange about the old skipper, something he couldn't quite place. "The pentagon has analyzed the samples of the upper atmosphere brought back in the space capsule. It tested positive. It contained more than ten thousand parts per million of Plutonium. As we feared, the North Koreans must have used the solar flare as cover for their own detonation of the thermonuclear warhead over the United States.

"I realize it seems improbable, to the point of incredulity, that Kim Jung Un would have launched an attack against us whose effect was going to be replicated exactly by the solar flare just seconds later. In other words, that North Korea's attack was unnecessary and redundant to the natural disaster which succeeded it. Nevertheless, we have our answer. No natural event known to man could have created the physical evidence captured by that space probe.

"All of this is academic, of course. What matters, the only thing that matters, is that we are now, for the first time in history, at Defense Condition One. From this minute forward, we will keep our nuclear missiles fueled and ready to be fired at seconds' notice."

Yes, something was strange, very strange, about the captain. Because the captain, today, was not himself. He was Major Kim Jigu, a woman and an enemy officer. Muratskian scanned the faces of his fellow officers. None of them betrayed the slightest sign that anything was amiss.

Chapter 8
Namaste

Zero Bardoff
Jackie Polish
A couple of seventh-grade boys
Kosoko Wright
Mrs. Vite

Meanwhile, in the refurbished cafeteria, the heartsick Jackie was thinking about giving the whole yoga thing a try. His would-have-been girlfriend Natasha had recommended it very highly.

He told Zero, "I'm thinking about giving this whole yoga thing a try."

Zero took a sip from his little pint-sized carton of chocolate milk. He pondered this for a moment, nodding his head. Then he said, "Yoga, huh? Hmm. Okay. Yoga. Let me ponder this for just a moment." He sat there very seriously. "Yoga, right? With the mats, and the outfits, and the incense?"

"I guess," said Jackie. Jackie was already regretting having even brought it up.

"Right. Just wanted to be sure, you know. That we were talking about the same thing. No point in having a whole conversation and then realizing we're talking about two different things. So you—you are talking about giving this whole yoga thing a try. That's what you said, ain't it?"

"A lot of basketball players do it. Kareem, Kevin Love...supposed to really help your game."

"Right! Well, that makes sense. Sure. Yeah. Because it can like improve your flexibility."

"Yeah. And your strength," Jackie said. "Plus, you know, I've been pretty stressed out, pretty anxious. This whole North Korea thing is a little intense, and then with Natasha—"

"Yeah," Zero was back at it. "So, why not? Yoga. Healthy body, healthy mind. I guess you'll get one of the little mats and carry it around. So that's kind of cool. I can see that. Maybe some of those yoga pants. A nice little pastel baggy tank top."

Jackie noticed at this point that Zero didn't quite look right. His tie was all crooked and off to the side. He looked a little sweaty. He was up on his feet now, pacing back and forth so that kids with their lunch trays had to stand clear.

"Funny thing, though, Jackie. I never thought of you as the religious type."

"Maybe because I'm not, dumb ass."

"Oh? Then I'm confused. Yoga is a word for various religious practices in Hinduism and Buddhism. But I guess you don't mean that kind of yoga. You mean the American kind of yoga, which is also 'spiritual' but in more of a dippy New Age way. Like, I guess we can expect to see you start like wearing little beaded necklaces. Maybe some crystals. Bracelets. Anklets! Sandals!"

"Oh, for Christ's sake, I'm not going to start wearing sandals. Jesus."

"Oh, okay. I was just asking since, you know, you're about to take up yoga. Toe rings? And you'll stop wearing deodorant and other shallow Western unspiritual shit. Materialistic shit. And I suppose you'll be meditating, too. Maybe saying *Om*. I'm sure you will. I think that's part of it, right?

"And that comes with a whole load of side benefits. I'm going to come in here next week and you're going to be one with everything. You're gonna be levitating above that chair, talking some shit about how in a past life you were a hermit crab, and talking about karma and the wheel of eternity.

"Forget reality. Forget science. Forget everything. You're gonna have it all figured out. There's no atoms or forces or whatnot. There's just you and your mindfulness and your inner peace. You're gonna start believing in chi and acupuncture.

"Fuck! Forget sandals, you're gonna be here *barefoot*. You're gonna give up your marbles and your gum and your baseball cards and all your worldly possessions.

"And I know why, too. Because the real world is scary. Bad things happen, and you can't just meditate them into oblivion. I'm failing out of school, my girl dumped me, Peter Graff got his head blown off, and the Doomsday Clock is at one second to midnight. But its' cool! It's all mellow, you know, *dude*."

Jackie had, early in this last monologue, gotten up and walked out. The only ones still listening to Zero were a couple of seventh-grade boys. One of them elbowed the other and pointed his thumb at Zero, like, "You believe this fuckin' guy?"

Later, Zero had the misfortune to run into Kosoko.

Misfortune, because Zero was in so ugly a humor he was hardly himself. And Kosoko wasn't exactly skipping down the sidewalk himself. It was getting dark out, and Zero should have been home already. Anyway, they barely looked at each other, and then Zero mumbled something about way to be a team player.

Kosoko, who had really put on quite a lot of weight by now from all the lying in bed and all of Birdie's mom's homemade jalapeño cornbread, and who was far from pleased about it (the weight), stopped short and looked up, straight ahead, like, "Okay. Here we go."

Then he turned to face Zero, who was already twenty paces toward home, and Kosoko said, "You say something, kid?"

The red-headed Zero, who acted in his own way like a tough guy and who was in reality scared out of his wits virtually all the time, also stopped short now, and turned.

Here you had the kind of situation that 99 times out of 100 would have had our boy whimpering for his mama, but right now with the yoga and the extra-credit F and with Birdie, well, he was still scared to death but he was also wicked pissed.

"Yeah," said Zero, straightening up his back for once in his life. He moved slowly toward Kosoko, with a strange confidence; his walk was almost like that of a young man instead of an old codger in a bread line. "Yeah, I said here comes the fuckin' team player himself."

Kosoko's eyes were wide now. He was almost too shocked to be angry, but, you know, still managed to nail the angry part. As in, he was furious.

"Boy, is you talkin' about *me?* Because I knew you were crazy, but I didn't think you had a *death wish.*"

"What's the matter, Kosoko?" Zero strode up right in Kosoko's face. "I guess you're the big man when you're not god-damn squiring around with your teammate's fucking *girlfriend.*"

Kosoko smiled. "Your girl? She couldn't handle a grown man like me. And she too little. She okay for you, right? But I need a woman, not some little girl."

Zero, rage flooding his eyes: "Don't fuckin' lie! You and her are cheating!"

He started walking away. He couldn't let Kosoko see him like this. Kosoko was so strong, so tall, so mighty as any statue.

"Let me ask you something, Zero. What the hell are you doing on my team anyway? You can't play."

That stopped Zero cold. And yeah, what Kosoko had said was cold.

"Why you on the team?" Kosoko asked again. "You can't run. You can't cut. We can't hide you on defense, your basketball I.Q. is the same as your name, Zero, and you never pass. You shoot every time you touch the fuckin' ball, and you can't even shoot! Any time we get you involved, the play dies with you. So why don't you quit? Find somebody who can play basketball and let him take your spot."

"I'm getting better," said Zero, barely breathing.

"The team was your idea," said Kosoko. "Don't you want it to be good? Don't you want it to succeed?"

Zero looked up. "What about you, Kosoko? Your leg doesn't look so bad. How come you don't come out and play again, if you're so worried about the team?"

"I'll tell you why, kid. I can't play with no girl on the floor."

"She's good."

"I didn't say she couldn't play. I said *I* can't play with her out there. I could run her over if I'm not looking, and put her in the hospital. Hell, no."

"Bullshit," said Zero. "Why are you really not playing? We're 10 and 11. We could make the postseason with your help."

"Fuck I care what you think anyway? If you don't care about the Liberators enough to quit, I'll get you thrown off the team. Who they gonna listen to? You or me?"

"You," whispered Zero.

"*You or me?*"

"You, Kosoko."

The magnificent Kosoko, magnificent even with his extra weight and his limp, stood and watched Zero disappear into the dark places between the street lamps. Then he turned and kept walking toward the cafeteria.

Fuck it. Didn't have enough problems, he needed some nutty white kid making claims? As far as Zero knew, Kosoko was completely innocent and had never laid a finger on Birdie.

Kosoko kicked a can that was standing there on the sidewalk. Kicked it hard. Only it wasn't a can. It was some kind of outdoor electrical outlet. So now the swift Kosoko stood on his bad leg, holding up his good foot and leaning on the cordwood fence, practically about to hop up and down with the pain. *Fuck that motherfucker Zero.*

"*God-damn it!*" said Kosoko. And he looked up and saw the librarian Mrs. Vite a few feet up the sidewalk. She looked pretty sore. "Sorry, Mrs. Vite," he said.

Kosoko figured then and there he wasn't taking any more shit from any of these clowns. If Zero wanted to start something, Kosoko would happily oblige. Fuck that weird motherfucker!

Chapter 9
A Prison Becomes a Home When You Have the Key

David Muratskian
Kim Jigu
Zero Bardoff
Frank Wright
Kosoko Wright

Muratskian was staring at his displays.

He was too numb to notice the way his fingernails dug into his wrists as he scratched them. The poor man seemed to have developed a kind of rash, and it seemed to cover most of his body that wasn't hidden by his clothes. Right now the locus of anguish was his left wrist. Anguish, of course, and ecstasy, because the misery before and after each scratching session was mirrored by the almost orgasmic pleasure when he scratched.

There was a fly on his forehead now, which he swatted at. Flies on a submarine are not rare, but they are particularly unwelcome. He felt the fly disappear, and then suddenly it was crawling down into his collar, onto the tormented flesh beneath.

So now Weapons Officer David Muratskian is so unhappy, twisting himself into a pretzel in a vain attempt to destroy the fly, that it was a relief when he saw the alert start to flash.

The sonar team had spotted a bogey 800 meters off the port bow.

It was a Sinpo/Gorae class diesel-electric submarine, one of the new NorKor ballistic missile subs. Her purpose was to launch missiles against land-based targets, but she was plenty dangerous in the water, too. The captain called for a zero bubble dive and silence fore and aft. On the 1-M-C, he ordered the crew to battle stations, rigged for ultraquiet.

Muratskian had an unfamiliar feeling just then, one he didn't recognize at first.

Here he was, dozens of meters beneath the Sea of Japan, evading an enemy attack sub, but he felt as light as a snowflake in an updraft.

And then it hit him: He was free. Free, when he hadn't even known he'd been caught. He listened to the captain's voice. It was his again, not the woman's.

Does anybody remember a much younger Zero?

One day, when Zero was seven or eight, he found himself alone at the middle school playground. He didn't go to middle school yet, but they lived very close by and sometimes he walked there. Anyway, he was the only one in the playground.

Playgrounds were a particular favorite of his in those days. He didn't go in for sports. None of his friends did. Theirs was a more creative, more imaginative style of play. They'd invent scenarios and then improvise them.

For example, in their fertile minds the swings might be transformed into X-Wing fighters. Or they might do battle with a dragon that others saw as an ordinary jungle gym. The reader will have noticed by this point that they were, if nothing else, extremely difficult to embarrass.

On this little solo excursion he found himself trying out a brand-new attraction: the spiral slide. It was a very choice slide indeed, brightly painted and as yet free of wear. One climbed the metal staircase up some ten feet, then hunched down on the diamond plate platform. Perhaps one inhaled the rarified air, and took in the whole expanse of creation. Then the action: Grab the crossbar at the entrance to the enclosed spiral, hurl yourself in, hurtle down though the winding helix into the sunshine at the bottom.

And as he began to climb those stairs, he entered the world of fantasy.

To anyone who had ever talked to a girl, this was a slide. But to him it was the bowels of a sophisticated prison. Crouching at the top, he was trapped in his cell. Or was he? A bolt on the structure proved to be a secret button, and when pressed the button activated a secret door to an escape chute. Seizing his chance, he slid down to freedom. And what did he find at the bottom? Naturally, a huge cache of gold bars.

But every time he was about to raid the treasure and depart the prison, he heard the approaching footsteps of the guards. Zero had to scramble up the slide back into his cell and wait for the authorities to move along.

Such was his predicament. He must grab all the gold he could carry and escape, but he had to time his movements perfectly to avoid detection.

If ever there was one, this was an occasion for a song. And sing Zero did, both in lamentation and utter determination. Imagine, if you can, his golden falsetto as it pierced the gloom of his cell.
The chorus went,

Oh! I must get the gold.

And the gold, it must be mine!

He'd just completed the second chorus of his anthem and was launching into another verse when he sensed something behind him.

There was a boy his age whom he had never met, standing at the top of the ladder inches from his face. Behind him, a line of several other kids waited for their turn.

And that boy said something to him that he'd never since forgotten. He said, "You like to sing, kid?"

The night before the last game of the regular season, a game which would determine whether the Liberators went on to the sectionals, April 16, 2017, there was another game.

It was an NBA playoff game pitting the Boston Celtics against the Chicago Bulls. And a remarkable night it was. For the great leader of the Celtics, point guard Isaiah Thomas, apple of Birdie's eye, had just the night before lost his baby sister Chyna in a car accident.

The Celtics held a moment of silence in her memory. There was idle speculation up to the last minute whether Isaiah would play. But there he stood at center court, all 5'9" of him, waiting for the tipoff. The camera zoomed in on his shoes, on which were written, "Chyna," "Rip Lil Sis" and "I love you."

Chyna had been 22 years old.

Birdie sat and cried throughout the game.

Isaiah was unstoppable—he had 33 points, six assists, and five rebounds—but the Celtics still lost.

Frank Wright had come home again to a wife who wouldn't say two words to him and a son who wouldn't come out of his room. The mayor was so tired, had so much god-damned weight on him. Dealing with FEMA, trying to get the town back up and running at full speed, all under constant threat from that miserable motherless fuck Elijah Hart.

Well, shit.

If he was going to get swept away by the currents at work, blackmailed into failure and obscurity, he damn sure wasn't going to get pushed around in his own house. Not anymore. He was going to take charge.

He took one look at Barbara, standing there in the kitchen with her cigarette, and realized that he should start with Kosoko.

Up the stairs, then! *His* stairs, *his* house, by Christ. Into Kosoko's room. Kid was watching TV. Didn't even look up.

"What?" said Kosoko.

Wright walked right up to that TV set to shut it off. This wasn't going to be the kind of chat you'd have with the god-damn TV running its mouth. That much was for sure, and— where the HELL was the power switch on this thing?

"Turn this TV off now, Kosoko."

Kosoko killed the TV with his remote control. And then he repeated his question.

"Well, son, I'll tell you what. You've been sleeping here all semester. You hardly talk at dinner, and it smells like you haven't had a shower in days. Your grades are slipping, you're missing classes—"

"I'm not missing classes," Kosoko said.

"Son, don't *tell* me you're not missing classes. Don't forget that Ms. De Bono is a personal friend of mine. If you think I'm not hip to everything that goes down at that school, you're out of your mind. So let's knock off the bullshit here and now.

"You got your mother worried sick—did you know she's smoking again? After what she went through in the blackout, you think she needs this from you? You limp around here with that hard look on your face like everybody else is to blame for your troubles."

"Old man," said the unsmiling Kosoko. "You're talking about yourself, not me."

Frank Wright was hearing none of this. *Hell* no. And now he stood over his son, real close, and he told his son the truth.

He said he knew Kosoko looked at him differently now, over all the shit with the union and the politics. He could see that lack of respect, and he wasn't about to stand for it. He told Kosoko what it had been like when *he* was coming up, in Boston in the 80s. Shit. He'd seen stuff back then that would reduce Kosoko to tears if Frank cared to talk about it. Kosoko thought he had it rough. Please. Kosoko was never even on the same side of the street as rough. He hadn't ever seen what rough looked like, growing up in this lovely quaint historic little city.

"Oh, right," Kosoko said, sitting up. The boy'd grown a double chin. "I forgot all the hardcore things you been through. Yeah. Like I suppose you seen a man shot in the face right outside your window, right? I suppose you seen a bone come right out through your thigh."

Frank stood there a minute. He knew the kid was right. Hell, he was just trying to help Kosoko. But his mind just wouldn't let him respond. He just couldn't find the words he needed.

Frank went downstairs. He felt beat up and beat down. It was dark downstairs. Barbara had gone off to bed. Frank didn't bother to turn on the light. He sat down in a plush chair and just looked out the window.

Then the hall light came on. "Hey, Dad." It was Mazi.

Good old Mazi. Look at him there, standing in his t-shirt and underwear. The whole world was falling to pieces all around him, and Mazi still had the same sweet smile on his face.

Mazi went into the kitchen and got a glass of water. He walked into the dark living room and sat down across from Frank.

"Dad, how was work?"

Frank smiled. The question belonged to another era in their lives, when it had really seemed like things were going to be all right.

"It was a good day at City Hall, son. You know what they say, right?"

"You can't fight City Hall."

"You got it," Frank said with a smile. Then he thought for a second, and then he said, "Funny thing happened at work, now that you mention it. Had a visitor."

"Oh yeah?"

"Yeah, some lady. Chinese, I think. She was asking about Peter Graff, where he was. I told her what had happened to Graff. She didn't seem too phased about it. And then you know what she did next?"

Mazi admitted he didn't know.

"She asked me about your coach—but not about him, about his *dog!* Can you believe that? She wanted to know where she could find the dog!"

"Presto," said Mazi.

"That's it. Presto. Absolutely unbelievable."

Mazi just smiled. He didn't think it was so hard to believe.

Chapter 10
A Burning Building

So the Liberators had a shot at making the sectionals. Nobody could believe it.

They were still a five-player team and still without their best player (though he'd promised he'd try to play). Never mind the asterisks. Never mind that this had been a shortened, and then bizarrely extended, and altogether convoluted season, with the playoffs happening months behind schedule. What did it all matter? It was a do-or-die game.

Somehow the Liberators had made it this far. The odds were ten-to-one against them to get into the sectionals, but consider: This was Lefty, who'd gone a little around the bend: Jackie, who was seriously down in the mouth over the Natasha situation: Mazi, who'd lived in his brother's shadow since the day he was born, practically: Birdie Love, who for all her skill was a battered and bruised 90-pound eighth grader. It was a miracle that they were in contention at all.

Two days before the game, the disconcertingly desperate Ms. De Bono had finally gotten through on the phone and talked to Mr. Watson.

Remember Mr. Watson? "Fast Eddie" Watson, former star player for Garrison, now some kind of internet billionaire or something.

And now, after literally months of trying, she'd got him on the phone. She almost didn't know what to say.

"Mr. Watson," she said, "It's lovely to hear your voice."

"Ms. De Bono!" he always sounded happy, both times she'd talked to him. She supposed being a billionaire probably wasn't the worst thing in the world. "How are you? How's my alma mater?"

"Well, I'm glad you asked," she said. "Thank you for asking. Yes. The school is on the razor's edge, Mr. Watson. It is on the very verge of shutting its doors forever this summer, after more than one hundred and twenty years."

"Hell, that's tough," he admitted. "Great old school."

"Sir," she said, pacing her office floor, "We've survived two turns of the century, the Great Depression, two world wars, two presidential assassinations, the moon landing, Korea and Vietnam. We even survived the blackout. But we've reached the end of our resources. That's why I wanted—"

"Ms. De Bono. Ms. De Bono, I have to cut you short here. I'm sorry. What you may not realize is that there are a thousand schools in the same predicament. Not to mention towns, cities, companies large and small... hell, the whole continent. To say nothing of my own company, which you can just imagine how the blackout and the data wipe affected an AI company. And I guess you can imagine what all of this did to my own personal worth, Ms. De Bono. My ability, therefore, to do the kind of philanthropic—"

"Sure," she said. She'd never been in storm-tossed waters desperately clinging to a lifeline, but she knew it must feel a lot like she did now. "But if you could please—"

"Tell you what. Talk to my controller. She handles all this kind of stuff for me. She's not exactly all smiles, but you tell her about your situation and who knows?"

Ms. De Bono settled back in her office sofa. The lifeline had snapped, and she was going under. This controller person was a dodge, a kiss-off. And she had just run out of options.

"Okay," she said. "Well, thank you, Mr. Watson. I do appreciate your time and consideration."

"Good, Ms. De Bono. Take care."

"Oh! Mr. Watson, do you know that the Liberators are contending for the sectionals two nights from now?"

Mr. Watson said he was damned glad, very surprised and damn glad to hear it.

The crucial game started ten minutes late.

Why do basketball games always start late? So strange.

Anyway, Harriman made a good speech this time. Kosoko was there, but he hadn't bothered to suit up. He said there was no point, the way his leg was hurting. Added to which he was drinking something out of a flask.

Garrison played pretty lousy in the first half and went to the break with a 15-point deficit.

Nobody on the team noticed it, but there was a little two-seat section with tape across it in the stands. "Reserved for Mr. and Mrs. Edward Watson." Written in Ms. De Bono's own hand.

She waited through the first half, just in case, then went home. It was too bad, because Watson actually did show up half an hour later. He and his wife had been delayed getting there from the airport. They sat down and watched the last five minutes of the game. They were both exhausted. They talked all through the game's end. In the last minute, the Liberators got two possessions, and somehow on both of them Zero got the ball and reflexively shot it. Both misses—one airball, one in-and-out.

So they lost. So much for the sectionals. Lots of people had left early, not just Ms. De Bono. Kosoko himself had left during halftime.

Mr. Watson shook his head. He scanned the room for any sign of the headmaster, not really knowing what she looked like. But it was obvious she wasn't there.

If you think missing a make-or-break shot is too trivial to cause a suicide, you don't know much about basketball, and you definitely don't know much about suicide.

The importance or triviality of a moment in time is like the climate of the world. There are areas of high pressure where the skies are clear. And there are pockets of low pressure, and into these flow all the storms and darkness. What's a basketball game? What's the end of the world? The mind sees as it sees, diminishing what should be great, enlarging what should be small. The mind is our one and only portal to the world. And the mind lies. And the game was finished, and could never be done over.

Zero was on the top floor of the Douglass building, the tallest building on campus.

He'd walked straight here from the game—hadn't even changed out of his uniform. He was floating along as though underwater, his body in slow motion, his eyes staring lifelessly. He followed the exit signs to the stairwell, whose doors read, "No roof access." Nevertheless, the stairway went all the way up, and he followed it. This time the door, which led out onto the roof, had a push handle across its middle that read, "EMERGENCY EXIT ONLY—ALARM WILL SOUND."

If this wasn't an emergency, what was? He'd lost the team its big shot. His family was broken and broke. He was about to fail out of school. He'd been traumatized by the sight of my violent death. He suffered from untreated major depression and anxiety. The world was on the brink of war. His girlfriend was probably sleeping with Kosoko, a man who was in every respect superior to himself, so superior that even though he blamed Birdie with all of his being, he couldn't blame her at all.

The image of Birdie and Kosoko in bed together played through his head on an endless loop, from the first moment he woke up every morning. He saw the pleasure in her eyes, the sweat on her back. He saw this as often as his heart beat, as often as he blinked. All the decent drapery of Zero's life was rudely torn off.

The alarm did sound when he pushed the exit door open, and it jarred him into full consciousness, but it stopped when the door closed behind him.

From the roof he could see all of Newburyport, and smell the fresh air of middle spring. All across the campus and the city beyond, lights were shining in the darkness. And behind every one of those windows was a life, a story, precious to itself and others.

But in those lights, in those windows, he could only see them huddled in their embrace. Birdie and Kosoko, multiplied by every window, every streetlight, every star in the sky overhead.

What Zero knew, and what those who've never chosen this path never knew, was that he wasn't angry. He wasn't disgusted with the world. He didn't even want to die, really. But to live, to persist, had simply become intolerable.

A man will jump from a burning building because to fall is better than to burn.

And that's what nobody understood. He walked around every day, apparently living a normal life like all the other students, but he was suffering the emotional equivalent of fourth degree burns, burns that went through the skin into the organs and muscles below.

But if his body could saturate itself with endorphins to slightly diminish the pain of a burn, it could do nothing to mitigate the pain of a disordered mind.

All he wanted, all he could do, was leap out of the flames into an empty sky. It was three weeks before his 15th birthday.

Zero knew what he was giving up.

The chance to explore those rooms and buildings and streets, the chance to learn those stories. The chance to see what the world could dream up next, if it survived. He was giving up the tiny chance of winning Birdie back, of feeling her against him once more. He was giving up his parents, his sisters, everyone he dearly loved.

For love was still in him, despite the horror.

It gave him pause, just for a moment.

And then he stepped up onto the ledge. He took a last look straight up and though he didn't know it, he was looking directly at Uranus.

"Death," he said. "Death, what can I do?"

He heard the alarm again as Jackie and Dr. Harriman busted out onto the roof.

At the same moment, Watson and his wife had reached the airport, having decided to helicopter back tonight, right after the game. It had been silly, sentimental of them to fly out here.

Plumb Island Airport was just a flat grass field with a few antique planes and a shack. The Watsons were walking over to the helicopter when I ran into them. Yeah, me, your humble narrator, the revenant Pete Graff, the ghost in the machine.

"Not a bad game, huh?" I said. "Too bad they couldn't close it out."

Watson looked like he was going to brush me off, but he stopped. "You saw the game? The Garrison game?"

"I never miss one," I said. "And I'll tell you what, my man. If you can stick around for another night, you can catch them again. See a whole game instead of just the final minutes."

"What? I thought the season ended tonight."

"Yeah," I said, "but the real finale will be tomorrow night at Filibuster Gym. Grudge match. They're playing an unofficial grudge match, a scrimmage, against their rivals Newburyport High."

Watson and his wife looked at me a minute. Looked at me pretty strangely. There was no way they could know about my getting killed a few months back. No way in hell. But they looked at me almost like they were on to me.

"What's your name?" said Watson.

Across town, at the Sea Level Oyster Bar, Mayor Frank
Wright was eating a very large order of baked oysters and a
coke and a glass of whiskey. It was 10:00 p.m. and Wright was
the only customer there—the only customer they would have
served after hours.

He knew damn well he shouldn't eat this late, with his acid
reflux disease. Eating late meant digesting while lying prone,
and that was asking for it. His stomach would have been sour
in any case.

Everything was sour.

Even this late at night the restaurant wouldn't let him have
a cigar. Even though they were officially closed.

Fuck it. He took a swallow of his whiskey, then looked up
to see Elijah Hart seating himself at the next stool.

"How the hell did you get in here?" said Wright.

"Is this the man?" said Elijah, with great good humor. "Is
this the man who took payoffs from the teamsters? Is this the
gentlemen who lined his own pockets and abused his power?
Is this the man who wrecked the buffet at the Harrow club?
Who disabled an unmarked unit—with a banana?" Elijah Hart
spoke at an indiscreet volume, and there were a good half
dozen employees cleaning up the restaurant.

Frank stared at him, hard, but he couldn't speak.

He heard the ice cubes rattling in his whiskey, and he tried
to steady his hand.

Was he sweating?

He knew he must take control of himself and the situation.
You don't walk into the Sea Level Oyster Bar and speak to a
man like Frank Wright like that. But he just couldn't get the
words out.

So Elijah went on. "Kidding aside, Frank, I was real sorry
to hear about your sons' losing tonight. To go from last place
to the sectionals; that would have been quite a thing. Quite a
thing. But you know what the man says. There's always next
year." And then this prick had the gall to put his hand on
Frank's soldier.

"Yeah," said his Honor Mayor Frank Wright. "But there's still one more scrimmage. Tomorrow night, in fact."

"That's right!" Hart said. "You know, I'd forgotten all about it. Our sons are going to go at it right there at Garrison, and may the best team win. Shame your older boy's still hurt."

Frank took out a cigar and unwrapped it, never taking his eye off his enemy.

"It's funny you coming in tonight, Hart. Because you'd never have guessed it, but I was thinking about you. Thinking about a lot of things. About the people I've been able to help as mayor since the lights came back on. About the FEMA dollars I fought for, and the emergency supplies, and how we got our grocery stores up and running—gas stations, too—up and running two weeks faster than any other town in Essex County. Two weeks is a long time for a family that's suffering, Hart. And yeah, speaking of the union, they've got a lot of members here, real good people, and they have something in common with me. They don't look kindly on being threatened."

"Hell," said Hart, "I don't—"

"I'm not finished, motherfucker. And as I was sitting here thinking on you and all of this shit, I started to form a conclusion in my mind. Would you like to know what this conclusion was?"

It was Hart's turn to stare back in silence.

"My conclusion was I think I'm gonna invite you to stick that evidence of yours straight up your ass. Not saying I've made up my mind, now. But the thought has a certain appeal."

"I'll tell you what," said Hart, smiling. "I'll tell you what, now. You—"

"Now I'd like you to get the hell out of here," said the mayor, rising to his feet.

"I'll tell you what," said Hart. "I got a proposition for you." He stood up, too. His affect was gracious, but he still looked mean. "A friendly wager."

"Are you shitting me?"

"You'll like this," said Hart.

"What did I tell you?" Jackie said to Harriman as they ran across the roof to Zero. "Guy's gonna jump off the roof! Hey, Zero!"

"Zero, get down here this instant!" shouted Harriman, running over to the ledge. He was heaving wind so hard it took him half a minute to catch his breath, 30 seconds doubled over, hands on his knees. Zero stood there on the lip of the building, shaking his head.

"Never would have thought I could feel sorry for someone else right now," said Zero.

"Sorry? For me?" Harriman straightened up. His eyes burned into Zero. "Horseshit. HORSE SHIT. Look into my eyes, boy. What do you see?"

"Well, alcoholism, I guess."

"Fuck that!" said the old man. "I fought a war! I faced down failure and rejection and humiliation again and again! I drank myself half to death, lost three wives to divorce, and damn near had a stroke when those god-damn ruffians set upon me! What you see in my eyes, Zero, is LIFE."

"Yeah, but you..."

"But nothing!" Harriman was rolling. He looked huge, but not in his usual way. Impressive. Colossal. "But JACK SHIT! You listen to me boy, and listen well. You think you're suffering? Good! You think your existence is intolerable? Tolerate it! Because it's now, at your darkest hour, when you look into that darkness, that you have to say one thing to the whole god-damn world."

"Fuck you?" said Zero.

"Close. And that's good. You'll have plenty of chances to use that. But no. The word you have to say to the world and to your life is YES. YES to the pain. YES to the misery, the heartbreak, the despair. You're here on this corrupt old world for one reason: to cling, like Ulysses, to the boards of your shattered bark. To defy the heavens to their worst. To strive with gods."

DAMN him, how the old man's voice boomed across the campus. By Jupiter!

Zero stepped down from the ledge. It wasn't that he felt much better, but it would have been awkward to leap to his death after such a fine speech.

"We love you, brother," said Jackie. "We're all holding onto you for dear life. Can you feel that? We're all crushing you to ourselves. Besides, we play Newburyport tomorrow. Last scrimmage. We need your three-point threat."

Two hours later, at the Carousel Lounge, Harriman sat in a booth by the pool table.

It was just after one a.m.

Presto lay at the old man's feet. Harriman was the kind of guy who brings a book with him to a bar. Presto was the kind of dog who lies on his back, waiting for someone to rub his tummy, when nobody's even paying attention. Harriman could read while drunk, which talent had gotten him his doctorate. He was reading Cicero's *Epistulae ad Brutum*. In the Latin, of course. If I haven't made this clear, Latin is a very difficult language. Difficult enough that even an old hand like Harriman had to really concentrate, so that he didn't notice the woman enter.

A moment later, she was sitting at a table next to his booth, facing him. She wasn't looking at him, though. She was looking at Presto.

"Thank you," said Kim Jigu, accepting her drink from the bartender.

Harriman cocked an eyebrow when he noticed her. In such situations he reflexively looked away, afraid of being exposed as a dirty old man.

Presto got up and walked over to Kim Jigu. He had his tail and his ears down, like he thought she was going to swat him. She leaned forward and began whispering, looking deep into the doggie's eyes.

"Quamquam et hunc, ut spero, tenebo multis repugnantibus. videtur enim esse indoles, sed flexibilis aetas multique ad depravanduin parati," Harriman read, before noticing he was reading aloud.

"I beg your pardon," said Kim Jigu. She gave him a look, as though he were interrupting.

Harriman was about to answer when I, the late great Peter Graff, entered the bar. Harriman was sober enough to sense that there was something odd about my being there at the Carousel Lounge.

Let him stare.

I had business with Jigu. She was as surprised to see me as he was. I took a seat across from her at her table. I didn't even bother to order a beer like a civilized person.

"I believe," said I, "I have the honor to address Major Kim Jigu, avatar of Gaia and officer of the Strategic Rocket Forces of the Democratic People's Republic of Korea."

She asked me how I did, etc.

"And to you," I continued, "I introduce Dr. John Harriman of the Garrison Academy."

Harriman's ears, already pricked up, now rose further with the man himself, and the floorboards groaned beneath him as he moved to sit at Kim Jigu's table.

Kim Jigu said that she was delighted, and gave Harriman her hand to kiss. He did kiss it, without too much awkwardness, and as he did, her eyes were on me.

"Dr. Harriman," I said, "is a student of our era. A classicist, and more to the point, a humanist."

"You expect him to change my mind," she said, her smile as pacific as the vast blue. "Very well, Dr. Harriman. I wonder if you'd be kind enough to settle a disagreement for us."

Dr. Harriman said he'd be very pleased to try.

"What we're hoping from you, Harriman," I said, "is an apologia, a defense of the human species."

Harriman straightened up in his seat. "A defense..."

"I really don't mean to pressure you," I said. "But please craft your answer as though a great deal depended on it."

Harriman lifted his glass to his lips and then paused, frozen. Then he put the glass back down and pushed it away.

"In our defense," he started, and then paused again. He was looking at Kim Jigu with some glimmer of comprehension. At Kim Jigu, and then at Presto, and then at yours truly. Harriman was thinking of the crisis on the Korean peninsula, the disposition of the U.S. Navy.

He spoke up at last.

"Ancient Europe had no gods. The Great Goddess was regarded as immortal, changeless, and omnipotent; and the concept of fatherhood had not been introduced into religious thought. She took lovers, but for pleasure, not to provide her children with a father. Men feared, adored, and obeyed the matriarch; the hearth which she tended in a cave or hut being their earliest social centre, and motherhood their prime mystery.' But children grow up."

He shifted awkwardly. Pausing for effect, or unable to speak? Then he continued.

"And who the devil is this child, man? A godlike paragon? A quintessence of dust? The universe's way of knowing itself?" he looked down into his drink. "Both, I should think, and neither..." he looked deep into the abyss of Kim Jigu's eyes. "Who is this man I speak for? One old, but not learned. Rich, but broke. Lucky but not grateful. Fearful. Violent. Curious. Searching."

He looked at me.

"For Homer, man was the one who dies. For Plato, the one who thinks. For Aristotle, the political animal. For the American Indian, the human race is one flesh. Kwame Gyeke said man was driven by a desire to use the munificence and powers of the gods for the promotion of human welfare and happiness. Mark Twain said man was the animal that blushes. But who else toils at art and science? Who writes the stories? Who creates mathematics, or language, or history? Man is a scholar, a creator, a philosopher, an athlete."

Kim Jigu looked over at me. Her face was weary. It was later than we thought.

"This man is too smart by a half," she said. "Too smart to stay in his niche. Unconcerned, mocking, violent. A despoiler of worlds. An exterminator of species, a killer of his fellows, a killer of children, a rapist, a weak, frightened, shallow bungler who destroys what he touches and casts everything into ruins."

Harriman seemed to have lost his thread.

I was surprised to see him slump down in the booth and stare under the table. The dog looked up at Harriman with gravity.

"Yes," said Harriman. "Yes. But man is unique and precious. Alone capable of irony, rationality, explanation, artistry, and universal observation. And if all this is not enough, there remains the example of Garrison."

"Where you teach," said Jigu.

"Yes," said the old man, clearing his throat. "And a noble institution it is. But I refer to the man, William Lloyd Garrison, that risible gentleman of the 19th century. For he was a man, take him for all in all, as human as anyone. Weak, frail, doomed, and never knowing when he was licked. He was an activist, of all things, which means a nuisance to everyone, loved by none. Yes, and blind to the facts, blind to his own chances, quixotic, petulant, gently inclined to treason, strongly driven in calumny, peevish, bilious, and a laughing stock.

In these respects he epitomized the human race.

But in one more respect, too: He sought after great things. He fought against slavery at a time when it was nearly unheard of, with an uncompromising determination and even violent obduracy. He fought for the equality of women, when even his fellow abolitionists opposed so far-fetched a notion. He did not equivocate. He did not extenuate. He was in earnest. He was hated. He was a fool for an idea. And he was a man. I daresay he and his legacy are the reason why this discussion should be taking place in his town of birth.

"I should therefore suggest," Harriman went on, "and you will agree, that like Garrison, man is a fool. Somewhat past his prime, somewhat fat (which is no sin), a touch lame, a touch sick." There were tears on his cheeks now. "A poor scholar, a poor coach, a lonesome rascal. A fool who wanted to be a hero and wound up trapped in his own vices. A fool bound by gravity who nevertheless let his mind range through the heavens. A man who tried to lead, but was led and was alone.

"And this is my defense, my catechism. This ember in the darkness, this man who fails while striving greatly, is great not despite but because he's lost. He inquires because he knows so little. He's wise, because he's a god-damned fool.

"Therefore banish industry, banish craft, banish all his works, but banish not man. Banish man, and banish all the world."

I couldn't speak for Kim Jigu, whose reserve was without bottom. But Harriman's words had moved me. He seemed like the guilty child who begs not to be beaten.

But his apologia—would it wash? The old man had given it his best.

And he knew it.

And now he leaned back into the booth and reached shrewdly for his whiskey. Raising a toast to us, he smiled at last and said, "Fuck it! You want my defense? Come see my team play tomorrow night."

He drank it at one swallow, and he and Presto walked out of the bar.

Kim Jigu and I stared at each other for about a minute. She burned with a volcanic rage that would scour away all of civilization, but she still brought out the old love light in my eyes. At last I said, "An Iliad?"

She laughed.

And I shook my head. "An Iliad without Achilles."

Chapter 11
The Final Scrimmage

The next morning, the day of the scrimmage, Harriman was awakened by a phone call.

"Dr. Harriman!" said the voice of Ms. De Bono, a voice no less elegant than her person.

"What?" he yelled into the receiver.

"Oh, I beg your pardon, Dr. Harriman. I hope I'm not reaching you at a bad time."

"You may hope, and hope in vain, Ms. De Bono, until the end of time. Now please tell me what you want. I'm very busy."

He could hear in Ms. De Bono's voice that she was trying to be brave.

"It occurred to me," she said, "that there are really two likely scenarios in the next few months, either of which should make you happy, Dr. Harriman. In the first scenario, by far the likelier scenario, Garrison will cease to exist. We're ruined, deep in debt and have no real prospects. Anyway, in the second, which is a kind of blue-sky scenario, we'll somehow come up with a grant that will recall us to life.

"Again, extremely unlikely.

"But should it happen, for reasons I won't get into here, I plan to place more emphasis on basketball in the fall. Yes, even to the extent of hiring a real coach. So you see, Dr. Harriman, either way you're off the hook. You can hang up your whistle at last. Now, Dr. Harriman, what do you think of that? Rather nice to hear, isn't it? Hello? Dr. Harriman, are you there?"

Dr. Harriman had gone back to sleep, but not for long. This would be a big night.

And when he woke up, he found that Presto had run away.

As the Newburyport-Garrison scrimmage went into halftime, Weapons Officer David Muratskian was standing at his console, struggling to read the data.

For days, the USS Nebraska had been on the 1-SQ, both hunting for and hunted by the NorKor submarine. On three separate occasions he'd come within a milligram of pressure on his trigger to firing his torpedoes. Each time the signal had faded.

"Broadband contact!" came the report. "Bearing 0-9-9."

"Emergency depth!" The captain shouted on the 1-M-C.

"Angles and dangles," said the missile technician to Muratskian's side, and the submarine inclined sharply. Muratskian grabbed two handholds and kept his eyes on his scopes. They were rigged for Romeo; red lights only, so that everyone was cast in that infernal light.

Did they know back home? Did his wife know? He knew she didn't. The news only had part of the story. They were in a shooting war now, and nukes would go up at any second.

The *Nebraska* started to level off and make its depth, and Muratskian lit a smoke.

For some reason—maybe adrenaline sickness, maybe simple fatigue—he suddenly found that he could really taste the smoke from his cigarette. How had he gone through so many packs without once experiencing the full flavor of the tobacco? He closed his eyes and indulged himself for just a moment, letting it swirl across his tongue.

It was absolutely revolting.

"Sir!" said the Missile Technician, "We've got torpedoes in the water! At least two torpedoes, and they're closing on us!"

Muratskian got on the horn. "Captain, we have two or more torpedoes on vector for our heading."

"Jesus Christ," came the disembodied voice. And then the same voice rang through the entire submarine. "Evasive maneuvers, left full rudder! Emergency speed! Prepare to launch countermeasures on my mark!"

And halftime in the Newburyport scrimmage was a time for the team to come together one last time before the summer.

The team, minus Kosoko, but with Birdie present and accounted for, was in the locker room. The players looked pretty down, pretty low.

Birdie had been terrific in the first half, boxing out on guys twice her size, shooting the lights out. But she was exhausted, and nobody could stop Hank Hart. Harriman felt even worse, of course. His dog was gone. Presto!

But duty, his sacred duty, was no respecter of Harriman's personal troubles. He rose to his feet with great difficulty and stood before his team.

"If there's a Garrison next year, which I'm obliged to doubt, I hope you'll play for this team again. I won't be your coach, of course. Ms. De Bono is going to find you a real coach, not a fat old drunken wizened carbuncled wheezing Latin instructor but a coach who understands the game of basketball.

You will have earned it, each of you. Not so much by the courage, the grit, and the heart you've shown in making it all the way to contend for the sectionals after so strange a disaster, no. Rather you've earned it by playing well.

You learned, you applied yourself, and you became basketball players. I know that wasn't easy, and I know I was of but little help to you, especially in the beginning.

Before our first game, I asked you to fail while striving greatly. Tonight..." the coach leaned forward on his crooked arm to hide his old face. He didn't cry, but hark how he fetched breath. "I don't know if you boys know this, but Presto has— well, he's gone, boys. My dog, my friend, is gone. He never got to see you play, you know. He saw you practice once or twice, but I know he would have liked to see you play."

"Coach," said Jackie. "You okay?"

"I was saying," said the old man, "I once hoped that you might fail while striving greatly. But if Presto...if Presto were here, he'd have none of that shit. None whatsoever."

Harriman stood and wiped his face off with his hand. Then he looked into the faces of every player on his team.

"So for Presto's sake, I'm not telling you to fail while striving greatly anymore. I'm telling you to do one thing, for Presto, for me, for Garrison. Win. *Win*."

With Birdie at the vanguard, the players ran back out onto the court.

At 5:30 p.m., Kosoko Wright had risen for the first time that day. He'd been sleeping in his Liberators uniform, which he did a lot.

He was up because his leg hurt. He didn't want to be up, but he knew he needed to walk on it. He put on his basketball shoes and headed downstairs from the dorm.

It was 50 degrees out, and he had on neither coat nor long sleeves. He turned to head back outside. But when he got to the staircase, he realized he was too weary to climb the stairs. He decided to go to the cafeteria.

It was a short walk to the cafeteria, short and cold and painful. The weather did his leg no favors. Every step on it felt like a mild electric shock, a small power surge that radiated out onto his lower back. He didn't like his fellow students seeing him limp. He didn't like the concern and pity in their faces.

When he reached the cafeteria, he stopped at the entrance. He felt a little bit warmer now.

He wasn't hungry, and he didn't want to see anybody. He especially didn't want to see his teammates. What did they want with him? Birdie had stopped visiting him weeks ago. Kosoko was pretty damned sick of carrying everybody on his shoulders. He was barely 16 years old. His father counted on him to score votes. His mother wanted him to be a credit to his race. The Liberators, including his brother, wanted him to kill himself on the court, maybe break his leg again, and for what? So they could brag to people, maybe to themselves, that *they'd* won the game?

Not including his brother, really.

He had to admit that much.

His brother had never complained. Mazi had just kept playing, kept pushing and scrapping when Kosoko disappeared and Birdie Love took over.

Even now, he knew, Mazi was in there playing his heart out in a hopeless battle that he himself hadn't bothered to show up for. He thought for a minute that Mazi was like a dog who kept licking the hand of a master who beat him. He was disgusted with Mazi for that, and disgusted at himself for thinking something so rotten.

He realized, indeed, that he was describing not Mazi but himself. And it was he who was rotten.

When Kosoko Wright fell into this kind of humor, his whole face would pucker around his mouth, and his gaze would fix on the ground in front of him. He could see the grass and dirt of the football field passing along beneath him. He could feel the fat of his thighs rubbing together.

He forced himself to look up so he could breathe.

In the middle of the field, with all the buildings shrinking in the perspective, he saw the sun had begun to set. The clouds were a ladder whose rungs stretched for miles to the north and south. They glowed with solar radiation, painted by the fingertips of the dusk, burning streaks in the mournful sky.

All the trees around him were shrugging, sighing. In the air the piping plovers were losing their strength and spiraling down to the ground in a narrowing pattern. The darkness was settling over Newburyport.

Kosoko stopped.

As his eyes adjusted, he saw he was looking straight at Filibuster Gym. And as he listened, he could hear the crowd inside reacting to the ups and downs of the Newburyport-Garrison scrimmage.

Whatever else this scrimmage might mean, it would have been his last chance to play Hank Hart.

Hart was a senior with just weeks before graduation. He hadn't thought about Hank in a long time. He tried to brush the thought of him away. Kosoko had never gotten the better of him. Four out of five times, Hank had frozen him out, blocking his shots or making him give up the ball.

And it wasn't Hank Hart's skill or athleticism that had shut Kosoko down on the court. It was Hank's contempt. He projected what is called "magnificence of mind," a just and perfect contempt, a disdain for challengers, a pity for the rest.

Now Hank was in there, in the Liberators' gym. And Kosoko knew as sure as life that Hank was dominating. And Kosoko's brother was in there getting killed, and Kosoko's parents were watching. It made Kosoko so ashamed that he could barely think of it.

But what could he possibly do now? The game must be nearly over. His leg was burning. He'd basically quit the team. They'd run him out of the building if he so much as showed his face.

He turned and headed back to the dorm.

The fact was, he'd put too much of himself into the game of basketball. And into the Liberators, and Garrison. He'd stuck his neck out too far. It was just as well he'd busted his leg. His mother was right about one thing: He needed to put childish things to one side and be a man now.

His father was probably going to lose the election, if he didn't get thrown out of office first. He might even be disbarred. This would lead to an expensive divorce, leaving his parents unable to afford Garrison. And that was fine, too. Because part of being a man meant doing without these luxuries, setting them aside as he had his crutches. He'd never been the letterman type anyway, the prep school type, the college type.

Of course, all of that was in the future. And he thought something as he grabbed the handle of the dorm building entrance: What if I started being a man now, instead of waiting for everything to fall apart?

What would it look like right now if I were to face my shit and deal with it?

What would happen if I shook this the fuck off?

Before he could think of answers to these questions, he noticed that he was running at full bore toward the gym. And now the cold air was biting into his lungs, trying to slow him down, and his leg was begging him to stop, to take it easy, to go the hell back to bed.

He burst through the gym floors and looked around. The game was well into the second half. Everyone looked at him.

Kosoko, terrified, feeling he should say something, limped over to kneel before the scoring table.

The crowd held its breath as one body.

Bobby Driskill scored along two for the Newburyport Clippers.

The ref handed the ball to Jackie, who inbounded it to Mazi. Mazi signaled for time out.

Kosoko climbed to his feet and headed onto the court, greeting his teammates with low-fives. They were, for the first time, a six-player team, which meant somebody had to go to the bench. Zero didn't even wait to be asked. Mazi bent Kosoko forward so he could whisper into his taller brother's ear. Kosoko told Harriman, and Harriman nodded. Then he whispered something to both of them.

Kosoko listened, then shook his head as he replied. Then he nodded his head.

He and Mazi clapped their hands simultaneously, and Kosoko said, "Okay."

Birdie just stood there, watching.

The referee announced that the time-out was over.

Jackie inbounded the ball to Birdie. Birdie took it up the floor, then passed it to Lefty, who touch-passed it to Kosoko. The court looked about a mile long.

Kosoko drove haltingly for the hoop right into the teeth of the defense, then went up for the lay-in. His collision with Hart wasn't terribly forceful, but it sent Kosoko sprawling to the floor. Again, silence in the arena.

Kosoko sat on the gym floor now, holding his thigh. He was wincing.

Mazi walked over to Kosoko and said something to him. Kosoko shook his head again, and with help from Mazi and Lefty, he got to his feet again.

The crowd exhaled.

For a moment, Kosoko surveyed the scene through the dancing lights of his vertigo.

He seemed to recognize each person in the crowd. There was Naomi, there were his parents, there was Ms. De Bono, there Natasha Reinhardt, Andy Tangent, Milo Potter, Brent Sanger, Rebekah Marigold, Tanya Roberts, little Fannie Romero, old Elijah Hart, and on and on.

In every face he saw the same feeling, a feeling at the crossroads of hope and despair. Strange, to think that so much and so many could depend on a friendly scrimmage of basketball.

The ref blew his whistle.

Birdie inbounded to Mazi, Mazi passed to Kosoko, who held the ball for a long moment before putting it on the floor.

The scoreboard read:

CLIPPERS: 45   LIBERATORS: 39   3:36   HALF: 2

A lion, his prey flushed out before him, will run into the deepest pack of them, choosing as he goes. The slowest antelope may yet be strong, though the weakest of his herd. He may be nimble. He may spring from one hard cut to another, evading his predator. He may come close to escape. But the lion's claw will find that slowest antelope, and then the lion's teeth will bite into his rivering flank.

So did Kosoko now slash through the Newburyport High School Clippers, avoiding the redoubtable Hank Hart and feasting on the smaller, slower players. He stole the ball from their point guard, streaked down court and finished with the jam. And when Hank recovered on defense and stopped Kosoko, that left Birdie Love open to slash her way to the basket. Kosoko blocked, he leaped, and Birdie bucketed ball after ball. The Liberators took the lead.

Then Hank Hart, beating Kosoko on the fast break, stopped and popped from the arc, burying a three-point dagger. The look on Hart's face when he released that ball would have frozen the blood of any competitor. Here was the boot in the face. Here was the oppressing hand.

And when the last seconds came, the Clippers, up two points, called for another time out.

The Clippers huddled up under their basket. And the Liberators came together at the bench. Everyone was silent. Coach Harriman produced, out of nowhere, a little dry-erase board. On it he had drawn a succession of exes and ohs the likes of which he'd never before attempted.

"Hark, my children," he said. "I have drawn up a play."

Bobby Driskill put the ball in, but a flash of light called Birdie Love streaked across, grabbing the basketball before it could reach Hank Hart. Birdie had a clear path to the basket, with six seconds on the clock, to tie the game.

Hart was so fast, though, that he managed almost to get in front of her. Instead, he inadvertently tripped her. She went down harder than she ever had before. When she got to her feet, shooing away her teammates who tried to help her, she was holding up her right hand with her left. "No!" she said, staring. "No, God-damn it!"

Her finger was bent back at a sickening angle, badly broken.

There was a commotion for a few moments, and Birdie was helped off the court to the bench.

Hank had committed a flagrant foul against Birdie. And since Zero must now come in to replace Birdie, he was the one with the chance to tie up the game with two foul shots and three seconds on the clock.

Lefty stood up from the bench, and said, "Guys, a basketball game shouldn't be the end of the world."

Zero's stomach hurt.

He shot the first free throw. He missed.

He dribbled the ball twice, as he always did when practicing his free throw. He looked up at the back of the basket, the part where the rim attaches to the backboard. He lifted the ball into the air with both hands; his right shoulder was at a perfect 90 degree angle to his trunk, and his forearm at a perfect 90 degree angle to his upper arm, and his wrist at yet another 90 degree angle, so that he looked like a waiter carrying his tray. The ball rested neatly in Zero's right hand. His left hand gently held it there. He exhaled, and shot.

The ball caromed off the rim and over the backboard into the stands.

Zero's couldn't look up. He just couldn't face his teammates. But he ran to his position and stood there, bouncing slightly back and forth.

The ref handed the ball to Jackie, who passed it in to Kosoko. And now it was the last three seconds of the game, with no more time outs, and the Clippers up two points.

Mazi Wright brought the ball up and passed it to Kosoko. This time Kosoko couldn't switch off his defender. There was no time. So there he faced Hank Hart, who was waiting for him in the paint.

Hank was daring Kosoko to get around him and score. He stood in his athletic stance, arms wide out to his sides. Hank's face was stern as the law, but his eyes were laughing.

Kosoko dropped his shoulder.

He charged at Hart at a full sprint.

In the instant before he reached him, Kosoko leapt into the air, bringing the ball up for the dunk. But as he and Hart collided, Kosoko was sent ass-over-teakettle, completely out of control, helplessly covering his head with his arms.

The clock ran out and sounded the end of the game.

Kosoko hit the ground hard. Harder than he'd hit it when he'd snapped his femur. He didn't break anything this time, but he was dazed. He'd have to be carried off. Kosoko lay back onto the cold hard wood, as Hank towered over him, staring.

But a thing had happened at the last instant as Kosoko was flying into Hank Hart.

Kosoko had brought the ball up to dunk it, but had instead hooked it down the baseline to the corner.

There it had been caught by Zero, who had instantly, unconsciously shot it.

And yes, of course, it had been a swish at the buzzer.

Victory.

The crowd poured out onto the basketball court in flood of joyful sound. They seized Kosoko and lifted him into the air. They grabbed everybody, Birdie, Zero, Lefty, Jackie, Coach Harriman. The crowd was deafening.

Still in the stands, Barbara Wright turned to her husband, beaming. She grabbed him close to her and looked into his eyes.

"Okay, Frank. It's okay. It's okay."

Jackie turned to see Natasha running at him. She leaped into his arms.

Lefty stood there with tears in his eyes. He understood everything now.

De Bono turned back to the stands. She saw the Wrights and Naomi and a few other stragglers who'd stayed in their seats, probably Newburyport High School fans.

And then she saw Mr. Edward Watson, sitting with his wife in the front row.

She hadn't known he was coming. Hadn't noticed him at any point in the game. Now he rose to his feet and strode over to her, offering his hand.

"Ms. De Bono," he said, "I congratulate you. Hell of a game. Say, you know, we're in town until tomorrow night. Maybe the three of us could have a little meeting. Talk about good old Garrison Academy."

"That would be delightful. More than delightful," said Ms. De Bono, her face flushed and glowing.

"Hell of a team," said Mr. Watson. "Really something. Hell of a coach, too."

De Bono started to laugh. "Would you like to meet him?"

"Could we?" said Watson.

She didn't see why not. Harriman was close by, at the bench, and the teammates were giving him hugs. He was a sweating, half-crazed old god-damn fool. He turned to Ms. De Bono with a fearful expression.

"Mr. Watson," said Ms. De Bono, "permit me to introduce our basketball coach, Dr. John Harriman."

Zero saw Birdie. She was smiling at him as she iced her hand. Not smiling at Kosoko, not at the scoreboard, but right at him. He blinked his eyes twice, and smiled back.

Kosoko was finally lowered from the crowd's shoulders and let down on the floor. There he felt his full weight settle back onto his leg. Pain shot through him in a cascade of spasms that jerked him like a puppet on a string. He bent over to catch his breath.

"Kosoko!" said Mazi. "You okay?"

Kosoko, still grabbing his knees, looked up at his brother. He smiled.

54981819R00180